ATTUNING

Attuning

A Novel

John Popielaski

Paperback ISBN: 9781965412237

Front cover art by Kyle St. George

Cover design by Jacob Arms
Produced in the United States
Published by Broken Tribe Press
Lawrence Landing Company
Raleigh, North Carolina 27609
www.brokentribepress.com

Broken Tribe Press is a proud member of:

Independent Book Publishers Association
 and

Community of Literary Magazines and Presses

BROKEN TRIBE PRESS

For this side and the other

"The earth hath bubbles, as the water has,
And these are of them."

—William Shakespeare, *Macbeth*

Chapter One: Monson, Maine

Albert Lesiak's tan shorts hang lower than is seemly for a man approaching fifty. His bald spot glows like a tonsure in the kitchen light. He delicately sets a light-green, transparent plastic bag on the counter. He removes the towel-wrapped Duvel glasses from the bag and unwraps them, carefully producing each glass from its cotton folds and placing each one on the counter so the Duvel lettering faces the little table at which Mary Lesiak and Chris Atwater, interrupted, sit with cups of chaga tea.

"We saw something you two might be interested in," says Albert as he turns the faucet on and intermittently inserts his index finger in the outflow to determine if peak temperature has been achieved. He runs a sponge beneath the faucet, squeezes out the excess water in the manner of a person seeking low-commitment stress relief, and applies a drop of dish soap to the sponge.

"You're using up a lot of water there," says Chris. She is wispy, coiled but at ease.

Albert runs a Duvel glass beneath the faucet for some seconds, fills it so the waterline is just below the rim, and sets it in the sink. He does likewise with the second glass and shuts the water off.

He picks up one glass, dumps the water, and applies the sponge to the interior. He rubs the remnant lacing and the stickiness. He rotates, and he rubs. He rotates, and he rubs.

Married to him, Mary, fair-haired, square, substantial, shakes her head.

The back door opens. Charlie Watts, a sleek chihuahua greyhound, runs in and greets Chris and Mary. AJ Blasius walks in and pulls the screen door closed behind him.

"Hey, AJ," Mary says.

"Hey, hey," says AJ. He is barefoot. His extensive black hair could be twisted into dreadlocks, but he lets it fly as though it were electrified.

"AJ, this is Chris," says Mary.

"Hey, hey." He admires a date, *10/18/72*, tattooed in blue ink on the vein side of her right wrist as she drinks her tea.

She notices his admiration. "The day the Clean Water Act was enacted."

AJ makes a fist and holds his own right wrist up, which is bare.

"Did you just smoke?" asks Mary.

"I have more," says AJ.

"I'm good. Want some chaga tea?"

"No doubt." AJ says to Chris, "Detoxify. Free radicals."

Chris wonders if he is commanding her to purify her body, or to get involved in revolutionary action, or to do them both without regard for drawing lines and relegating major life decisions to compartments.

Albert finishes his thorough rinsing of the second Duvel glass and turns the faucet off. He holds the glass upside down, by the stem, to get what clinging droplets out he can. He sets a segment of the glass's rim on a towel on the counter, and he leans the glass so that a segment of its base makes contact with the backsplash. He determines that the angle of the lean is in agreement with the angle of the lean of the adjacent Duvel glass whose segments he already situated likewise—rim to towel, base to backsplash. He turns around and notices the others watching him.

"Prevents spotting," he explains. He pulls up the bottom of his shirt and dries his hands.

"Would you move already?" Mary asks. "I'm trying to get your friend some tea."

"We're not friends?" asks AJ.

"We're friends, AJ. We are friends," says Mary.

"Cool."

"So what did you see?" asks Chris.

"Show her," Albert says to AJ.

Communication lines of some vitality have recently been severed.

"The pictures on your phone," says Albert.

"Right, right," says AJ, happy with the speedy restoration of the lines. He pats his pockets. "Be right back."

Mary sets AJ's tea on the counter and steps into the living room to check on Jake and Ryan.

"You know where Bottle Brook is?" Albert asks.

Chris sips her tea and thinks a moment. "Off the road to Russell Mountain."

Albert nods.

"It's spring fed," Chris says. "Flows under Route 16."

"It's possibly a candidate for advocacy."

"We know about the aquifers around there, but there's basically no population impact."

We've seen no signs of development activity."

"It's flagged."

"Flagged?"

"Surveyor's tape from the Old Mountain Road through the woods to Bottle Brook."

"Stakes?"

"No stakes."

"How'd you find this out?"

"AJ heard."

"You saw?"

"With these bespectacled eyes."

Albert pours himself a cup of chaga tea and leans against the counter. "Problematic, right?"

"Potentially. Potentially," says Chris, the repetition amplifying her perception of potential.

Chris and Albert contemplate the plotting forces possibly arrayed against them.

The grass-roots activist, discrete and minuscule, infrequently the beneficiary of imposing legal counsel, not much bolstered by the intricacies of the Republic's apparatus, is a creature always struggling to persuade and marshal and deploy and bring to light the machination business and raise funds to get the inglorious legwork done, and is, by nature and accrued experience, defensive and suspicious and perpetually approaching limits past which patience, stamina, and hopefulness are rarefied, endangered, qualities that prod the grass-roots activist to think up means, for once, to get out in front of the intrusion, the development, that he or she intuits could be catastrophic to a way of life, to a biota, to who knows how many denizens, civilized and wild, deemed hostile or indifferent to the benchmark economic growth rate.

"Could be related to the East-West Corridor," says Albert.

"Could be related to a lot of things," says Chris.

"Are any of them good?"

"Could someone just be putting in a camp back there?"

Albert sips his tea and shrugs. "I need to check the Registry of Deeds to see who owns the property. Actually." Albert puts his teacup on the counter and takes a seat, opening the laptop on the table. "I probably can find that out right now."

Mary walks in and says to Chris, "So what did they see that was so interesting?"

"Maybe nothing," Chris says. "Waiting on the pictures still."

AJ walks back in, his phone in hand.

"Did you just smoke again?" asks Mary.

"You want?" asks AJ. "Clementine Wreckage. Very mellow. Citrusy. Cerebral. Boosts perception. Elevates your creativity."

"I'm good. Your tea is on the counter."

"Much obliged and gratified," says AJ, stepping toward the counter. He arrests his motion and reverses his direction. "Here you go," he says to Chris, handing her the phone. "Scroll that way." He steps back toward the counter, studies Albert's cup, then his, and picks up the full cup. He sips and nods. "Right on, Mary. You're an alchemist."

"What am I looking at here?" asks Chris, holding the phone across the table toward Albert.

"A small hole in the ground," says Albert. He stands a moment, gets his teacup, and resumes his seat. "There were twenty-four in a line."

"Spaced out how far?"

"Fifteen, twenty feet, I'd say."

"Someone did a seismic-refraction survey," Chris says.

"What's that for?" Albert and AJ ask in unison.

"In this case, probably to gauge the level of the water table. Probably to characterize subsurface aquifer geometry."

AJ whistles.

"I doubt that anybody would conduct a seismic-refraction survey just to put a camp back there. You're right," says Chris. "This is possibly a candidate for advocacy."

"We got that process started," Albert says.

"What do you mean?" asks Mary.

"First rule of monkeywrenching as expressed by George Washington Hayduke: 'Always pull up survey stakes. Anywhere you find them.' Weren't any survey stakes, so we took down the tapes."

"That isn't helpful," Chris says. "What does that accomplish?"

Albert thinks about the book he left in AJ's truck. He takes a moment to arrange the words he wants to quote from *Ecodefense: A Field Guide to Monkeywrenching*. "It must be strategic, it must be thoughtful, it must be deliberate." He pauses, focusing. "The Earth warrior always asks, 'Will monkeywrenching help or hinder the protection of this place?'"

"You're not an Earth warrior," says Mary.

"We didn't ask that question," AJ says, exuding nonsectarian contrition.

"No, we didn't ask that question," Albert says, confirming failure to adhere to codified procedure. "We let moral indignation cloud our judgment." He sips his tea.

"It's no big deal," says Chris.

"We showed a lack of Earth-warrior discipline," says AJ.

"That's because you're not Earth warriors," says Mary.

"First of all," says Chris, "we're not sure this is anything. It could be a routine USGS updating of the aquifer maps. And second, even if this does turn out to be a situation, I don't think we want monkeywrenching Earth warriors directing it. They're good for garnering publicity but not for changing policy."

"I disagree," says Albert.

"Name one long-term success that monkeywrenching has achieved," Chris challenges.

"Earth First! and ELF have done a lot."

"Like what? Name one long-term success."

"Can I check the internet?"

"No."

"Name one long-term success that *your* approach achieved," says Albert.

"The decommissioning and removal of the Veazie Dam and powerhouse."

Albert's powers of rebuttal won't respond to summoning. He checks the internet.

"A coalition got that done," Chris says, "not monkeywrenchers. Environmental groups, Penobscots, government agencies, local businesses, and citizens accomplished that through negotiation and legalities. The process took years. Slow, fraught, and unromantic, but it was the only way. If ELF or Earth First! had monkeywrenched, it would have added years or shut the whole thing down."

"Julia Butterfly Hill," says Albert, looking at his laptop.

"What about her?"

"She was a success. She occupied that redwood for 738 days with Earth First! support. She saved the tree and got a preservation zone around it that extended two-hundred feet."

"A limited success," says Chris. "All right, I'll give you that one, but it doesn't change the fact that monkeywrenching in that case perpetuated animosity. Does your source there say what happened after the agreement?"

Albert scrolls down and stops. He reads to himself. With minor facial rearrangements, he expresses dirge-like consternation with how far mankind has come since pre-Fall garden imagery. He reads aloud, "According to Tree Weaver, vandals later cut the tree with a chainsaw. A gash in the two-hundred-foot-tall redwood was discovered in November 2000 by one of Hill's supporters. Observers at the scene said the cut measured thirty-two inches deep and nineteen feet around the base, somewhat less than half the circumference of the tree. The gash was treated with an herbal remedy, and the tree was stabilized with steel cables. As of spring 2007, the tree was doing well with new growth each year." He pauses. "2007? I wonder how she's done since then." He searches, searches, and reports, "According to sanctuaryforest.org, 'Though the experts had predicted that Luna would soon show signs of die-back, in 2016 the canopy continues to look green and strong, and every year shows signs of new growth.'" Albert sits back. "What the fuck is wrong with people who would do that to a thousand-year-old tree?"

They contemplate the scope of human wrongness and the vulnerability of trees.

"We all have blood on our hands," says AJ. "So to speak."

Albert stares at AJ for a second and intuits what he means.

"Do you know how many trees are felled to make the books sold each year in this country?" Albert asks Chris.

"Thirty million," says Mary.

"Thirty million," Albert says. "Three hundred million in a decade. About..."

"About a billion and a half since he's been on the earth," says Mary.

"About a billion and a half since I've been on the earth," says Albert. He facilitates a lull. They all attempt to visualize that many trees and fail.

"When you factor in domestic manufacture of dimensional lumber, plywood, toilet paper, copy paper, toothpicks, cabinetry, and so on," Albert says to Chris, "who knows what the number is. AJ's right. We're all complicit. We're selective when it comes to moral indignation."

"Take it easy," Mary says.

"Grandeur worked in Luna's favor, as it should have. But a minor alteration in perspective shows us that a hemlock is as grand. A poplar is as grand. So why is no one sitting in the thirty-million trees condemned for annual domestic book production? Where's the hemlock's Butterfly Hill? Where's the poplar's?"

"Right on," says AJ, holding up and out his teacup to make public ideological accordance. "It could be you."

"Anybody in the mood for watermelon?" Albert asks.

AJ elevates his hand above his head and looks around. When Chris and Mary indicate that they are in no watermelon mood, he puts it down.

Albert opens the refrigerator and takes out a watermelon more or less the size and roundness of a regulation dodgeball. He sets it on the cutting board and lays his left hand on its top so that it doesn't roll while he unsheathes a chef's knife from its block.

"Big tree, small tree. Old tree, young tree. No tree wants to be reduced to a commodity," says AJ, veering toward a lilt.

"What is that?" Chris asks. "A song?"

AJ shrugs and sets his teacup on the counter.

The sound of a substantial severance dominates a moment and is over when the blade hits the cutting board. The watermelon is bisected.

"Probably the boys will want a piece," says Albert.

"Probably," says Mary, sitting in the seat that Albert left.

Albert bisects each half, wondering in that brief time what differentiates meiosis from mitosis, and then lays the chef's knife in the sink without producing a metallic clink. He takes a stack of four plates from a cabinet and extends the stack toward AJ, who accepts the top plate.

"Help yourself," says Albert.

Appraising each slice, concave and reminiscent of an ineffective wedge, and suddenly not wanting to seem greedy or excessively self-deprecating, AJ chooses that slice which appears to occupy the watermelon median, a designation rendered on the basis of such fine distinctions as to make him wonder if the median is an illusion and his choice in fact is an offense against his friend and host, a violation of an ancient code, and sets that slice on his plate as though the act of setting is no longer in his hands. Observing furtively the other faces for a sign that verifies he has transgressed and recognizing none, he realizes he is somewhat bugging out and chuckles.

"What's so funny?" Albert asks.

"I'm bugging out."

"About what?" asks Albert, setting Jake and Ryan's watermelon slices on the next two plates.

"The hospitality code."

"The ancient code of hospitality," says Albert, as if longing for a simpler time.

"Xenia," says Chris.

"What?" asks Mary.

"Xenia is what the Greeks called it."

"How many Americans do you suppose are bugging out right now because of xenia?" asks Albert.

"It's over. It was low intensity," says AJ, picking up his share of the watermelon with his right hand. He assesses the logistics of consuming it with just the one hand while his plate is in the other, sets it back down on the plate, and says to Mary, "Mind if I sit?"

"Tell us why you bugged out over xenia."

Albert leaves with one plate of watermelon in each hand and can be heard expressing fruit-based salutations in a mellow register, affectionate and stable.

With the language of the body, AJ says okay to Mary's stipulation. He sets his plate on the table, sits, picks up his watermelon share in both hands, and takes a bite that to politer sorts might seem uncivil.

"Greenhouse watermelon?"

Mary nods.

"Delicious."

"Thank you."

"AJ," Albert says, reentering the kitchen.

"Albert."

"Xenia should be a reassuring thing," says Albert, leaning back against the counter.

"Right on."

"And it wasn't?" Albert splits his watermelon into two pieces.

"No, it was," says AJ. "Mary welcomed me and gave me tea. You gave me first pick of the watermelon. You honored me. No questions asked. Except when Mary asked me if I just smoked weed, no questions asked. You both held up the host end of the covenant." He shark bites his watermelon. "First I thought I might be violating my end. I was focused too intensely on propriety. As you know," AJ says to Albert, "weed's intensification properties I take to be a form of insight. Like miniature ecstatic revelations. So I really focused on what I believed the weed was trying to communicate to me about the scope of code violation. If I choose the big piece, am I expressing a regard for self that's opposite to what a guest should stand for? If I choose the small piece, am I saying that I think your hospitality needs circumscribing, and, in so presuming, doing you dishonor? That's how the bug-out started."

"But the watermelon pieces seemed of equal size," says Chris.

"Eventually I came to that conclusion," AJ says.

"That's it?" asks Mary.

AJ shakes his head. He gets down to the rind on one side of his watermelon. Holding his allotment of the gourd fruit with both hands still, he says, "You know how weed will sometimes lead you down a false path, giving you a tour of some illusion, when, without you understanding how, you find you're on a true path where the meaning of reticulating leaf veins or whatever suddenly is crystal clear to you?"

"The Quest of the White Stag," says Albert.

AJ points the nibbled rind end of his watermelon at Albert to express not rudeness but acknowledgment of the ethereal and heretofore unspoken for ideas and energies that bodies otherwise distinct discover sometimes they are similarly receptive to.

"Yes," says AJ. "Xenia was my white stag. It tempted me to bug out, and I fell for it." He pauses, working on the watermelon flesh and contemplating how temptation could be spun as a survival mechanism, an advantage that biology or God or forces yet to be revealed selected for. "How long ago could it have been when xenia wasn't even possible because the business of survival made it so that hospitality was too big of a liability?" He has the eyes and beard and head hair of a man approaching holiness or wisdom on a mountain that is not conveniently accessible. "How long ago could it have been when xenia began to feel right, when a guy decided to extend a piece of watermelon or whatever to a guy he wasn't obviously connected to because the unconnected guy just looked like he could use a piece of watermelon or whatever?" AJ shakes his head and takes a bite. "Was that the beginning of morality and empathy? Was that when we decided it made evolutionary sense to share a little in the name of hospitality and mutual defense? That's when it hit me. Xenia these days has got to have an interspecies application. When you look at it objectively and through the eyes of, say, a opossum, all we do is take." He takes a bite of watermelon flesh and nears the rind. "And this is where I think my bug-out ultimately was leading me. I realize that watermelon size is just a quibble in the grand scheme, and I realize you can't just give a piece of watermelon to a opossum and believe that really fixes anything systemically. I mean, yes, you can put a piece of watermelon out at night and probably a nearby opossum will accept your hospitality and show some sign of opossum gratitude that will remain invisible to you. I mean." He pauses. "What I mean is xenia these days between the species, meaning human xenia extended to the other species, can't just be about that sort of hospitality. It has to be preemptive or restorative. Without the native habitat intact, what good is one fourth of a watermelon? Juicy, yes. Refreshing, yes. But nothing when it comes to long-term sustenance and an unbroken, opossum-centered homeland."

"That was beautiful," says Albert through a mouthful of watermelon.

"Clementine Wreckage seems to have linguistic benefits," says Mary.

"It does optimize," says AJ. "And another thing that bugging out made clear to me. The Luna situation and the situation with the Veazie Dam are not analogous. The parties that extended xenia to the Penobscot River and its various dependents through the legal process, noble parties though they were, were free of certain pressures. For example, they were not confronted with machinery designed to fell in no time what it took a thousand years to grow. If Julia Butterfly Hill had held out hope for civil remedy and didn't monkeywrench, then Luna would have been cut down. No doubt. My point here being that extremity is necessary sometimes. Even maybe violence in the interest of preempting some injustice or beginning to restore what done injustice ruined and extending by the one way or the other xenia to Mother Nature and what we forget, because we have been schooled to so forget, are our cohabitants, endowed with certain rights no matter what the Constitution says or doesn't say."

"Even if extremity is detrimental to the cause?" asks Chris.

"Who's to say what's detrimental to the cause until the dust has settled?"

"I think you're looking at it," Albert says to Chris, "from the perspective of a product-driven person."

"Something tells me I should feel offended."

"All I'm saying is you're operating under the presumption you'll be around to see the outcome of your efforts. You expect and sort of need to see your goal achieved. Not everyone is working under that presumption."

"For example."

"For example. *For* example," Albert dallies, trying as a self-respecting former English teacher to enlist applicable canonical support. A minute passes. Then he seems illuminated by the process of retrieval. "For example, in *A Tale of Two Cities*, one half of a revolutionary married couple fears he won't live long enough to see the revolution realized. The other half is certain that their efforts and their sacrifices have already helped to make the revolution inevitable. As far as she's concerned, it doesn't matter whether they're around to see it. They already laid the groundwork, targeted who needed targeting. If they get imprisoned, so what? If they get beheaded, so what? They are not the movement. If the movement can't survive them, how substantial can the movement be?"

AJ looks up from his rictus of a watermelon. "If you love it, set it free."

"It's a pattern that's been repeated immemorially. Identify a grievous injury, seek civil remedy if you believe that sort of thing is viable, experience the disillusion that afflicts the patient seeker of redress, go dark, get organized, direct collective energies toward something that the fellow travelers agree on more or less, decide on methods, strategize, get right with how long the odds are and what you are willing to put up with loss-wise, which, if you're commitment is legitimate, is everything, put all of it in motion, and keep going even if it starts to seem like in your time things probably won't break your way." Albert pauses as if mentally performing simple math. "Like John Brown. Was he detrimental to the cause of abolition? Did politer abolitionists denounce his tactics? Whether you agree or not with his decision to use violence, you can't say he didn't have a nationally transformative effect on which way ultimately the thing would go. The guy was not a masterful tactician, but you can't deny he was galvanic."

"Galvanic?" Mary asks.

"Galvanic. Galvanizing. Like he roused the population through a process that was metaphorically electrical."

"Why?"

"He hated slavery."

"I mean why use that word."

"It came to me. I had no reason to reject it." Albert finishes his second watermelon half and sets it next to the other on the plate beside the sink. He wipes his hands and says to AJ, "When you're done with that, I'll take the rind for compost."

"Done," says AJ, handing him the plate.

"I lost my train of thought," says Albert.

"John Brown," says Chris.

"Galvanic," Mary says.

"John Brown was a cocklebur," says Albert like a person whose conclusion has been peer reviewed. "He grabbed the country's consciousness and held on with a prick's tenacity. You ever see a picture of him? Basically a human cocklebur."

"A galvanic human cocklebur," says Chris.

"Is there a Civil War without him?" Albert asks, ignoring Chris's wonderment and mockery, though privately he tells himself the wonderment proportion is ascendant. "Probably. When, though? 1880? 1900? AJ's right about extremity. Selectively employed, extremity is no transgression, or at least is less of a transgression than whatever it's selectively employed against."

There is a period of quiet and refocusing on chaga tea. The onomatopoeia violence of a vintage Mickey Mouse cartoon transmits more clearly from the other room.

"Fetishizing violence," Chris says, "as the last hope of the righteous and believing that, if you could only slightly overtop the violence the unrighteous have been perpetrating, you would have the means to rid yourself of the unrighteous worldview and install and propagate your own have been repeated immemorially, I'll grant you that. But they're irrational."

"Do you believe the Queen of England is irrational?"

Chris squints at Albert with the quizzical expression that sequential conversationalists reserve for those who seem to value the non sequitur for its disruptive force alone.

"Explain to me how Queen Elizabeth is technically the owner of one sixth of our planet's land mass," Albert says.

"Is that true?" asks AJ.

"I believe it is," says Albert.

"You're trying," Chris says, "to equate the violent means available to grass-roots movements with the basically unlimited coercion power of the state and multinationals. It's asymmetrical. A false equivalency. That's why I'm saying it's irrational. If your opponent is the state or some big multinational like Nestlé and you think that violent tactics will advance your movement, you're irrational."

"So if a grass-roots guy is violent in the name of forest preservation, he's irrational," says Albert. "If a royal is violent in the name of wealth consolidation, then it's veneration time and a parade is held to celebrate her rationality."

"Fucked up," says AJ, swirling tea dregs. "Not cool."

"Behavior that is rational to someone working for a certain interest of the state and with the backing of the state would be insane to someone working for the rights of nature. The state actor operates within prescribed parameters but deviates when risk seems manageable. If managing risk requires violence and if violence makes the shadow people money, violence that the levelheaded person would regard as emanating from irrational decision-making is forgiven as a hazard of securing democratic freedoms or excused because of unforeseeable conditions on the ground or not discussed at all or flipped around to make it seem the levelheaded person is irrational and doesn't have the policy chops or the connections or the regional immersion or the mental nimbleness to understand what's been achieved. You take a monumental fuck-up, what should be reported as the sort of dictatorial irrationality America is famous for despising, and you use what tools your government affords you and you complement your sponsor's apparatus and you spin until the levelheaded people can't keep up and get exhausted with believing there will be accountability and quit to care about more life-affirming things."

"Sounds like Iraq," says Mary.

"Iraq, Afghanistan, Libya, El Salvador, Nicaragua, Vietnam, Korea. Pick a country. All you have to do if you're the U.S. is mention national security, our way of life, and freedom preservation, and you're covered. Who's above the U.S. for accountability-enforcement purposes? The U.N.? The Hague? The Geneva Conventions? Who can get away with what the U.S. government can get away with? Not El Salvador. Not Libya. So why would anyone believe a monkeywrencher can? What matters is what you can get away with. That determines whether what you tried to do was rational or not." She pauses. "It's a childish perspective in a sense, but it's instructive. Look at what the U.S. did to North Korea on the pretext that it was a Communist domino: bombed cities, dropped canisters of plague-infected flies, bombed hydroelectric dams and flooded everything, destroyed the means of food production, killing all told a quarter of the population. By standard after standard, these are war crimes. Crimes against humanity. But to this day the U.S. has acknowledged nothing. No wrongdoing. No accountability. Not even a symbolic gesture to suggest we've come to realize that we fucked up."

"Plague-infected flies," says AJ. "That's a special sort of evil."

"But was it irrational to do it knowing you would get away with it? And not only get away with it but benefit from it."

AJ, Mary, and Albert contemplate the interplay of geopolitics and rationality and abdication of humane essentials. They wonder if morality becomes a luxury for public servants of a certain grade and if foregoing it is noble, a condemnatory sacrifice such people make because what's tangible to them and central existentially is capital and country.

"Are you familiar with the Nimbus Dam?" asks Chris. "In California?"

Head shakes, pursed lips, downcast eyes, and repositioned body parts express to Chris more powerfully than words that AJ, Mary, and Albert feel the shame the unenlightened who are oriented toward improvement-seeking are supposed to feel when they are confronted with a clear and inescapable conclusion of their ignorance of something as essential to the healthy coursing of their nation's rivers as their nation's hydroelectric infrastructure and its water-management philosophy and its relationship to all things riverine.

"About ten years ago," Chris says, "a guy named Eric McDavid and three others, one of whom turned out to be an FBI informant, planned to blow it up. McDavid later said in court they weren't sure if, once the deed was done, they would attribute it to ELF or not, but they were certain that the risks of blowing up the dam, including possibly, collaterally, the death of innocents, were worth restoring water quality and fish migration routes. The sentiment was noble. I want water quality restored. I want fish to migrate freely. But his means were violent. Whether any human would have died or not, his means were violent. Violent means beget responses that are violent. It's just microcosmic warfare, and it's not restorative. His ends were unrealistic. Even if he had the demolitions expertise to breach the dam, what then? Did he believe the federal government would say, 'Okay, ELF got us. Let's just let the river flow'? McDavid and his two conspirators, who testified against him, were irrational."

"They testified against him?" Albert asks. "That's exactly why Dave Foreman says that monkeywrenching should be individual."

"It doesn't matter, Albert," Chris says. "Even if they didn't testify and even if there was no FBI informant and even if McDavid had the demolitions expertise and even if he breached the dam, it wouldn't have achieved what he envisioned. Radical idealism not moored to reality is as destructive as what the idealist is hoping to remove."

"So what?" asks Albert.

"So McDavid went to federal prison. He got out on a technicality, but still he served like ten years. The Nimbus Dam is still intact and operational. So nothing."

"I mean what's the alternative. Do nothing?"

"Organize. Advocate and educate. Build coalitions. Pressure legislators. That's what got the Veazie Dam removed. That's what McDavid should have done. And if you have to and you can, you sue."

"What happens if you lose?" asks Albert, arms crossed.

"You just lose," says Chris.

"You just lose."

"It happens," Chris says. "You regroup."

Albert shakes his head. "Historically, extremity has been the next step."

"Right on," AJ says.

"Eras change. Conflict-resolution models change," says Chris, examining the tabletop with an intensity that seems inspired by the uniformity and variation of its wood grain coexisting as if uniformity alone would be unnatural, as if variation only would be insufficient witness to the grandeur of the organizing principle. "You know how many dams have been removed from U.S. waters in the past hundred years or so?" She looks up from the tabletop but does not pause to leave room for a speculation period. "One thousand four hundred ninety-two. Eighty-five percent of those were removed in the last thirty years. Eighty-six dams were removed last year, and American Rivers, which was instrumental in the Veazie Dam removal, had a role in fourteen of those. And not a single one was the result of someone like McDavid blowing it up. Zero."

"Those statistics are impressive," AJ says. He then inserts his corresponding index finger in his right ear and reciprocates it lightly and at no great depth before removing it without examination. "Never underestimate the power numbers have to moderate emotional responses seems to be the lesson here."

"You're saying no extremity at all in defense of the environment ever," Albert says.

"That's what I'm saying."

"What about a baby-Hitler situation?" Albert asks. "If you could travel back in time and kill the baby Leo Henrik Baekeland, would you?"

"Who was he?" asks Chris.

"He made the first synthetic plastic. He invented Bakelite." When this information yields no recognition glimmer, Albert says, "Assuming the production of synthetic plastic dies with him, would you humanely kill the baby Baekeland?"

Chris's eyes move in a manner that reveals interior consideration and a moral inventory newly underway.

"No plastic gyres in the oceans," Albert says. "No microbeads. No dead whales stuffed with plastic bags. No straws impaled in turtle nostrils. Cancer rates on land would plummet. Think about the suffering across the species lines that killing baby Baekeland would eliminate."

A game-show tension builds up in the kitchen.

"You aren't dealing with reality," says Chris.

"It's just a thought experiment. A parlor game," says Albert. "Nothing bad will happen to you in the afterlife. Your answer can't be used against you in the matter of damnation."

"Kill him," AJ says.

"You have to kill him," Mary says.

The four of them are silent, and the silence briefly fosters the impression that an actual infanticide is on the table here.

Chris puts her hands to her face as if to be concealed from observation while she struggles with the moral code and puts her elbows on the table. Nodding twice, she takes her hands away and shows her face.

"I do," she says. "I have to kill him."

"So you concede that violence sometimes can eliminate a greater evil," Albert presses.

"Hypothetically," says Chris.

"I take no pleasure in this victory," says Albert.

"Victory?" Chris asks. "You're using an impossible scenario to come to a conclusion that is almost always false when you apply it to the real world and an individual or small group against a force that is beyond them."

"I disagree. It's called extrapolation."

"Extrapolation is when you proceed from something known and then hypothesize from that. But you proceed from a hypothesis that's based on fantasy and leads to nothing known."

Albert isn't sure if her extrapolation definition is of dictionary quality, but her delivery suggests it is.

"I think John Brown would disagree," he says.

"John Brown didn't free the slaves," Chris says with the exasperation of a person arguing with someone she believes enlisted in the ignoramus army voluntarily. "The government did. The state did, and it didn't travel back in time and kill the baby who in real life grew up and brought the first slave to the New World."

"Does anybody want a brandy?" Mary asks.

"How old is it?" AJ asks.

"I don't know."

"Okay," says AJ.

"Why not," Chris says.

Albert gets four snifters from the cabinet, aligns them on the counter, gets the brandy bottle from the cabinet, and observes the four pours with an intensity that indicates a personal investment in equivalency and shared experience. He serves each snifter, placidly and solemnly, as if the substance it contains is unifying and liturgical, the sort of distillation in the sort of vessel one would be remiss to take as cavalierly as a whiskey shot. Accordingly, each snifter is received with the humility that characterizes gracious registration of an incommensurate exchange. They swirl their snifters and inspect the brandy fumes with focused nasal inhalations.

"Love that smell," says Mary. "We should have heated up the glasses."

After several seconds, the initial swirling and olfactory-inspection period concludes.

"To," says Albert, holding up his snifter and extending it in an inclusion gesture toward the middle of the group.

The other three do likewise, and the four of them, positioned thus, say nothing for some seconds, wondering what object to supply that preposition with.

"To Ram Dass," Albert says.

"To Ram Dass," they repeat as they clink glasses and imbibe.

The four of them are silent as their throats and torsos warm. They breathe as though the respiration process has been consciously renewed.

"Is he alive?" asks Chris.

"He is, I think," says Albert. "I believe he's still on Twitter."

AJ puts down his snifter and consults his phone. He says, "From Ram Dass eight hours ago: 'The predicament is that truth doesn't actually have form. Everything that's in form is really only relatively true.'"

They sip their brandies, breathe out, and consider.

"Could you read that one more time?" asks Albert.

AJ reads Ram Dass's tweet again.

"Everything that's in form is really only relatively true," says Albert.

"Everything that's in form is really only relatively true," says Mary.

"Everything that's in form is really only relatively true," says Chris.

They sip their brandies, breathe out, and consider. Meaning is elusive.

AJ scrolls and says, "I overlooked Ram Dass's use of an ellipsis.

'Everything that's in form is really only relatively true.' Ellipsis, double space, and then he ends with: 'Words are just the Vehicle.' Capital V."

"Then what are actions?" Albert asks.

"Just a vehicle," says Chris. "Only relatively true."

"Then what is anything?" asks Albert. "What's the point of human agency?"

"Can I see your phone for a second, AJ?" Chris asks.

AJ hands it over.

Chris taps and scrolls. She stops and reads in silence. "Here we go. Ram Dass says, 'Our relationships with each other can be vehicles for our unity, and they can be vehicles for our entrapment...In my relationship with you, who I think I am affects who I see you to be.'"

"His worldview seems to tend toward the vehicular," says Albert.

"Who do you think you are?" Chris asks.

"Who do I think I am?"

"Who do you think you are?"

Albert feels directly challenged to articulate a creed or to account for his existence in a way Ram Dass would approve of, meaning in a way that joyfully embraces the illusion of the body and assuredly anticipates how beatific it will be to recognize the spirit as the universal entity, beyond vehicular restriction and unbounded. But articulation and accounting do not flow, and he is on the verge of saying something humorous and snide, deflecting their attention from his present inability to speak transcendently but plainly, truly, as a guru or an unaffiliated wise man in this situation would. Instead, he sips his brandy, keeps the snifter near his lips as though another sip is imminent, and wonders who he thinks he is.

"Well," Chris asks, "why'd you go to Cooper Brook today?"

"Trail Magic," Albert says, his snifter now chest high.

"Why do that?"

Albert shrugs. "I've been a Trail-Magic beneficiary."

"You were grateful for the kindness?"

Albert nods and sips.

"So *you* performed a kindness?"

"I suppose."

"So, on some level, would you say you think that you're a kind person?"

"Generally."

"Why else go to Cooper Brook?"

"Are you using the Socratic method on me?"

"Why else go to Cooper Brook?" Chris asks.

"I like the woods."

"What about them?"

"I don't know. You know. They're peaceful."

"So, on some level, would you say you think that you're a kind person who likes peace and nature?"

"I would say that's fair to say."

"So why let your relationship with an external force entrap you into acting counter to your self-perception?"

Albert thinks about the nature of the human personality and the survival value of interior cohesion and exterior aggression that betrays the self's ideal parameters, but, as he repositions his posterior against the counter and begins again to elevate his snifter, Albert realizes that survival value is, in application, merely biological, concerned with preservation of the body, the corporeal extensions, offshoots, when what Chris appears to have in mind as an alternative to the entrapment vehicles the self unwittingly abets is something more holistic and more difficult to put the earthly finger on. He can't at present answer, so to stall he sips his brandy.

He reads aloud the wording on the light-green bag from which he took the Duvel glasses.

"'This bag is our commitment to the environment. Reusable, recyclable, and biodegradable. Reduces landfill volume.'" He pauses. "Well, I guess I'm someone who doesn't believe a word of this."

Chapter Two: Garland, Maine

This morning Albert and his family enter H.C. Haynes Incorporated's minor property across the discontinued road from their cedar-shingled camp. He says disciple-wise, "A man is rich in proportion to the number of things he can afford to let alone." He says this, expecting no response because he quotes this passage from Thoreau each time he walks through here with them. He used to explicate, but now he champions the source quotation's gnomic quality by saying nothing further. Albert says this when they enter H.C. Haynes's property as if his saying so out loud will ward off something the adult in him acknowledges must someday come, and in that sense it is no different than his solitary, verbalized petitions for familial stasis, for the family health and happiness and harmony to be by incantation and divine reception and the blessing protocol indemnified as long as possible against the ultimately unsettling trajectory.

This morning Albert and his family enter H.C. Haynes's property across the discontinued road because the cycles of selective logging have improved it such that there are skidder trails on which to stroll, a dirt road leading to the Cemetery Road, and relatively unadulterated sunlight of the sort that is not to be had in Albert's unlogged woods. As Albert quotes Thoreau, they pass the slash piles and take the skidder trail that leads them past regenerating cedars, pines, balsam firs, and hemlocks to the apple orchard that H.C. Haynes Incorporated left alone.

Watts runs ahead and pauses, nose down, sensitive to the diversity of passages. Jake and Ryan follow Watts's lead and pass by Albert and Mary. They walk in silence, flanked by evergreens primarily. The flanking gives their stroll the air of a procession.

The sunlit bower quality responsible for all the tingling going on within their torsos as they amble down the skidder trail gives way to atmospheric openness and orchard, apple-blossom whiteness, broad green lanes, and radiance it would be sacrilege to gauge exclusively in watts. They take the only trampled lane, the one that they have taken many times before, and follow it to where the formal, lineal apple-tree plantation ends.

"Johnny Appleseed became a vegetarian in later life," says Albert.

"I know."

"The only Swedenborgian that I can think of," Albert says. "Aside from Swedenborg."

Mary doesn't reply. She has heard this all before.

"Divine communion through the agency of contemplation."

"Like plant meditation," Mary says.

"According to what Swedenborg revealed about his personal communications with the angels, I would say his most important mystic revelation is that someone's inner nature in this life becomes that person's being absolutely in the afterlife."

"Johnny Appleseed is with the apple trees."

"He is. And if your inner nature in this life inspired you to frack, then in the afterlife you're stuck with your proprietary fluid and whatever fossil fuel was dearest to your inner nature."

Mary looks around the meadow, at the apple trees organically disseminated, at the boys, at Watts who hops through high grass, disappearing, reappearing as he goes. She says, "I'd like to think this represents our inner nature in this life."

"That would be nice."

Albert and Mary sit down near an apple tree on grass that has been flattened due to visits such as this one. Mary slides her backpack off and takes a thermos and a pair of matching camp cups out. She pours a cup of chaga tea, extending it to Albert.

"Thanks."

She pours one for herself. They sip and watch the boys, who follow Watts from tree to tree and deviate occasionally to entertain some notion.

"He planted Rambos," says Albert.

Mary sips and elevates her eyebrows.

"Johnny Appleseed. The last known survivor of the trees he planted still produces apples somewhere in Ohio."

Mary watches Jake and Ryan studying the texture of a trunk.

"I realize it's probably because in market terms they're relatively worthless," Albert says, "but I admire H.C. Haynes for leaving these."

"Me too."

"A man is rich in proportion to the number of things he can afford to let alone," says Albert.

Mary says, "I haven't heard that one before."

Watts sniffs at the apple tree they sit by. Jake and Ryan close in.

"You guys want some tea?" asks Mary.

"Yes, please," Jake says.

Ryan, Jake's twin, nods.

Mary pours two cups and hands them out.

"When you guys finish that, we'll do a tick check," Mary says.

Albert looks across the meadow at the line of evergreens.

"Three trillion trees on Earth," says Albert, "and we need a trillion more to neutralize a decade's worth of carbon spewed."

"Let it go," says Mary, indicating via facial drift that Albert's talk of insufficient forest density and how it factors into the expanding ecological catastrophe might trigger in the boys the stressful sense that personal control from childhood on up is a delusion.

Albert says, "I wish I could. I know the Buddha says all suffering arises from attachment, but does that suggest the Buddha, in the present circumstances, wouldn't plant a trillion carbon-neutralizing trees if it were possible? As long as he was stuck here, how could he not plant? You see my problem."

"Let it go," says Mary. "Drink your tea."

He does not let it go, but he says nothing. The domestic compromise. She watches him askance and waits for him to speculate if what must be the Buddha's natural tree-plantation inclinations would invalidate what he has said about attachment, suffering, the self, and all the rest, but Albert sips his tea and looks across the meadow at the line of evergreens.

The boys sit on the grass with Watts and sip their tea. They scan the high grass for the turkeys that they know strut through here. Jake puts down his cup and from his pocket takes a turkey call. He rasps the top slate several times against the two strips of slate beneath and waits. He rasps again and waits. A turkey gobbles in the distance. Ryan sets his cup down and extends a hand to Jake, who shares the turkey call. Ryan rasps the top slate several times against the two thin strips of slate beneath and waits. The gobbles multiply. He rasps again and waits. The gobbles multiply. The upper portions of the turkeys surface in the high grass at the meadow's edge, where the transition back to evergreens begins.

"Make sure Watts doesn't chase them," Albert says.

Jake clips the leash to Watts's collar.

Ryan rasps again. The turkeys mill and gobble.

Mary studies Jake and Ryan's skin, what patches she can see without intruding on the magic of the turkey interlude. She searches for a dark dot that is on the move or for a dark dot, camouflaged by stillness, that a hasty, non-maternal glance might overlook as harmless mole or freckle.

Suddenly, the turkeys vocalize distress and run in two lines to the cover of the woods.

Above the tree line, an unnatural object hovers.

"What the hell is that?" asks Albert, pointing. "Is that a drone?"

"Looks like a drone," says Mary.

"What the fuck?" says Albert.

"You're not supposed to let external circumstances take control of your emotions," Jake says.

"My apologies," says Albert. "Thanks for the reminder. I've regained control."

"It is a drone," says Jake.

They watch the drone, maintaining elevation, steadily advancing toward them. It stops above them, humming, hovering, and then continues toward the discontinued road and disappears beyond the trees.

"I'll try to follow it," says Albert, standing.

"How?" says Mary. "Sit."

He sits.

"I wonder who would fly a drone through here," says Mary.

"*Why* would someone fly a drone through here is what I'd like to know," says Albert.

"Maybe it's just recreational," says Mary.

"People use these things for topographic surveys now," says Albert, looking where the drone last was. "Like for the East-West Corridor. This could be for that."

"We would have heard."

"It's been too quiet. Like the Mother Kite said, 'There is something ominous behind the silence.'"

"What's that from?" asks Mary.

"Things Fall Apart."

"You're paranoid."

"What's paranoid?" asks Jake.

"It's like when you're afraid, but there's no reason you should feel afraid," says Mary.

"You're not supposed to let external circumstances take control of your emotions," Jake says.

"I'm not letting them," says Albert, looking where the drone last was. "I'm in control."

Mary, Albert, Jake, and Ryan take turns with the turkey call, although the turkeys do not reappear or call back.

They sip their chaga tea.

They listen to a meadowlark and do not try to undermine the singularity of what they hear. They snack on natural foods and do not really gather how to give the antioxidants their due.

The drone does not return.

They leave the meadow and the scattered apple trees. They pass the ordered apple trees and take the skidder trail past cedars, pines, balsam firs, and hemlocks, through the sunlit bower quality that, organ-wise, affects the ambling family more profoundly in the going than it had affected them in the coming.

Where the skidder trail becomes the clearing, Watts rigidifies and growls at two people standing by a Forester's open hatchback. One is male and wears a button-down short-sleeved shirt and khaki pants. The other, female, holds a drone flight controller, gets distracted for some seconds by the growling, and refocuses on the controller. The man, observing Watts, comes from behind the hatchback and approaches, casually, assuredly, as though he's carrying a firearm, which he is not.

When he sees Albert and the others in the clearing, he stands still and says, "Good morning. I apologize, but this is private property."

"We own the camp across the road," says Albert.

The man says nothing and appears to wait for further information.

"You with H.C. Haynes?" asks Albert.

"No, sir." Balding and bespectacled, the man is nearing seventy.

Albert now appears to wait for further information. Then he says, "We have permission from the owner."

The man says, "H.C. Haynes no longer owns this property."

"Since when?"

"A few months back."

Albert looks more closely at the man, and he remembers.

"You're Harold Brown," says Albert. Then he glances at the woman, and he wonders why she looks familiar. He has seen a photo of her on the internet. It comes to him. He recognizes her as Eva Desjardins, the CEO of Waterloo and Kirk Renewable Natural Resources.

"I'm sorry, have we met?" the man asks, polite but guarded.

"I was at your Dover presentation back in February," Albert says.

He chuckles. "Not a friendly audience." He eyeballs Albert, trying to remember if he stood and spoke against the East-West Corridor proposal.

"No, it wasn't."

"You're opposed," probes Harold.

Albert has not read Sun Tzu, but he imagines what Sun Tzu would do in such a parley.

He decides Sun Tzu, to misdirect and lull his enemy, would lie.

"I've kept an open mind," says Albert.

"That is all we ask," says Harold, easing. "Harold Brown," he says to Mary, Jake, and Ryan, waving to acknowledge them as interested parties. After introductions, Harold says, "So let me ask you. What are your concerns about the project?"

Albert's certain that anticipating your opponent's moves is central to the Sun-Tzu way, yet Albert failed to see the question coming.

As he tries to formulate a misdirection worthy of Sun Tzu, Mary says, "For one thing, one map shows it coming right through here."

"I heard about that map," says Harold. "It was bogus. We would never circulate a hand-drawn map."

"The Corridor isn't coming through here then?" asks Mary.

Albert struggles to respond to Harold's inquiry as he imagines Sun Tzu would.

"We don't know all the route specifics at this time," says Harold.

"Yet you bought this property," says Mary.

"Yes, ma'am," says Harold.

Mary opens wide her eyes, conveying her awareness of the obvious.

Albert wants to ask if Harold bought it on behalf of Eva Desjardins, whom Albert knows bought properties through Black Bear Forest LLC, Penobscot Forest LLC, and Kennebec West LLC along the length of the potential route. Albert wants to tell him that he did the deed searches and he knows that Eva Desjardins and Black Bear Forest bought the property off Route 16, west of Abbot, on the road to Russell Mountain, where the seismic-refraction survey was done. But Albert tells himself Sun Tzu would have advised him not to tip his hand so early and so easily.

"And one of our concerns," says Albert, channeling the coolness of a general of the Eastern Zhou, "is no one's made an offer on our property."

Mary, disbelieving, stares at Albert.

"Well, as I said," says Harold, "all the route specifics haven't been determined."

"But the drone's determining the ones you don't know?" Albert asks.

"It's helping, yes," says Harold.

"So you can't say if we'll get an offer?" Albert asks.

"At present, no," says Harold, "but I can say, if you were to get an offer, it would be extended by July." He hands his card to Albert.

"July," says Albert, studying the information on the card.

"Mid- to late July," says Harold. "Good to know an offer interests you."

"I guess my interest would depend on what the offer is," says Albert.

"As it should," says Harold. "As it should."

"We should be getting back," says Mary.

Departure words and niceties ensue.

The family walks across the discontinued road to its imperiled camp and eighteen acres.

"What the fuck was that?" asks Mary in a whisper.

"I think he just confessed the Corridor is coming through here."

"I mean what's with your interest in an offer."

"Earth warriors don't say what I just said to Harold Brown. If he believes I'm interested in an offer, then he has no reason to suspect me as a monkeywrencher," Albert says.

"You're not a monkeywrencher, Albert."

"That's exactly what I want him to believe."

Chapter Three: Big Wilson

Experiments have proven that the Himalayan salt lamp doesn't negatively ionize the air, but Chris Atwater thinks there's something science must have missed. The sense of wellness that she gets when she sits in its presence is a sense she'd be a falsifier of the highest order to deny.

She's willing to concede that in the wasteland of the lab the Himalayan salt lamp's ionization powers have not been observed. She isn't anti-science. But she's willing to concede that sensitivity and intuition have their own ways of revealing truth. In the Himalayan salt lamp's case, her sensitivity and intuition tell her some phenomena are similar to social beings and require complements and kindred to fulfill their activation roles.

She sits before the salt lamp's pink glow, breathes as if the heated Himalayan salt and temperate she, combined, are ionizers. Outside, day breaks on the lake. The season of the open windows.

The lamp's salt was extracted from the Khewra Salt Mine, which one of Alexander the Great's horses, in the midst of that king's Hellenizing everything from Anatolia to India, reputedly digressed to lick, discovering a resource that has been productive for one potentate or other ever since.

A beneficiary of extraction and combustion all her life, Chris wondered at the time of purchasing the lamp if its reputed ionizing properties and its connection to the wisdom of the Himalayas justified the toilsome extraction efforts and the fuel burned overland and oversea to ship the salt from its primordial home in what for now is Pakistan. She told herself the salt would come regardless of her single purchase and in fact had come already, fully formed, a Himalayan salt lamp sitting in a warehouse somewhere in her country. Since that purchase, she has wrestled more than most Americans with the decision-making implications of the cog mentality.

Chris has Google Earthed the Khewra Salt Mine many times, and each time she is briefly comforted to see that the effects of over two millennia of salt extraction do not seem dramatically disruptive from the satellite's perspective, even when she zooms. But when she leans in and imagines what has gone on underground for over two millennia, she sees the surface calm as indispensable illusion—like the stand of trees that hides the clear-cut from the road or like the brook that Poland Spring employs to advertise that it would never mine what's not eternally renewed.

She sits before the salt lamp's pink glow, eyes closed, breathes what heat releases from the Himalayan crystals, and lets go. The breeze in from the window, and the barest lake-slosh in. The come and go. The give and take. The agitation and the soothing. Every day, the go-round, the suffusion. Caffeinated. Ionized. What difference does it make? She has imbibed the tonic somehow. She's awake.

She comes back to her eyes and clicks the salt lamp off. She looks around the kitchen. Is it time to keep a modest animal? The big hand on the clock above the table ticks to 12. The little hand is on the 6, the house wren. Birdsong. Chris looks at the twelve birds on the clock face and remembers how the celebrated ornithologist and naturalist got each of them to stay still long enough to represent its species in a painting.

"Humans, humans, humans," Chris says as she rises.

She goes into the living room and checks her backpack, slings it on, and looks around for an omission or a light left on.

She heads back to the kitchen, opens the door, and stands a while, half in, half out, looking at Lake Onawa, illuminated, calm, a ripple here and there, the trestle bridge above the trees.

On certain mornings, as on this one, she recalls the famous book that taught her how to see the basic objects of the world as code for the eternal confrontations of the mind. Where Chris once saw an ordinary door, the book said see the sanctity of the threshold, see the sacredness of the passage. So she saw the sanctity and saw the sacredness, but it was hard to live her life that way: to every day be stunned and humbled by the lintel, two jambs, and the doorsill framing the transition zone she passed through on her supposedly heroic way to what, when all was said and done, would be her Life; to recognize the little death and rebirth each departure and return were; to release the time or place or being that was put behind her on the other side of each closed door and to embrace what she now sided with.

People sometimes told her, "Live each day like it's your last." She thought the problem there was similar. As simple as it sounded, the imperative could not be followed faithfully. She thought of the insurance premiums that would go unpaid, the toenails that would go unpolished and unclipped, the prophylactics that would go untaken, the bacteria and plaque that would build up, the skin discolorations that would go unchecked, the exercises that would go undone, the lawn care that would go undone, the home repairs, the haircuts, the essential commerce and the inessential—everything that isn't what you'd want your last breaths spent on, everything that isn't what you'd want survivors to remember that you chose to do as you ran out of time, you would not do. You cannot live your life that way. Not really.

But one day, as she touched the knob and pulled the kitchen door toward her, she looked beyond that threshold at Lake Onawa, the light, the calm, the fleeting eddy of a threshold-testing pickerel, and the trestle bridge above the trees, and saw that the analogy did not align. She told herself that "Live each day like it's your last" was more or less the adage of the simpleton, the citizen of limited horizon, one who did not see the range of what could be. You did what you desired, and you died.

She told herself a threshold isn't that way. It is not one way. It is a way in and a way out, an end and a beginning. There's a line between the inside and the out. A line between this life on earth and something else. A line between the earth and all the water. A line between what humans are and woods. A line between what's down here and the sky. A line between the light and dark. A line between the sober and the high, the rational and the ecstatic. Lines bend. Lines blur. Everywhere a threshold separates what Chris Atwater knows and doesn't know, and every threshold is a separate invitation. Sounds like Eden.

Chris Atwater crosses over, locks the kitchen door, drives west a few minutes on the Valley Road, then south along the west side of Borestone Mountain. Just before the Montreal, Maine, & Atlantic Railway crossing, she pulls into a gravel lot and parks. The lot is empty otherwise, but soon a pickup crosses the track and parks beside her Subaru.

Mary Lesiak gets out and asks, "Have you been waiting long?"

"Just got here," Chris says. "Perfect timing."

"So the plan is hike along the rail bed for about two miles, take the AT down to Big Wilson Stream, and see if we can find some chaga."

"That's the plan," says Chris as she puts on her pack.

"The clouds supposedly are coming in," says Mary as she puts on her pack. "Forecast said it might rain later."

"You have rain gear?"

They walk on the rail bed for not quite a mile, Chris on one side of the track and Mary on the other, just the sound of agitated gravel and a pair of ravens to the north. Flanked by conifers, the track extends into the distance, blurs and curves, disappearing altogether into woods.

"We should take this all the way to Montreal," says Mary, shifting to the railroad ties and lengthening her stride.

"And then what?"

"Watch the Quebecois make condescending faces when I try to speak French."

Chris laughs. "It is a beautiful city, if you like that sort of thing, but I don't think I'd even make it to Lac-Megantic."

"Where the oil train blew up," says Mary.

"Too far," Chris says. "And anyway you've got the obligations."

"The obligations."

"You can't leave them all of a sudden and start speaking gringo French in Montreal."

The ravens fly down toward the railway corridor and watch them from the trees.

"The obligations wouldn't miss me for a day or two if there was food."

"Of course they would," says Chris.

They independently consider love's provisional and unconditional proportions.

The ravens fly across the railway corridor and watch them from the forest on the other side.

Mary pretends for several railroad ties that if she misses one and touches gravel she will break her mother's back.

"You heard about the alewives?" Mary asks.

"They went upriver to where they were born. To spawn."

"A bunch of them got caught up in the turbines at a dam," says Mary, switching to the rail bed, shortening her stride.

"What? Where?"

"Near Orono."

"The Stillwater Dam." Chris shakes her head. "How many died?"

"Bushels," Mary says. "I think it said a hundred-something."

Chris shakes her head. Her face contracts.

"How many in a bushel?" Mary asks.

"A hundred thirty-five."

A raven croaks.

As if to let the numbers sink in, they say nothing for the span of several railroad ties. But it is more a period of mourning or acknowledgment. They do not really bother with the math.

"At least the Ellsworth Alewife Harvester is happy," Chris sighs.

Mary looks at Chris to see if she will clarify.

"Brookfield Renewable's Mortality Event Plan—and you can bet that, if the owner of a dam is legally required to file a Mortality Event Plan, then everyone involved, from government officials all the way down, expects at some point a Mortality Event." She takes a breath and, in a flatter tone befitting someone who has seen this sort of thing before, continues, "Their plan stipulates that, in the event of a Mortality Event, the Ellsworth Alewife Harvester will be provided with the alewives the Event killed. For lobster bait."

They do not discuss the institutional deployment of the euphemism to express what was foreseeable catastrophe in language that declines to get hysterical and sidesteps the unpleasant process of assigning blame, allowing the community and everyone affected to move calmly forward to a time when what the messy past has taught us has been implemented operationally, which should be all the solace humans need to not get mired in the omissions, indiscretions, errors, negligence, what have you, of a time we all have worked so hard to leave behind.

"We told them this would happen, which was wasted breath since *they* knew this would happen. We've been trying to get that fucking dam on the decommission list for years."

Mary looks to the forest on the right side of the track and points to a white blaze on a tree.

"The trail south is just ahead," says Mary.

"I know the arc of the moral universe is long, but how long does it have to be before whatever's at the end doesn't feel like justice anymore? How long does nature have to wait?"

Chris studies the track's progression to the distance. Curvature, then disappearance. A raven croaks and flies north across the corridor. The other waits some wingbeats and then follows.

"If this track is the moral universe, then where does it bend toward justice? Up ahead where we lose sight of it? At Lac-Megantic? Montreal? By the time you get to Montreal, or even Lac-Megantic, do you really care about the alewives anymore? You're just so tired."

"Do you want to find a tree and meditate?" asks Mary.

"I can wait. The alewives and the track just got me thinking."

"No, it's my fault," Mary says. "It made no sense to mention it. It's not conducive."

Chris points to a white blaze on a hemlock to their left.

"I'm fine," she says. "It's just as likely that the arc bends this way."

They leave the rail bed and the vista. They lean slightly backward as they head into the drainage ditch and slightly forward as they leave it.

Past the blaze, the shade intensifies. The trail is root-slick, rock-slick, mud and duff and solid ground. Big Wilson Stream, unseen, sounds from this distance like a steady breeze through branches, needles, leaves. The world is interwoven, a community of greens and grays and browns. The pupils dilate, and the world seems older, grander, fable-bound, dependent on the ancient ways but willing to let slide the past offenses, finely tuned yet formless, open but bewildering, a consciousness that no cartographer has ever charted and no scientist has been admitted to or truly parsed. And there is life here that would captivate the outside world if it were found on Mars. The slugs cling. The mosquitoes rise. The fungi and the algae vitalize the lichen. And there's death here. Everywhere are passages. And there are smells.

They moderate their pace and step more carefully as they descend. Each slip on root or rock or mud reminds them that the earth is willing, briefly or for good, to let them go, but neither falls.

"A little wetter than I thought it would be," Mary says. "That could bode well." She looks around. "I have my doubts."

"About there being chaga here?"

"About there being chaga here. About a harvest in July. I've only ever scouted in the summer. Then I'd come back in the fall for the harvest."

They continue to descend. The air cools and humidifies as they get closer to Big Wilson.

"In certain chaga circles, summer harvesting is an offense. Like poaching. The tradition is to let the chaga grow in spring and summer and to harvest in the fall and winter when the water concentration in the chaga's at its lowest and the betulin is highest. Plus, it's easier to find the chaga when the leaves are down and easier to reach it when the ground is frozen and the mud is gone."

"What's betulin again?"

"A natural chemical compound found in birch. Especially paper birch and yellow birch. It's anti-inflammatory, antioxidant. Extremely beneficial for the liver. And the heart and pancreas. But really beneficial for the liver."

"Harvest only in the fall and winter then."

"I could. But in progressive chaga circles," Mary says, "the thinking is the summer chaga offers something that the fall and winter can't. More melanin. Which, if what you're looking for is third-eye activation, more melanin is what you want."

She holds a closed fist to her forehead and then opens it as though it blossoms.

The density of shade has been progressively diminishing. The light ahead proclaims the forest yields. A bounded luminance. A lit zone. Irresistible. The solar draw.

They take their packs off in the light and sit on separate rocks beside Big Wilson.

"Moderately high," says Mary.

"Not too bad. Knee-high at the most."

Two dragonflies on nearby rocks observe them as dipterous configurations swirl around apparent axes in the light.

Chris takes out Tevas. Mary takes out Crocs. They take their boots and socks off, stuff each sock in its companion boot, and double-knot each pair of laces so each pair of boots, thus linked, can be transported as a single unit in the crossing. Chris and Mary slip their fording footwear on. They stand and put their packs on, and the dragonflies return, atilt, to their patrols above the stream.

The women ford Big Wilson and emerge.

They take their packs off, sit on separate rocks beside Big Wilson, and undo the double knots.

The dragonflies alight on separate rocks.

One Teva is removed. One Croc.

They slip a sock on, then a boot.

Another Teva is removed. Another Croc.

They slip another sock on, then another boot.

They pull the laces, tie the knots.

They dip their fording footwear in Big Wilson, shake the Tevas, shake the Crocs, and stow the fording footwear in their packs.

It's like two versions of themselves, divided by Big Wilson and the small expanse of fording time, are close to simultaneously existing, but it's hard to notice confluence just missing when you're looking from the one side at the other and the view's too buggy or too gauzy at so close a range to make you wonder if there are degrees of threshold exclusivity.

They stand and put their packs on.

"Ready?" Mary asks.

They leave Big Wilson and the light. They take the trail into the woods, ascending slightly.

"So," Chris says. "More melanin."

"The market seems to want more melanin."

"Instead of betulin."

"It doesn't have to be an either/or, I don't think," Mary says. "They're both there. It comes down to a person's concentration preferences."

"But if the market had to choose."

"More melanin."

"To activate the third eye."

"You make it sound just mystical."

"It's pretty mystical."

"It's also biochemical," says Mary, slowing where the trail begins to gradually descend. "It's also environmental." Mary peers into the woods on both sides of the trail. "Have you seen any birch yet?"

"Any chance that chaga grows on evergreens?"

"I hope not. That would really fuck the market up."

They ease into their former pace, and they say nothing for a while. They listen to the woods.

As if she's still discussing the dynamics of the chaga market, Mary finally says, "It isn't really mystical. Our pineal glands are calcified. They're actually encased in a hard shell made of phosphate crystals. Actually encased. The pineal gland is so important to our physical and mental health, but it's more calcified than any other organ or tissue in the body. And what's more fucked up is take a guess what mainly causes calcification."

"Fluoridated water."

"Yes."

"I think I've heard of some of this before but never followed through."

They both feel somewhat dimmer than they had before the subject of the calcification of the pineal gland came up.

"It's natural not to follow through," says Mary, "when the problem staring at you is so tough to get a handle on."

"It isn't that," says Chris. "In Defense of Water looked at fluoridation rates in Maine a couple years ago. Just under half the state relies on public water systems, most of which are fluoridated. Private wells we didn't worry much about, but since then we've seen studies indicating that potentially a quarter of the private wells are fluoridated, probably because of public-water fluoridation and some sort of cross-contamination. Either way, the science says in proper parts per million fluoride's beneficial. So we really only concentrated on the public systems that exceeded parts-per-million guidelines."

"The science," Mary scoffs. "It says it's beneficial for the teeth."

"That's right."

"But what about the risks?" asks Mary. "Does the science say how toxic fluoride is? Does the science say that fluoride is an endocrine disruptor and a calcifier of the pineal gland? A bone destroyer? Does the science say that fluoride is a cancer risk? The health department's science really doesn't. But the other science does. The problem is the citizen too often has to dig a while to find the science that she wants. The science that has no agenda."

"That's sort of what I meant about my basic sense of fluoridation not progressing to a level you could characterize as knowledge—not progressing due to lack of follow through."

"There's only so much one environmental NPO can do."

They wonder how much one environmental nonprofit organization can ideally do to make the water-fluoridation forces reach the endpoint of the moral universe's arc toward justice, but the period of wonderment is short because its object is impossible for them to quantify without comparative analysis. The period is short because the practicalities of movement on no uniform terrain pull rank as Chris and Mary step, prioritizing in the stepping the continuation of their species' upright and bipedal ways. They hear Big Wilson in the distance, though, and feel its regional centrality, and they do not abandon their consideration of the water's cause and every being, irrespective of inclusion in the sentience records, whose cause is the water's cause.

"It makes no sense," says Mary. "Think about it. What's the warning on the toothpaste tube? 'Call Poison Control if swallowed.' Yet we swallow fluoridated water every day."

"You let Jake and Ryan swallow fluoridated water?"

"Hell, no. I meant *we* like *we, the people*," Mary says. "*We* as in *me and Albert* get our well water tested twice a year. We have reverse osmosis."

"That's dead water," Chris says. "It's mineral deficient."

"Yes, but eating right makes up for the deficiency. Detoxify the water first. Then you can find the lost minerals elsewhere. So we filter out the arsenic, fluoride, and the other shit, and then we make up for the lost minerals by careful vegetable selection mainly."

"Your third eye should be activated then."

"I basically drank fluoridated water from when I was in the womb until I learned about the fluoridation issues, which was what? About a year ago. My poor third eye is probably so calcified I can't imagine how much melanin I'd need to chip away at what's built up in there." She shakes her head as if to expedite the chipping process. "Once again it goes to show you can't accept the science. Not uncritically. At first the science says don't worry about the pineal gland because it's just vestigial, but then the science says the pineal gland produces melatonin, which the science says is vital. Then the science says fluoride calcifies the pineal gland and calcification fucks with the production of the vital melatonin, but the science, some of the science, says we should go on drinking fluoridated water." Mary shakes her head as if the expedition of the chipping process via head shake is impossible. "It makes no sense."

They walk in silence for a while, questioning what we have so far done with what we so far know.

"If you make chaga tea with fluoridated water for the purpose of third-eye activation," Chris asks, "isn't that a wash?"

"I make it with reverse-osmosis water."

"But if someone doesn't have reverse osmosis."

"It would be a wash, I guess," says Mary. "But it doesn't have to be. If I diversify my product line and market better, label better, everything becomes much clearer, and a wash becomes a matter of an informed consumer's choice instead of something I'm complicit in if someone seeking third-eye activation buys my chaga but has no idea that fluoridated water calcifies the third eye."

"I didn't mean to imply that you're complicit or deceptive."

"No, I am," says Mary. "Unintentionally, I am. But truth in advertising, clarity in advertising, marketing, whatever—truth and clarity eliminate complicity and make the whole transaction more transparent for the customer. So let's say you're an alcoholic soybean farmer who's religiously and socially conservative. What you want chaga for is to protect your liver, and you probably don't want to hear about the third eye being calcified by fluoride. So to you I'd recommend the winter chaga with the higher betulin content, and I'd have the website's product info and the packaging say something like 'Although reverse-osmosis water isn't necessary to derive health benefits from winter chaga's higher betulin content, common toxins found in private wells as well as public water systems could reduce those benefits, especially if your intent is to detoxify your liver or improve immune-system, heart, or pancreatic function.' Maybe not so wordy, but you know exactly what you're getting. In the package and in terms of preparation. Everything is clear."

"So winter chaga is the one line?"

"Yes. And if we ever find some, summer chaga will become the other, marketed toward the consumer who's not feeling psychically or spiritually at home and wants a chaga that will stimulate what she can somehow feel has been a stunted consciousness for too long."

"And you don't think the alcoholic soybean farmer wants that?"

"No, not really."

"Isn't your job as a marketer to make him want that? To make him feel he couldn't live without it?"

"I'm not really a marketer."

"But you believe in summer chaga's third-eye-activation possibilities."

"I do."

"But you don't think the alcoholic soybean farmer might be worthy of those possibilities?"

"I made him up for illustration purposes."

"But if he wasn't made up. Don't you think his third eye would be calcified?"

"I don't see why it wouldn't be."

"And wouldn't you be helping him if you got him to buy a product that would activate his third eye whether he believes or not in third-eye activation?"

"Yes, but how am I supposed to sell him something that's supposed to help with something that's ridiculous to him?"

"Consider him."

"I have."

"Consider him."

"I will." As if beginning the consideration process forthwith, Mary walks in silence, squishing, for some minutes down a stretch of slickness. Then she asks, "Is there an alcoholic soybean farmer in your life?"

"My uncle. On my mother's side."

Mary waits for painful family history to be related.

"Let's just say that he could use another eye."

Some time elapses to allow for dissipation of the statement's cryptic aura.

"If we find some chaga," Mary says, "I'll give you some to give to him once it's prepared. Just tell him if he wants to maximize the melanin's potential he should use reverse-osmosis water."

"You don't have to do that."

"Maybe I can hook him with a free sample," Mary says. "Free melanin."

"Free melanin," says Chris as though momentum builds for a resistance movement unimagined hitherto.

"Free melanin," says Mary, looking with the radical longing of a liberation theologian at the woods. "We free the melanin from the birch trees. We prepare the chaga, and we drink the tea. The melanin begins to free the melatonin and the DMT. The third eye is freed. We see as we were meant to see. Free melanin," says Mary, calmly, as if the negotiation window has been shut and it is time the sympathetic captor let the hostage go.

"Free melanin," says Chris.

"I think I found my tagline for the summer-chaga line. *Free melanin and see.*"

"*Summer chaga: See as you were meant to see.*"

"I like that," Mary says. "That's it."

They do not speak of marketing again.

They look more closely—to the one side for a while, then a swivel to the other—at the older trees and the undaunted understory, at the dense arrangements and the infinite particularities, the mutualities and offshoots, the relationships and intimacies they can't begin to comprehend or enter into. The intellect inserts itself at first, the questions surge, impediments to meditation and botanical reception, to communing with what chaga keepers might be out there: Who depends on this one tree? What kinds of insects? Does this forest shelter towhees? Is it true that moss grows only on the north side? Can that vine entwine that tree without becoming parasitical?

Because no answers come, they try to let the questions go. A process not so natural for the average Western rationalist begins. A layer of their Occidental being gives a little at the edge and curls back slowly as the cover of a paperback will do in high humidity, a product of semantics and alignment yielding primitively to pressure in the atmosphere, to airborne moisture that consorts with mildew. Chris and Mary are not masters. They do not control the pace or progress of the process. They conclude they do not want to, which conclusion is in some traditions step one on the master's path. They look and do not look. They focus on not focusing, and a capacity that isn't so rigidified and differential is revealed, a spore that has been nurtured in the depths of the sporangium that has been in them all along. They see the forest for the trees. They hear it, smell it, feel it in their nostrils, on their tongues. They sense how porous are the planes. They channel what they can.

"There," says Mary, pointing to a white birch standing in a dense bed of long beech ferns that extends, frond after frond, into the forest to their right as far as they can see.

"No chaga, though."

"We sort of have to let it come to us. We have to sort of let the forest lead us. I say we try in here."

Chris surveys the expanse of green.

"I'm game," says Chris. "It's been a while since I've bushwhacked."

"I don't like to bushwhack," Mary says. "I try to take the path that's there already. I don't like to trample. There's a path in there." She scans the ground around them and picks up two sticks, both slightly gnarled at one extremity and not exceeding standard cane length for two people of their stature. "We just need to be receptive."

Mary hands a stick to Chris.

"If we lift the fronds like so," says Mary, "we can see what's down below and leave the fern stalks, frogs, and all untrampled."

"Leave no trace."

"And do no harm. It's slower going," Mary says as she negotiates the fern stalks and proceeds, "but slower going through the ferns, I find, helps put me in a meditative state of mind, you know? The motion of the fronds. Fern green in all directions. I don't know. The green does something to my insides."

"It's a primordial affinity," says Chris as she lets down the fronds she passes and uplifts the next ones with an orchid keeper's tenderness. The fronds close ranks behind her, and the wake of Chris's passage shimmers for a while and subsides, a forest phosphorescence once again, subjected again to common agitations. "It's pre-Christian. Pre-religion probably."

"How I feel about fern green?" Mary asks as she performs a path diversion, giving wide berth to a fern-stalk cluster territorial in its expansiveness and density.

"Primordial. Genetic. At our core, we know we're of the earth. We're natural. We have always known this to be true. So why do we feel separate from it? Who knows when, but human depredation hit a tipping point. The curse of dominance and feeling separate from the earth. Like we existed outside nature or beyond it. First just barely. Like we weren't sure."

A pileated woodpecker does its jungle cry.

"Our sense of separateness intensified. We started feeling sort of supernatural. As if we were up here looking down on what we used to be a part of, looking down on what we knew we had to still be part of. But we couldn't *feel* a part of it the way we used to."

"Toad," says Mary. "Hang on." She gets lower, reaches, and the toad hops, disappearing into cover. "Clear. But we couldn't *feel* a part of it the way we used to."

"We repressed an integral component of our mythos and identity. In Eden or wherever. We gave license to disunity. We drew a borderline. A lot of borderlines."

They move more fronds and pass in silence, pondering delineation and the troubled history of borderlines.

"But what you feel when you see fern green," Chris says, "is the earth reminding you that separateness is an illusion."

"I believe that's true."

Chris pans the fern expanse.

"That feeling's like your Green Man," Chris says.

Mary isn't clear on who the Green Man is. She isn't willing to admit this. Then she is.

"I don't know what that means," confesses Mary.

Chris explains the Green Man as a pagan representation of a foliated male, the disappearance of a borderline, an intertwining of the plant world and the human, coalescence, oneness in two forms.

"Like Dionysus and the vine," Chris says.

They see another white birch and do not remark on its not hosting chaga.

"What's weird about the Green Man," Chris resumes, "is that he's carved all over medieval churches. Catholic churches." She considers. "On the other hand, I guess it isn't that weird when you think about the vegetation myths. Same cycle: birth, death, rebirth. Jesus kind of is a vegetation god. 'I am the vine. You are the branches.' All the seed talk. 'What you sow can't come to life unless it dies.' Same cycle. Who knows. Know what else is carved all over medieval churches? Vulvas."

"Vulvas?"

"Look up *Sheela na gig* when you go home and tell me what you think she's doing."

"What *is* she doing?"

"Showing you where babies come from. And she isn't shy about it."

"Maybe Sheela needs to meet someone," says Mary.

"Maybe she's been sending signals to the Green Man all these years and he's been too self-conscious to acknowledge them because his looks are unconventional."

"The separateness illusion is persistent."

"Yes, it is."

As matters of interiority will coincide in people of accorded sympathies who tiptoe through a forest's fern zone after they discuss depictions of imaginary figures whose depiction in a slowly yielding medium and on the buildings of an institution whose enormous shadow colors to this day the way those people view the world makes those imaginary figures more substantial than so many figures whose incorporation was a miracle of far more delicate material, what Chris and Mary think and feel about what's carved in stone and who's to clarify a symbol's vulvar ambiguity aligns without expressed coordination. Not a word.

They lift each featherweight and let it down as delicately as people who appreciate the vulnerability of being rooted so must do. The forest's baseline silence and the found path's rhythm pass to Chris and Mary powers of exquisite sensibility and intuition. Thoughts of adamantine symbols and mysterious aesthetics disappear as though the fern zone filtered them, correcting for imbalance in the air.

They see another white birch in the middle distance. And another farther on. And others. They approach each one like pilgrims whom the pilgrimage is teaching to be patient and content to leave the blessing they desire in the offing, where its sacredness is in no danger and not anxious for untested souls to come. They touch each tree, aglow and papery and cool. They look up slack-jawed at each height. No wound. No scar. No chaga. They are not dismayed. They wish each tree long life, no injury, and do not feel compelled by mere commodity to move on this serenely through the ferns.

They raise the fronds and lower them and do not see another white birch in the middle distance or beyond. The forest's white-birch distribution logic is beyond them. They imagine the immense intelligence that they are in the presence of in terms that they suspect are code for the unknowable, and they accept not knowing as the crucible of true belief. Serenely through the ferns they move, attuned, attentive, softwood people, soil people, people of the silent passage, of the deepening remove.

A rumble from the west rolls in and unifies the region. It requires shared awareness, holds the regional attentions, crests, and breaks, the quiet of subsidence in its wake, the ever-present undertone.

The treetop breeze picks up.

No mention of the rumble as they move.

No mention of the distance they have come.

No mention of no chaga or return.

Another rumble. And again the breeze.

No mention of how much impends.

Serenely they move on. A quarter mile more.

Toward the quarter mile's end, a long-lived river birch resides, deep-rooted, widespread, high, surrounded like a forest sage by long beech ferns.

Mary points.

"That's not a white birch," Chris says.

"River birch," says Mary. "Black birch. See that black knot?"

"Chaga."

"Chaga," Mary says. "Or black-knot fungus."

Mary moves on toward the river birch. Chris follows. Lift, let down, move on. Lift, let down, move on. The rhythm of the pilgrimage continued.

Mary lifts, looks down, and screams.

A man's inverted face, its eyes at first closed when she lifts the fronds, awakens as she lets the fronds go and obscures the face again. She jumps back, saying, "Shit, shit, shit," because she must say something quickly.

"What?" yells Chris. "What? What?"

"There's a fucking man down there," says Mary.

"What?"

"There's a fucking man down there."

The fronds, so recently released, still quiver.

Chris and Mary tightly grip their sticks but do not brandish. Tensed, they watch the quivering diminish.

"Hallo," a voice says from beneath the fronds. "I am no harm."

Chapter Four: Cosme Esperanza

A rumble. Breeze.

"I rise now," says the voice.

The air is ionized.

Two hands rise slowly through the ferns. They turn to show two empty palms. They turn to show that nothing sinister is on the backsides. They invite a brief inspection and then disappear beneath the cover of the ferns again.

The fronds begin to rustle.

The man's form, back first, breaches. Then his head appears. He stands. He is not tall. Five-six, five seven. His lower face is stubbled. He seems free of malice and designs. He must be forty-five or fifty, but his hair is dense and panther black. He is compact and limber, versed in the economy of movement. He keeps both hands on his chest as if to prove he is material.

A rumble. Breeze.

"My name is Cosme Esperanza. Hallo."

"I'm Mary."

"Chris."

"Are you from Colombia?" asks Mary.

Cosme's eyes go wide. "Colombia!" he says, as though the notion of Colombian origination is preposterous.

"Your shirt," says Mary, pointing to his t-shirt on which is the image of a tree around whose canopy the word *Colombia* is arced.

Cosme looks down at his shirt and chuckles as he studies it.

"No, no. I see why you might say." He looks up from his shirt with an expression of good humor. "You may say our eyes cannot be always trusted. I am of Peru."

"Peru?" says Mary.

"But, if I am true, what I am really of is Ucayali."

"In Peru?" asks Chris.

"Ucayali is before Peru. Before the nations." Cosme nods. "Where I was born was by Fanacha, which flows into Ucayali, which flows into, you may say, the Amazon. If I am true, that is what I am of. And you?"

"And me?" asks Chris.

"What are you of?" asks Cosme.

"Onawa. Lake Onawa. Not far from here."

"Onawa. What is the meaning?"

"*Awake.* Or *wide awake.* It's from the Chippewa. Ojibwe."

"From the native."

"Yes."

"And you are Chippewa?"

"No."

"Ojibwe?"

"No. My family came from Scotland long ago."

A rumble. Breeze.

"And you?"

"Not native either," Mary says.

"This matter," Cosme says. "Natividad. What we are of. It is less simple now. But you? Not far?"

"Not far. A town called Monson. South of here."

"I crossed a road in Monson." Cosme thinks a moment. "Yes, I crossed a road in Monson."

"Are you a thru-hiker?" Chris asks.

"I am hiking through," says Cosme. "To the mountain. Katahdin."

Chris and Mary glance at one another, at the ferns, and back at Cosme.

"Where's your backpack?" Mary asks.

He crouches slightly, reaching one hand down below the ferns and bringing up a backpack he holds toward Chris and Mary. "These colors? Each one, hand-dyed. This? Hand-woven. Much work. Much work."

"That is beautiful," says Mary.

"It's exquisite," Chris says.

"Yes. A woman I relieved of pain took care in making this for me."

Chris stares intently at the backpack.

"You wonder how I come this way with only this. You wonder is it waterproof," says Cosme.

Chris feels caught in the commission of an indiscretion.

"Many people tell me I am ill-equipped," says Cosme. "Many tell me how I travel is too light. But feel."

Chris takes the pack and holds its modest weight for several seconds. Mary takes it next and does the same. She gives it back to Cosme.

"I think not too light," says Cosme, setting down the pack.

"You're Ayahuasca," Mary says. "My husband heard of you. He works at Shaw's."

"In your tradition of the trail name," Cosme says, "I have been named so. I do not accept the name. What ayahuasca teaches us and shows us is not possible for me to teach and show. It is, I think, a sacrilege to name me Ayahuasca. Ayahuasca is the mother of tobacco, and the mother of the mother of tobacco is a snake. The people who say I am Ayahuasca do not know this. So I come."

"The mother of the mother of tobacco is a snake," says Chris.

"The mother of the mother of tobacco is a snake," says Cosme. "Yes."

A rumble. Breeze.

"So who's the mother of the snake?" asks Mary.

"You may say the mother of the snake is God. But she is more than that," says Cosme. "Language cannot make this clear."

"What can?" asks Mary.

"Ayahuasca," Cosme says.

"Do you have ayahuasca?" Chris asks.

"And tobacco. Socks," says Cosme with a shrug.

"I'm sorry," Chris says. "I don't mean to pry."

"It is okay."

"No food?" jokes Mary.

"No food."

"You have no food?"

"I do not *carry* food," says Cosme, spreading out his arms as if to welcome in the selfless forest. "But, as you can see, I do not starve. I am protected."

"What are you protected by?" asks Chris.

"The forest. Ayahuasca," Cosme says. "My spirits."

"You have spirits?"

"Yes, of course," says Cosme. "You do not have spirits?"

Chris and Mary say they do.

"Of course," says Cosme. "So you see." He pauses, studying their eyes. "I see you do not see. I ask. Why have I come here?"

"To Maine?" asks Chris.

"To *here*," says Cosme, pointing downward. "To this place that is before Maine. To this time."

No answer.

Cosme listens to the river birch.

"It's okay. What I have seen and been told is almost never everything."

A rumble. Breeze.

"Before the new year, I ate nothing. One week. No food. When that week was over, I drank ayahuasca every day. For thirty days. I saw great wonders. Many things that deeply frightened me. Each night I saw a forest spirit, reading to the smaller forest spirits, warning that the forest needs their fierceness to defend the forest and the beings of the forest. Each night I saw the fires in the forests of the world. Each night I heard the crying of the trees because of what appears to come. Each night I fought the witch who tried to lure the mother of the waters into evil. Many times, for thirty days, I could not breathe and feared I would die. My spirits were strong. When I was able, I sang as I have never sung." He pauses. "Sometimes you believe your visions are behind you when the ayahuasca's power wears off. Not true. They go on without you."

He points up at the river birch.

"One night, in my visions, was this tree, a tree not of the Ucayali jungle."

"You saw a river birch?" asks Mary.

"This tree is the tree I saw," says Cosme.

"How can you know that?" Mary asks.

"How can I know you are not her?" asks Cosme, gesturing toward Chris but looking at the upper reaches of the river birch. "You look a way. You move a way. You sound. You emanate. It is the same with trees," says Cosme, looking from the upper reaches to the black knot halfway down the trunk. "This black knot was positioned in my visions as it is positioned here." He nears the river birch and lays his right hand on the knot. "I have been with this tree for three days. I have fasted with this tree for three days. This is the tree."

"You've been here three days?" Chris asks, looking from the knot to Cosme.

"Yes."

"You haven't eaten anything for three days?" asks Mary, looking from the knot to Cosme.

"You see then how I know."

They focus their attentions on the black knot.

"In my ayahuasca visions," Cosme says, "the black knot spoke to me. One night it said, 'There is a mountain.' I saw only Ucayali jungle beyond the tree. Another night the black knot said, 'There is a mountain.' I looked at the jungle as the owl looks. Only jungle still. Another night the black knot said, 'There is a mountain.' I looked at the jungle as the owl monkey looks. Still jungle only. I began to fear this was a sorcerer's deception. Still I looked because I know that sometimes visions do not end well."

Rumble. Breeze.

"A line materialized." He extends his right hand at approximately the level of his chest. He glides it to his right and angles it in order to accommodate ascent. He flattens it a moment and then angles it again for steep ascent. He flattens it at the imaginary peak and glides it over the imaginary ridge. He angles it in order to accommodate the steep descent and then the softening. "The outline of a mountain." Cosme puts his right hand to his side. "And then the mountain. Trees like these below." He points to pine and spruce and hemlock. "Green and blue and gray. I felt it cool the jungle. In the trees below the mountain was a white house. And below the white house was a rainbow. In the rainbow's color bands were blue and purple berries. Millions. In each band of color, black bears ate the berries. And below the rainbow was a lake. And in the lake two snakes entwined and told me it was time to go. But where is what I did not know. The snakes said nothing more."

Light rain begins to fall. The forest whispers.

"Often, yes, the answer we desire does not easily or quickly come. Would you mind if we sit?" asks Cosme.

Each of them begins to part fronds and inspect the ground. Each sits, legs crossed, the fronds, unparted, closing ranks again so that each person seems to be just head and partial shoulders.

"Next night I drank twice the ayahuasca. All was absence. Never was the dark so. Never was the silence. Nothing. Sometimes, yes, there is delay. I waited. Long. I drank more ayahuasca. Twice more. Nothing.

Then. The sound is almost no sound when the panther comes. I could not move. Approach I knew but not direction. I was powerless to run. The panther in the air. My throat no longer was my throat. I could not breathe."

He holds two tight fists above the ferns. He waits a moment and then opens them to indicate explosion or the sudden blossoming of something.

"Blood sprayed from my throat and lit the sky. The jungle glowed. I saw the chainsaw spirits and the spirits of deforesting machines attack the spirits of the trees. I saw the final monkey clinging to the final tree as one of many loggers stood below. I saw the oil spills expanding into where the jungle always was. I saw the multiplying cattle lapping oil and destroying soil where the jungle always was. I saw the multiplying soybean spirits chase the forest spirits toward the cities. All this time, my blood was airborne. All this time, I died."

Rumble. Breeze.

They feel the rumble rise up from the ground, the low vibration in the viscera now that the three of them are sitting.

The ferny undulation does not last. Its calm transference lingers. In the river birch, two phoebes land and make what sense they can of three heads hovering above the ferns before one flies and the other follows.

"Each drop landed. Fire burst. What I described before all burned. From every, if I may, corpusculo a fire. The separate roars combined. The separate smokes. I closed my eyes to die. I thought I heard a countryside guitar. But I could not be sure. The roar. I opened them. A white thread hung in front of me. It shivered from the heat. The energy. The shivers made the sounds of countryside guitar. I held the white thread with both hands. As if very high, I held. I felt my powers flowing into me again. I felt no wounds. I sensed no panther. Energy surrounded me. Protecting me. But what is personal protection when the jungle burns? What good my body then? I held with both hands. Sunrise came. The thread let go. The roar died down. The smoke cleared. Ucayali jungle as it always was. I thought this was enough. I told myself no more would I drink ayahuasca. I sat in the jungle, wondering about the sun. By afternoon I understood. Control and no control must coexist. So that night I drank ayahuasca. And the panther came. My blood. The fire. Smoke. The white thread. I held on. Energy protected me. I doubted. Sunrise. Same. Control and no control must get along.

"The next night I drank four times more. If absence can be four times deeper than another absence, this was four times deeper than the absence of the night before. The dark was four times deeper. Nothing. Not a panther. No sound. No scent. No touch. No speck of light. Atomic isolation. Such that I could not be. I had nothing to relate to. I was nothing. I could not remember. How long I was like this I am powerless to say. It was not earth time."

Cosme closes his eyes and bows his head.

Chris and Mary wonder how to file all that he has so far said.

"A spaceship I have seen in other visions was a light year from me," Cosme says, with raised head and open eyes. "Its speed is infinite. Its sense of distance is not ours. Its suddenness of coming and its brightness overwhelm. Our senses cannot handle all at once. I closed my eyes. The particles came through. The waves. I heard the spaceship hover. From no sound to this. No light to this. I held the white thread with both hands and told myself to hold on and hurry up. Adjust. The spaceship will not hover there forever to deliver what it came to tell. A little at a time my eyes I opened them. The spaceship light was like the sun. I blinked much. I adjusted. I held on and watched the spaceship hover. Circulating stillness. Underneath it was the mountain I have told you of. I hung above the mountain by the white thread. Such a forest was below the mountain and in all directions. Water bodies. Bogs. Alluvia and soils. Needles. Leaves. Bacteria. Mycelia. I saw who take the carbon in. The flux and equilibrium. I saw the checks on fire. Control and no control. A mile high or higher, I saw the invisible world. A microscope was in me. Yet I saw the outward grandeur, yes? The largeness. Mile after mile were the muscles of the world. You see how ayahuasca is the microscope and telescope combined?

"I saw the wise ones everywhere. The teachers. Ayahuasca teaches many things, and one of them is who the teachers are. I looked down at the wise ones. How they are ignored. I wept. I wanted to let go of the white thread and become the mountain, the bacteria, the soils, the alluvia, the trees and plants, the bogs, the waters, the mycelia. To become a wise one. I held on because I thought this could be sorcery. An evil spirit tricking me to death. I did not think this true. But there is good and evil. This we know. I held on and watched the spaceship hover. To determine good or evil."

"I have grip," says Cosme, opening his hands and closing them above the ferns. "My forearms, you may see, are not appropriate for someone of my stature." Cosme holds his forearms up as though he has just scrubbed for surgery. "The visions. People underestimate what they require from you physically."

His hands and forearms disappear beneath the ferns.

Raindrops land like distilled amphibians on fronds that quiver with each landing, shimmer for durations fixed by forces mathematical and otherworldly, and let go like beings who from time to time prefer the long goodbye.

"I held, and from the spaceship came a light. It spiraled in the air across from me. It shared my altitude. I focused. It said nothing. Sometimes saying is up here," says Cosme, tapping twice his forehead. "I prepared my mind to listen. I have seen the old ones come in ships like this one. I have seen the old ones. But I knew this was not them. This was not their spaceship. Not their light. I held. The white thread spun. I spun. At first at no great speed. The spinning harmed my listening. I feared each turning from the spiral light. I did not know if when I came around each time it would be with me still. The spinning got so fast my fears could not keep up. Now nothing was distinct. I saw no spiral. Only light. I felt my center bulge. The pressure. I could not breathe. The pressure in my center. I was spiral. I could not let go. I did not think my body could continue in one piece. I believed it would explode. I could not tell one revolution from the next. I held. I vomited my soul. My soul spun out from me beyond a light year. Then the spinning stopped. I held. I breathed. I saw my soul extend beyond a light year from me. My soul was spiral. Clear and cloudy. Bright and dim. I breathed. I understood what is inside us is out there and what is out there is inside us."

"We are stardust," Mary says.

"You see division is illusion," Cosme says.

They listen to the rain fall, feel it on their scalps, their necks, and watch the ferns bob.

"The spaceship light began to sing. A beautiful song. Inexpressible. I tried to learn it as I held the white thread. From the light a white man formed. He did not have much hair. I did not like his tone. Too much the man of method. Jacket, collar, tie. A city man. An inside man. We stared at one another. I forgot the spaceship. I forgot my soul beyond a light year from me. I forgot the white thread. In his face were not the banker's pores. Not the churchman's. In his eyes was simian tranquility. The jungle peace. How could this be? We stared. I understood that the song being sung was his. Was him. He did not move his lips, and yet he sang the beautiful song. It flowed from him. It was him. The song's power strengthened me. I sang. I knew that this song and this being would be my protection for what was to come.

"Then the song stopped. His lips moved. 'I am Percival,' he said. 'To pierce the valley.' From a pocket he removed a pipe and put it in his mouth. He took a matchbook from the pocket, lit the pipe, and puffed. He blew tobacco smoke on me, and I knew what it felt like to have wealth. It felt to me a burden better for a healer not to know. He blew tobacco smoke on me again, and what I knew of what it felt like to have wealth was lifted. From the man a mountain formed and rose behind him. 'I protected this,' he said. It was the mountain I have told you of. Below the tree line were the trees and white house I have told you of. The rainbow and the lake. The beauty of it all reminded me of the song. Then I saw a person trample alpine flowers on the mountain's tableland. And then another person. And another. Hundreds trampled. Thousands. 'It is time to go,' said Percival. I asked him where. 'There is a path,' he said. 'Tell people what the flora know.' He disappeared into the spiral light, which disappeared into the spaceship, which had gone beyond a light year by the time I could ask him more. Then all was darkness. Silence. Still I held. The sun rose. I had been let go. I was sitting in the jungle. Just a pinpoint in the universe. A molecule."

Cosme sings a while to the river birch.

"You know this tree communicates," he says. "These ferns communicate. Do you know how?"

The rain falls.

"Through senses. Signs. Symbols. There is something else. What you may say is extrasensory," says Cosme. "Ayahuasca translates. It removes what hinders. Teaches us the language. It is more than language, but you see my meaning. Ayahuasca teaches us to be more sensitive receivers. Healers who have practiced long and learned from ayahuasca often understand the plants without ayahuasca. I often understand the plants without ayahuasca. Each plant is particular. Each situation. Sometimes what you seek to understand the plant will not teach. Sometimes what the plant will teach you will not understand. Receiving, teaching, you may say, are two-way. Understanding, two-way. Sometimes it takes seconds. Understanding. Sometimes years.

"I felt the sunbeams gather. I saw orchids near me. Heliconia. I breathed. I took them in. I greeted them. I did not place them in an order for the story humans often tell themselves up here." He taps a temple. "I accepted. I received. It sometimes is as simple as receiving what the plants have always offered you. A scent. A pattern. Signs of infinitesimal design. Of infinite design. So small that grasping seems not possible. And yet you grasp. So grand that grasping seems not possible. And yet you grasp. But sometimes it is not so simple. Sometimes plants communicate by other pathways."

"Plant meditation," Mary says.

"You see," says Cosme. "So I sat. The jungle warmed. The sun set. I did not drink water. I was still. I sat in darkness. I did not drink ayahuasca. I took in the jungle. Animals came near. I did not fear. The orchids guarded me. The heliconia. I felt the force of Percival in this. I sang the beautiful song as the sun rose. I let go.

"The jungle warmed. An orange orchid petal fell. No breeze. No agitation. Yet the petal let go. As we all must, no? The slight resistance that its surface gave the air as it descended was no match for gravity. It landed softly on the puka allpa, which in Quechua means *red dirt. Red earth.* I thought about these colors. How the one fell on the other. How the one, unmoved, held up the other. Ants passed by the petal, which appeared to not be there for them. Why was this sequence interesting me? I studied the relationships. I tried to see connections. Patterns. Symbols. I tried to receive. Can interest be coincidence? Illusion? I believed I had to drink more ayahuasca after sunset. Then an orange heliconia petal fell. Two orange petals on the puka allpa. Two plants telling me the same thing. Ants passed by the second petal as if on the puka allpa was no second petal. Was no petal in the first place. Then I understood. I let the petals go. I left the jungle.

"I took the boat next morning to Pucallpa, where I lived for years when I was young. It is a city on the Ucayali. It was not so much a city then when I was young. But it is big now. I avoid the city. I have had my troubles there. But you see why I had to go. *Pucallpa. Puka allpa.* I was like an ant who searched the red earth. I searched here. And now I searched there. You cannot always choose what you may see or not see. Where you may be or not be. That is the lesson of the poor.

"I walked around the city like an ant until the middle of the afternoon. It did not feel productive. I was just an ant, I told myself. I had no views on productivity. I took a few steps more. I looked up. *Avenida San Martín*. This sign was something. Even for an ant in my position it was something. On my mother's side, you see, I am of San Martín. I walked the Avenida like an ant. Inspecting, pausing, moving on. Of course, you say, association of a street name and maternal lineage may be coincidence. Just chance. How do you differentiate between a confluence of signs that leads you somewhere from two signs that lead you nowhere? I do not pretend to know. You differentiate, or you do not. The signs are confluent, or they are not. You see the light, or you do not. I told myself that for an ant I thought too much."

The rain lets up. Becomes a drizzle mist.

"I crossed the Avenida. I inspected, paused, moved on. The same. This side did not feel different from the other. Sidewalk, buildings, shops. On this side, though, forgive me, I had now the need to urinate. I did not want to use an alley. The police might question me, and I was not sure of my status in their eyes. Most bathrooms in Pucallpa are not free. I had enough for boat fare. To return me. Not much more. I did not want to spend three quarters of a sol, perhaps a sol, to do what I have always done for free. I walked. Preoccupied with urinary matters. I assumed that I was missing signs I would not see again. We often think the body complicates the way. Its vessel qualities elude us. The assistance that it renders to the soul."

The forest drips.

"Ahead I saw was a façade. Concave. Curved inward. This was not here when I was a boy. The Biblioteca Municipal. I thought perhaps. I entered. On an easel was a painting resting lengthwise. In the left side of the painting, three green leaves appeared to be descending. To the right of those leaves, top to bottom, was a tree trunk gripped by two huge hands. No forearms. From the wrists extended green roots, twisting toward the greenness and the darkness of the background, the impression of the forest. In the middle of the painting was a blue sky and a distant tree line. In the right side of the painting, top to bottom, was the profile of a man's head facing what I have described. His mouth was open wide. Concave. Curved inward. Filled with sky. The top row of his teeth against the sky. His nose against the sky. His chin against the distant tree line. Eyes shut tight. The man was screaming. Pained. Across his neck and face and hair branched yellow lines. Like leaf veins. Or like fissures in a thing that does not have much longer. Everywhere, except where there was lightened sky, were dashes, vertical, like points of light stretched slightly. An illusion of terrestrial perception maybe. Star-like. Spirit-like. No pattern maybe. Scattered maybe. But they formed a line that curved around his ear."

Cosme's index finger runs along the helix of his left ear.

"And held the line until his temple."

Cosme's index finger angles toward his temple, which it taps in quick succession twice as if to emphasize an elemental point about cognition of the human kind.

"Where they scattered into maybe randomness again or maybe into an arrangement it would take more time to see. It fascinated me. This painting. Like a vision. This was something."

"How can you recall such detail?" Chris asks.

"I paint. I have the eye," says Cosme. "More importantly, my memory is photographic."

"Did you go?" asks Mary.

Cosme seeks an answer.

"To the bathroom," Mary says.

"I was relieved," says Cosme. "Yes. A woman saw my interest in the painting. An employee. She described the painting as traditional indigenous visionary art. She said it represented the collective native fear of forest loss. Of culture loss and forced assimilation. Loss of biodiversity. I did not say the native fear is my fear. I did not say I live in a forest village. Even many city people who have forest sympathies prefer a line between themselves and forest people. Many people who do not have visions are uncomfortable with those who do. And many people who do not believe the plants are teachers feel superior to those who do. I did not ask her views because I had to use the bathroom. And I knew. She asked if I was there to join the counseling program in Information and Communications Technology. I knew. I do not like to lie. I said I came for information. 'Excellent,' she said. 'Please follow me.' I asked if I could use the bathroom first, and she directed me. No fee. I was relieved."

The phoebes land in the river birch again. They listen to the humans in the ferns. They watch.

"When I came back, she led me to a white room with computers. No traditional indigenous visionary art. I sat at what she called a station and filled out a form she gave me. As precaution, you may say, I answered incompletely. The computer was already on. It hummed. She showed me how to enter, to create a username, a password. She said I was going on a web quest. I did not object. The web, she said, had engines that would search for me and find me information. Virtually, she said. She taught me how to use one. What if I was not sure how to say what I was searching for, I asked. 'Uncertainty,' she said, 'is part of any search. Refine your search.' She shared refinement secrets with me. Then she handed me a paper. 'Practice. Get a sense of what is out there. See what you can find,' she said. 'We live in an extraordinary time.' She said she would return to check my progress.

"The paper said imagine moving to a new place. Where would I decide to go? Who would I like to meet there? What would I like to see? How would I get there? What would it be like to be a stranger in this land? I closed my eyes. Imagining. I saw the mountain. I saw Percival. I saw the alpine flowers. I heard Percival. 'There is a path.' I did not feel a stranger there. I kept my eyes closed. The computer hummed. I opened them. I saw the engine on the screen. I spelled the keywords. *mountain Percival alpine flowers path*. I entered all of them at once."

The phoebes fly.

"The first result," says Cosme, eyes wide with guidance possibilities. "*Mount Morgan and Mount Percival Loop—New Hampshire*. I examined several photos of Mount Percival. It was not the vision mountain. But I felt the power of this engine. How it reached."

A raven croaks.

"The next result. *1-minute hike: Mount Percival in Northport. Maine*. How was this possible, to hike a mountain in a minute? I examined photos. This Mount Percival was also not the vision mountain. I consoled myself. I told myself elimination was refinement. An approach. I sat back in my chair and looked at other people. Staring at the screens. All searched. For what? Why here?

"I leaned back in to read the third result. *The Appalachian Trail*

Reader—Page 272. An excerpt from a book. I saw no photo, but I read a sentence that made less uncertain what I searched for. 'Percival Baxter, governor of Maine, calls out for a vast protected state park of which we are the beneficiaries.' I went to my engine, and I spelled the keywords. *Percival Baxter*. Entered. It was him. The vision Percival. I stared for some time at his photo to confirm. And then I read. 'On an August day in 1920, Percival P. Baxter found himself crawling across a knifed-edged arête as he approached the summit of Katahdin, which rises out of the north woods of Maine.' I spelled *Katahdin* in the engine. Photo after photo. No uncertainty. 'There is a mountain,' Percival had said. And here it was. The vision mountain."

Cosme is about to say more but then shuts his mouth and smiles at the river birch, at Chris and Mary, at the ferns. He takes a deep breath and exhales, a deep breath and exhales.

"The ordinary is sublime, and the sublime is ordinary. Separation is illusion. I have told you these things. I must sometimes tell myself," says Cosme, as if in apology. "My counselor returned to check my progress. I considered her an interruption at that moment. My consideration was not just. She oriented me. She pointed to Katahdin on the screen. 'Is that where you would like to go?' she asked. I nodded. 'Excellent,' she said. 'Keep searching. Find everything you can about the place. What does the word *Katahdin*, for example, mean?'

"Probably you know it means *main mountain* or *greatest mountain*. From the Eastern Abenaki. From the native." Cosme pauses. "What perhaps was sacred in the native the interpretations do not feel. Translation loses something, you may say."

They contemplate the mysteries of the transmission of the sacred, of the line that separates the partial from the total loss.

"I searched as I was counseled. Do you know what *Abenaki* means? It is important."

Neither Chris nor Mary knows.

"*People of the Dawnland*," Cosme says.

The solar-orientation nomenclature quiets them a while. An admission of the sacred.

"You know I am talking of Penobscot, who are Abenaki. But *Penobscot* means *descending ledges*. Like my people, they are river people. Forest people. Driven from the river. Driven from the forest.

They resisted. Like my people. They reclaimed. Adapted. They run businesses. They manage. They remain. But no one fluent in the native language is alive. Imagine what is lost."

Cosme takes a moment to respect the passing.

"My people. We are lucky. We have Quechua. Spanish pressures. English pressures. Quechua fends. My parents taught me Spanish for society. The missionaries taught me English. I am glad now, as I speak to you, but learning English felt unfaithful. Learning Spanish felt unfaithful. Quechua is the mother tongue. How many tongues can one mouth hold before the mother is forgotten? Two, for some, may be too many. How can the mouth go on without the mother tongue? How can the mind? The soul? The spirit? The Penobscot have gone on. Their dance of resistance is as it must be for them. Mine is as it must be for me. I searched.

"For many years, for almost all their history, they would not climb Katahdin, which was sacred and whose sacredness Pamola guarded. One day white men wished to climb Katahdin. Their Penobscot guides said they would die. The white men climbed without them. Below the mountain, waiting, the Penobscot guides were certain no white man would make it down. The white men, who did not accept the mountain's sacredness or the existence of the spirit guardian Pamola, made it down. The guides could not explain their safe return. Was every place for man? Was nothing natural sacred?

"When I read about this, I remembered. In my vision, thousands trampled alpine flowers on Katahdin."

Cosme pauses to allow his listeners to picture the commission of indignity.

"A tradition, a belief, is like an alpine flower. It may be resilient in a harsh environment for many generations. It may thrive in the environment's severity. Adapted perfectly. And yet it may be trampled by an upstart. In a second, crushed. By the indifferent or the hostile. It may be the taproot still remains. Connection may be there still. But expression does not come. No power to inch closer to the sun. No bloom. Vitality is stifled."

"On the first days of September, the Penobscot climb Katahdin to perform a ritual in honor of the mountain. This is not the old tradition. Not the old belief. The world changed. Upstarts swarmed. Enormous numbers. The Penobscot changed. Adapted. They run businesses. They visit modern doctors. Still they hold to what they can. It may be this is how we move on. How we find our way back. How recovery begins. How what the taproot is connected to becomes again the teacher of us all."

They feel the last cloud pass, the storm now to the east, and see three rays of sunlight beam through small gaps in the canopy. Each ray is in relief, both of the forest and not of. No-see-ums whirl in each shaft, orderly, coordinate, cyclonic but serene, ecstatic but adherent, almost stationary but revolving in one body, honoring a center that appears to have no earthly means to hold. Each ray lights on long beech ferns, illuminating water beads and fronds, intensifying beadiness and greenness and conferring on them the capacity to tingle human torsos in their presence. It is like an otherworldly force, desiring the water beads and fronds, entranced by the no-see-ums, meant to beam these beings up but cannot find the heart to take them from this forest where the temperature is just right and the ratio of light to shadow is just right, the colors as an entity for good would have arranged them, and the water concentration of the surfaces and air is just right and there is no lamentation for the fleeting lifespan of no-see-ums since what is occurring at this moment is a form of perfect life, which lasts despite what must come after.

"Three of them," says Cosme. "Three of us."

"And what do you believe that means?" asks Mary.

The no-see-ums whirl in shafts of light.

"What we feel here," says Cosme, laying his right hand on the center of his chest, "when we are in the presence of such wondrous things, which always, you must know, we are—what we feel here is what it means."

"I was expecting more," says Mary.

"What more?" Cosme asks.

"Equivalency, I guess," says Mary. "I would like to know what three of them and three of us is meant to equal."

"You would like the mystery removed," says Cosme, chuckling.

The no-see-ums whirl in shafts of light.

"That is what I have somewhat come for, I suppose," says Cosme. He points to the no-see-ums whirling in the shafts of light. "We equal these."

"The shafts of light or the no-see-ums?" Chris asks.

"The no-see-ums in the light," says Cosme.

They examine the no-see-ums whirling and consider the components of equation.

"Do you not feel we are whirling, you may say, around a center that has drawn us here?" asks Cosme.

Chris and Mary do not answer.

"Do you not feel we are drawn, like these no-see-ums, to illumination?"

Chris and Mary do not answer.

"Let me ask you. What has drawn you here?" asks Cosme.

Chris and Mary ponder separately.

"You do not think that everything is accident?" asks Cosme.

"Chaga," Mary says. She points up at the black knot on the river birch. "What drew us here was chaga. Probably."

"You saw the tree as I did in a vision," Cosme says.

"It isn't like that," Mary says. "I meditate. I try to let the forest guide me, but I don't have visions."

"Yet this tree. It drew the two of you. As it drew me."

"I'm no healer," Mary says.

She tells him of her business selling chaga, of botanical reception, of the winter harvest and the benefits of betulin, of the summer harvest and the benefits of melanin, of water fluoridation and the calcification of the pineal gland, of third-eye activation, of her wish to help her customers across the threshold of the higher consciousness.

"You are a healer," Cosme says. "You must advise the people you give chaga to. The giving must be face to face. You must prepare them for what melanin might show them. Many people are not ready for the third eye to be opened. Many people are not ready for what is across the threshold. Do you think you are prepared to introduce them to the spirit world?"

"But this isn't ayahuasca," Mary says. "It's only summer chaga, and I haven't even tried the summer chaga yet."

"Let me tell you something. Ayahuasca, long ago, was everywhere and powerful because the forest of the Amazon was everywhere and powerful. The spirits of the forest of the Amazon were everywhere and powerful. Then the invaders came. The missionaries came. The roads came. Loggers. Ranchers. And the spirits of the plants were driven deeper in the forest. It is sad. Retreat. Attrition, you may say. The strongest teachers left and must be sought by paths one did not have to take to seek before. Impure intrusion they will not abide. You cannot find them, you cannot be taught, unless you are prepared, unless there is the purity in you."

Cosme scans the forest.

"Let me ask you. Do you think, in all the world, the only teacher of the things that we have spoken of is ayahuasca in the Amazon? If so, then how could people far away be taught? How could the distant poor be taught? Are people far away supposed to not know what the plants may teach them? What the forest? No, no, no. The world is not that way. The universe is not that way. Tobacco is a teacher."

"The mother of the mother of tobacco is a snake," says Chris.

"And ayahuasca," Cosme says, "the mother of tobacco, is a teacher, stronger than tobacco. There are other teachers. Maybe not as strong. But maybe strong in ways tobacco is not strong. Or maybe even strong like ayahuasca. Where, then, are these teachers? If they were, where are they now?"

Cosme scans the forest.

"You may not perceive this, but the forest moves. It moves away when threatened. And the spirits with the forest move. The teachers with the forest move. Away from cows. Away from chainsaws and machines. Away from roads. Away from houses. But," says Cosme, finger raised, "this movement, you may say, is not one way. The teachers want to teach. The spirits want to show us what we coexist with, what we are beside. They signal to us. Who will listen? Always we are whispered to. Who listens goes to deeper places. Where the forest is not fractured so. Where plants know there is time before what certain humans call development discovers them. This does not happen only in the Amazon. Look here," says Cosme, glancing at the black knot on the river birch. "I do not know your chaga, but it seems that it retreats. Yet you are here, and you are here, and I am here. The spirit of the river birch has drawn us here. The spirit of the chaga, as you said, has drawn us here. We share an understanding, yes, an intuition. We are whirling, you may say, within the same illumination source. You said before, 'It's only summer chaga.' It may be that chaga was as powerful a teacher once as ayahuasca. It may be the only difference is how far the forest has retreated here. And it may be the space between the teacher and the novice weakened both. It is not one way, this relationship. The novice needs the teacher, true. But it is also true the teacher, in some ways, is as dependent on the novice. Rifts affect both sides. It may be you," he says to Mary, "who is meant to bring the teacher and the novice back together. As they were before the saws. Before the roads. When everything was forest."

"I'm not even sure that this is chaga," Mary says.

"You must know," says Cosme.

Mary stands and finds a path beneath the fronds that leads her to the river birch. She puts her face close to the black excrescence and inhales, internalizing something she could otherwise not know, and breathes out, externalizing something otherwise not known. She does this with closed eyes for minutes. Eyes still closed, she feels the texture of the black excrescence, tracing certain fissures to its juncture with the trunk and certain fissures back to its extremities, its brittleness communicating to her fingertips a softness just below, a goldenness not far below. She feels for minutes, understanding in a manner she could not if she were looking. Mary traces one crack to the juncture of the trunk and black excrescence, puts her closed eyes closer to the juncture, taking in what is there to be taken in, and opens them to see what she already knows is there: an orange-golden seam, like caulk applied by an abiding dryad who, by virtue of exquisite application and apparent absence, trumpets craftsmanship and fluid gender roles and anonymity.

Mary finds the path beneath the fronds that leads her back to Chris and Cosme. She resumes her place among the ferns.

"It's chaga," Mary says. "But I don't feel the harvest vibe."

"You do not have the merchant's sensibility. You have the healer's," Cosme says.

He points to the no-see-ums whirling in the shafts of light.

"How long do you believe they have to whirl here?" Cosme asks.

"Not long," Chris and Mary say in unison.

"Do you believe they will whirl elsewhere?"

No one answers.

"What we feel when we observe them. It is something?" Cosme asks.

"It's something," Mary says.

"It's definitely something," Chris says.

"Can you tell me what this something is?" asks Cosme.

"No, not really," Chris says.

He appeals to Mary.

"No," says Mary. "But it's definitely something."

"You have never harvested the summer chaga?" Cosme asks.

"No," says Mary.

"But you believe in it? That it has powers?"

"Yes."

"And you believe?" asks Cosme, addressing Chris.

"I think so. I'm inclined to. I do."

"Why?" asks Cosme.

"Mary seems to know a lot about it."

"She has never tried it."

"I know, but."

"Mary, why do you believe in it?" asks Cosme.

"Why would someone lie about the benefits of melanin? Of all the things there are to lie about, why lie about the benefits of melanin?"

"You trust there is a force for good," says Cosme.

"Yes, I guess I do," says Mary.

"Do you also trust there is a force for bad?"

"Yes, I guess I do."

"And you, Chris," Cosme asks, "do you trust likewise?"

"I believe I do. I do."

The three of them look up at the no-see-ums whirling in the light.

"Sometimes, when we look at things that make us feel as these no-see-ums do, we do not trust so much there is a force for bad. We understand up here perhaps," says Cosme, tapping his left temple, "that this force is out there, but we do not feel it *here*." He moves his tapping finger to his torso. "We see radiance, and we trust radiance. Or it may be the other way. We see destruction, and we trust destruction. See," says Cosme, pointing at the phoebes landing on the river birch. "What we felt when we saw these birds before diminished when they flew away. Perhaps the feeling disappeared with them. As if their leaving took a part of us and left a hole or something bad behind. Why should that be? You may say our horizon, what you may say is our range, is limited. Expansion is not easy. That is why so many people do not want to be a healer."

Chris and Mary watch the phoebes in the river birch. They wonder why the phoebes' previous departure felt like absence, like a hole, like loss when, in the presence of the phoebes, there was never any question of possession.

"When you see them, do you not feel curiosity, a fragile awe? Do you not wonder?"

Chris and Mary quietly agree.

"Those feelings," Cosme says, "they call to us. They tell us just beyond us is what we might call extraordinary. It is very near, but we perceive it barely. We prefer to think that what we see and hear and touch is what there is to know. We are among the wonders. Look around. Why should there not be more? What animates what we already are among? What causes all of this? Where is it from? What is it all connected to?"

The phoebes flap their wings with pure concision. Where they had been perched is now a slight vibration, which a little time diminishes and stills. The no-see-ums whirl in shafts of light as though they are embodiments of constancy.

"You may say that ayahuasca teaches us that being *in* the light is truer than observance *of* the light, and ayahuasca teaches us the light will let us in if we let go. Of ego. The remove of the observer. We may call what must be let go many things. This also is what ayahuasca teaches us about the world. The world does not hold us remotely from the world. We hold ourselves remotely from the world. This is why people who are rich build houses on the highest hills. This is why people who feel small when they look at the houses on the highest hills believe their troubles would be over if they could afford to live in such a house."

Chris and Mary wonder how far back in human history goes the desire to reside in fine homes on the highest hills.

A phoebe flies above the three of them at so low an altitude they hear the flutter of the phoebe's wings. They feel how fluttering propels.

"We see the bird fly," Cosme says. "We understand how critical to flying are its wings and feathers. How important are its shape and eyes. But there is more to flying than the bird. More than the bird's anatomy."

Cosme does not say what more there is.

Steam rises from the forest moisture. Heat becomes a presence.

"To be a healer took much time," says Cosme. "Healing is not always what the tourists who come to the Amazon in search of ayahuasca think it is. It is not simply peace and love. For people who have turned away from the tradition and religion they were raised in and seek meaning in the jungle by ingesting ayahuasca, evil often feels imaginary. Like a veiled force in a fairy tale. But ayahuasca teaches us that evil is not fantasy. That is why ayahuasca is, you see, no trifle. Ayahuasca will not kill. What it reveals, however, may. The healer understands this danger, but this danger is not easy to convince the tourists of unless they have experience with ayahuasca."

The no-see-ums gyre in the shaft light.

"In a vision, I have seen the seven lights. Six light the goodness and the wisdom of the world. When I was young, a spirit of the fifth light, bathed in blue and turquoise, healed my failing heart. This being is a beauty words cannot describe. But even those who have not taken ayahuasca, when they feel between them and the world the thinning of the veil and when they sense dimension past what they assumed existed, what they sense and feel is one of those six lights, and maybe even more than one, illuminating them at low intensity. The seventh is against the six. But it is not so simple as the six against the one. It is not given that the guardians of goodness and of wisdom will withstand the beings of the seventh light. It also is not given that the beings of the seventh light will overcome the guardians of goodness and of wisdom."

Cosme doesn't look away from the no-see-um gyres in the shaft light.

"You may ask is this not like the struggle with the body and the blood. The Christian struggle with the world. But it is not much like. The Bible, you may say, prioritizes man. The Bible tells us God gave man dominion over everything on earth. To have dominion means that you subdue. What you subdue must suffer. Ayahuasca teaches us that man is just man. Ayahuasca teaches us that man is insufficient to withstand the beings of the seventh light, and ayahuasca teaches us to not subdue, to listen to the river birch and the no-see-um and the light. It teaches us to listen to what we perhaps were taught could not be heard, to see what we perhaps were taught could not be seen, to feel what we perhaps were taught did not have substance. Ayahuasca teaches us that in what we call signs there is the way beyond the beings of the seventh light."

Cosme does not look away from the no-see-ums whirling in the light.

"Before I left the Biblioteca Municipal, I sat in front of the computer screen and thought about what Percival had told me in my vision of the spiral light. I listened. Percival had told me, 'I am Percival. *To pierce the valley.*' I told myself I would pierce the valleys on my way. I listened. Percival had told me, 'I protected this.' I told myself that somehow I would see what he protected. What he still protects. I listened. Percival had told me, 'It is time to go.' I told myself that somehow I would go. When I had asked him where I was to go, Percival had said, 'There is a path.' I told myself the Appalachian Trail must be the path. I asked myself should I walk toward the People of the Dawnland or away. I told myself on such a journey it is good to know the People of the Dawnland are ahead. And do you know what also is ahead?"

Cosme leans and from his pocket takes a map, which he unfolds and orients so Chris and Mary can see what he points to.

"In my vision of the mountain, you remember, was a white house. On this lake, I have been told," says Cosme, pointing to the east end of the lake, "there is The White House."

"There is," they say.

"You see," says Cosme.

"It's about a two- or three-day hike from here," says Mary. "You should stop there. It's expensive, but the food is good."

"I do not plan to eat for some time," Cosme says, "but I would like to see The White House from across the lake."

Cosme folds the map and tucks it in his pocket. He takes out another and unfolds it, orienting it so they can see the features he will point to.

"In my vision of the mountain was a rainbow, you remember. On Map 1, see what is just beyond The White House. Rainbow Stream. Rainbow Deadwaters. Rainbow Lake. Rainbow Mountain. Rainbow Ledges. Do you know what grows in millions on the Ledges?"

"Blueberries," Chris and Mary say.

"You have been there," Cosme says.

"Yes," they say.

"You see. As in my vision. And from there to where the alpine flowers are is not far."

Cosme folds the map and tucks it in his pocket.

"Percival said to tell the people what the flora know. Before I left the Biblioteca Municipal, I promised I would tell."

Chapter Five: Bind Them In Bundles To Be Burned

Harold Brown peeks out his window.

6:15 a.m., the Sunday of the third week in July.

At the bottom of his driveway, careful not to trespass on his property, three women and three men have arrived to uphold six signs. They are the early risers, or, as Harold likes to call them, the fanatics. More will come. This is the fifth day they have gathered at the bottom of his driveway. They are silent, peaceful, getting better, day by day, at drawing here adherents who believe that civil disobedience still has the power to induce in someone such as Harold Brown the empathy or shame to catalyze an alteration, a reversal of what seems a certain course.

When Harold left his house the Monday of the third week in July, the bottom of his driveway was unpopulated, signless. But when Harold got to Chinco's Pittsfield headquarters, he was hindered at the entrance to the parking lot. More than a hundred people wielded signs and shouted slogans at him as he tried to enter. Gradually they parted. Harold had expected this reception.

On the Friday of the second week in July, he had announced by press release that Chinco had, in all but one or two negotiations pending, reached agreements with the owners of the properties abutting the proposed route of the East-West Transportation, Utility, and Communications Corridor and that, beginning Monday of the third week in July, he would hold town-hall meetings in the six towns where the interchanges would be built. The purpose of the meetings, the release had claimed, was to establish full transparency and good faith, to present the final route specifics, to address remaining citizen concerns, and to transition from the planning and deliberation phase to the construction phase, the phase of building, after ten years, the foundation of Maine's economic future.

After the release, the Corridor opponents took the weekend and coordinated their response. They understood that occupying Chinco headquarters, or at least the public property immediately outside its bounds, would illustrate the David and Goliath sort of mismatch grass-roots activists preferred to illustrate because the optics of the mismatch rarely worked in favor of Goliath. They decided therefore on at least a week-long occupation, and they notified the media.

When Harold got to Chinco on that Monday of the third week in July, he saw the picketers, the media among them, and the Chinco building—pillared, windows darkly tinted, Brutalist in spirit—looming in the background. He discerned at once the mismatch optics. Harold therefore waited, not impatiently and not indignantly, to be admitted to the parking lot that morning, and he therefore waited, not impatiently and not indignantly, to be allowed to leave the parking lot that afternoon.

The Tuesday of the third week in July, the same.

On both days, Harold felt the atmospheric discontent, the fervor in the air. Although an unassuming bodyguard went with him each night to the town-hall meetings, Harold wanted to pass through the steadfast opposition by himself each morning on his way in to the Chinco parking lot and wanted to pass through it in departure, unprovocative but unafraid, aware the optics of aloneness in this context, with the building looming, served him better in the long run than the optics of untouchability, the optics of advantage. Impassivity, politeness, and civility were his defense. These qualities, he understood, outlasted discontent, outlasted fervor. Harold held that movements founded on emotional reactions were sustained by sources unreliable and fleeting. Discontent and fervor were emotional reactions, Harold reasoned, and could thus be managed by whomever did not operate according to their dictates. Managed properly, they petered out.

The Tuesday evening of the third week in July, the picketers, among them Chris Atwater, tired, footsore, absolute in their allegiance to the cause but feeling somehow smaller after picketing a monolith for half a day again, dispersed and found their vehicles. They stowed their signs in back seats, truck beds, trunks. Some in departure beeped. Some waved or flashed the sign for peace. Some shouted out the open windows a resistance phrase. Some simply drove away, as if in the imperfect stillness, the imperfect silence, was the crucial charge, the slow replenishment of energy that half of Tuesday had consumed, the slow replenishment of energy already pledged to half of Wednesday.

Chris Atwater had attended Monday's town-hall meeting and had heard about the new developments from Harold Brown directly. Things, she had admitted to herself, looked grim.

As she drove home the Tuesday evening of the third week in July, Chris reconsidered her decision to sit out the Tuesday town-hall meeting. Someone else had been appointed to attend the meeting in her place and represent In Defense of Water, but resistance did not lend itself so easily to delegation. Chris believed that she, as Maine Coordinator of In Defense of Water, should be there as well because resistance, tenuous by nature and too often done in spirit only, drew strength from each body present and depended on each present body to impress upon the force resisted, always measured, always rational, the corporal weight of solidarity. That was why she herself was on the picket line each day. She felt the moral counterforce of being there. She also felt the moral counterforce of being there was insufficient. On the picket line, Chris kept in contact via cell phone with In Defense of Water's legal counsel, but environmental statutes, always slippery, semantically duplicitous, demanded the attention of a stationary agent. So, instead of adding one more moral body, one more injured voice, to Tuesday's town-hall meeting, Chris held steady and drove home to Onawa to seat herself and Skype with legal counsel, hoping that another close examination of the statutes, one more dialogic parsing, would reveal with epiphanic clarity the path that had been hidden in the language all along.

As Chris approached Route 6 in Guilford, where, according to the map that Harold Brown had shown the town-hall audience the night before, a section of the Corridor will be imposed, she pictured this side of the walled-off toll road, offering no passage north except the narrow overpass. She pictured concrete topped by metal fence, unbroken but for six relenting interchanges, penitentiary defensiveness extending for 220 miles east and west, a barrier unnatural, a geographical affront.

As she drove through Guilford, crossing Route 6, she envisioned rising on the overpass and seeing from its apex nothing, neither east nor west, but barren Corridor, exclusive habitat. She tried to picture from that vantage what had been chopped down, uprooted, drained, filled in, paved over, steamrolled, gutted, and made refugee for this restriction, this advance. She pictured from that elevation wetlands, forest, deer yards, burrows, hives, nests, warrens, dens laid bare, eviscerated into nothing east and west. She pictured habitats arboreal and habitats terrestrial and habitats aquatic ruptured, ruined, gone. She pictured hordes of tandem trailers speeding, hauling their commodities, the deadline always looming, more pollution, mile after mile. The noise and the exhaust. The altered pressure of the air. The long, wide scar. 220 miles by 500 feet. She tried to picture what could not be pictured from the overpass's apex, what could not be pictured even from its lowest point. She tried to picture what was underground.

The night before, at Monday's town-hall meeting, Harold Brown had spoken of a pending expedited-permit application for the installation of a pipeline, subterranean and out of mind, within the right of way, to carry fresh Maine water east to tankers that would ship it to the arid regions of the world. "Remember," he had forecast, "future wars will not be fought for oil, but for water. Maine will be positioned for that future. Maine will do its part to keep the peace."

Chris pictured Maine's position in that future, and she saw no path back from the economics of depletion.

As Chris passed Guilford and continued north to Onawa, she understood the Corridor was an invasive species and its highest-profile propagator, Harold Brown, though born and raised in Livermore Falls, a lifelong resident of Livermore Falls, was in his marrow an invasive species. They were purple loosestrife. They were Asiatic bittersweet. They were Eurasian milfoil. They were emerald ash borers. They were browntail moths and hemlock woolly adelgids. She thought of Albert and what he had often said when they got on the subject of invasion: "Even the wild animals resisted the destruction of their homelands under the hordes of invading livestock." How much worse the Corridor would be than livestock. As she neared her home, as she neared Onawa, Chris saw it was no use to picket Chinco. The resisters must go to the home of the available invader and demand he take back what he had introduced. They must demand he take his loosestrife back, his bittersweet, his milfoil. Harold Brown must take his borer back, his moth, his adelgid.

Before she conferenced with In Defense of Water's legal counsel that night at her home in Onawa, she emailed her confederate resisters and explained her rationale, her change of course. She urged them to descend like civil locusts on the home of Harold Brown next morning and five mornings after.

Harold Brown turns from his window.

6:16 a.m., the Sunday of the third week in July.

He tells his wife, who monitors the percolating coffee, "The fanatics are assembled."

Harold sits down at the kitchen table on which Klara sets two saucers. Harold fiddles with the one in front of him and mulls. He stops when Klara comes back with the cups.

"The same six?" asks Klara.

She, like Harold, is bespectacled and nearing seventy. She wears a light-green sweater though the temperature today is forecast to be high.

"They look to be," says Harold.

Klara pours the coffee, sets the pot back on the stove, and sits across from Harold.

"Say what you will say," she says, "but they are punctual."

He sips his coffee, holds his cup close to his lips for longer than the norm, and sets it on the saucer when the measurement of his proposed rejoinder has been taken and approved.

"What purpose does it serve to stand in front of someone's private property by 6:15 a.m.? What good is punctuality when all it expedites is idleness?"

"They're punctual is all," says Klara. "This makes, what, five mornings in a row."

They sip, and in their sipping is not easily observed the toll of siege. The cups and saucers clink.

"I thought they might take Sunday off," says Klara.

"I forgot to get the paper," Harold says. He takes a deep draft that suggests his journey will be long and sets his cup down on the saucer. He stands. "Excuse me."

Harold slips his shoes on by the front door and goes out.

His ranch house, tastefully proportioned, spreads at leisure on a modest hill. There are no other houses near. His driveway gradually declines. A hundred yards. Two hundred. He proceeds and sees that, since his turning from his window, ten or twelve resisters have been added to the ranks of the fanatics. Harold thinks about how rapidly they multiply. Like cane toads. Mice. He sees their vehicles lined up along each shoulder of the road. Each one a carrier of known pollutants. Each a fact of exploitation. Each dependent on the hard truth of the road. These people know these things. They picket, but they know. Resistance, Harold thinks as he comes to the bottom of his driveway, is an easy way to shift the blame to those who make the hard decisions, those, like him, whose work provides necessities like infrastructure, those who take the necessary sins on their own heads so the resisters and the critics, beneficiaries of the tough calls, can indulge the fantasy of opposition, can believe that activism washes them entirely, absolves them of complicity.

"Good morning," Harold says as he takes his paper from the box.

"Good morning," some of the resisters say.

"You realize it's Sunday," Harold says as he stands straight again.

"Are you implying we hold nothing sacred?"

"Miss Atwater, you are free to rest or not rest on the seventh day," says Harold as he heads back up his driveway. Halfway up, he looks down at his *Morning Sentinel* in its transparent plastic bag and notices a sticky note appended to the front page. Through the plastic, Harold reads the flowing hand: "Our relationships with each other can be vehicles for our unity, and they can be vehicles for our entrapment. In my relationship with you, who I think I am affects who I see you to be."

He walks the last half of his driveway in the manner of a country gentleman observing his possessions and goes in. He slips his shoes off by the door and says, "It's very mild out this morning."

"There's another note, I'm guessing," Klara says.

He lays the paper on the table and sits down across from her. He slips the paper from its plastic bag.

"There is," says Harold, who then peels it from the front page of the *Sentinel* and passes it to Klara.

After reading it, she says, "She isn't wrong about relationships. I think she's reaching out."

He doesn't look up from the front page when he asks, "To what end?"

"I don't know. To smooth the waters maybe."

"Who I think I am affects who I see you to be," says Harold.

"That sounds right to me."

"The Corridor is happening," says Harold, lowering the front page to accommodate a meeting of the eyes. "Who she sees me to be means nothing. Chris Atwater doesn't know me. We have no relationship." When he says this, he is not impassioned.

"There is some relationship," says Klara, reaching for a section of the paper. "Superficial maybe. Maybe adversarial. But there is some relationship. You do communicate."

"She's adversarial," says Harold as he flips to page three of the *Sentinel*. "That's true, but she is not an adversary." He is not impassioned. "What she has at her disposal, instrumentally, is incommensurate to what I have at mine. If she is reaching out, she's not an adversary. She's a suppliant. These notes are her petitions. She is asking me to undo what for ten years I have done. Whatever this note says or any of the others, she is asking me to not do what I know is an approximation of the greater good." He sips. "Imagine her equivalent had prevailed against the Interstate in 1941. Imagine her equivalent had prevailed against the Dead River Dam in 1949. I know two villages were flooded. I know lives were changed. I'm not insensitive to local tragedy. But is there anyone today who would undo it all and live without electric power? Chris Atwater, would she give electric power up? Would she give up the Interstate and only drive on secondary roads and backroads? Going backward isn't natural. Stasis isn't natural."

Harold's color does not redden, and his voice does not sound tremulous or strained, and his extremities and essential systems do not feel the outer world encroaching on the usual somatic calm.

"Her heart is in the right place," says Klara.

"A lot of people's hearts are in the right place. Mine is."

"Yes, I know it is."

"But there is more to acting in the world than where the heart is," Harold says. "Where's the stomach? Is the stomach in the right place? Where's the spleen? The brain?"

They look at one another.

"Let's enjoy the paper," Klara says.

They raise their sections of the *Sentinel* and read in rustling silence, cups and saucers on occasion clinking, as if people outside aren't multiplying in defiance of what Harold swears is rational and good.

At 7:30, Harold gets the door for Klara. Tenderly he helps her in. He glances down the driveway as he walks around his Forester to the driver's side.

The picketers exceed a hundred now. The signs they hold exceed a hundred. Those resisters who obstruct the bottom of the driveway part as though respecting the approach of a procession. Harold passes. They do not confront him as they did at Chinco. They say nothing, but they glare at him and face their signs in his direction. Harold drives away. The language of the signs is backward in his rearview. No resister follows him. None cheers his riddance.

Harold, old enough to feel nostalgic for the custom of the Sunday drive, drives at a speed conducive to appraisal and remembering the good old days. When country yields to town, he turns his Forester onto Church Street, drives another mile, turns into the small lot on the northeast side of Eaton Memorial United Methodist Church, and parks, exhaling as if in proximity to neo-Gothic architecture in the service of the inexpressible is his relief.

He gets out of the car and walks around to Klara's side, opening her door and holding out his hand to help her rise. When she is out, he crooks his arm, which Klara hooks with hers, and they proceed, opposed appendages entwined, toward Church Street.

They turn right on Church Street and walk past a neo-Gothic tower, squared and bricked, its roof pyramidal and steep, a tapering of slate. The tower is identical to two companions at the building's rear. This trinity of similarity solidifies the theme of structural submission, of coordinate proportion in the name of something higher, of humility's aesthetic. But the tower toward which Harold and Klara walk is different. It is higher, spired. It was built to raise all passing eyes toward God. So Harold, still approaching, raises his. So Klara, still approaching, raises hers. They feel the spire glance is the beginning of the service, their acceptance of the invitation to go in. They feel the shadow sense of transportation, of what one day they believe their spirits will go through. Their eyes come down to earth and look at the announcement board outside the entrance.

The Calling
July 23—The Seventh Sunday After Pentecost

The Calling—Matthew 13: 24-30, 36-43

The Gathering begins, the greetings, the announcements.
Then there is the hymn, the opening prayers, the praise.
A member in the front row rises and walks to the lectern.
"Good morning. A reading from the book of Genesis, chapter 28, verses 10 to 19." She reads about Jacob going toward Haran and stopping for the night. She reads about the stone that he repurposed for a pillow. She arrives at the transcendent passage: "And he dreamed that there was a ladder set up on the earth, the top of it reaching to Heaven; and the angels of God were ascending and descending on it." After reading about this place, once Luz, that Jacob renamed Bethel, she returns contemplatively to her front-row seat.

Another member in the front row rises and walks to the lectern.

"Good morning. A reading from Psalm 139, verses 1 to 12 and 23 to 24." He reads about the inescapability of God, beginning with "O Lord, you have searched me and known me. You know when I sit down and when I rise up; you discern my thoughts from far away. You search out my path and my lying down, and are acquainted with all my ways" and ending with "See if there is any wicked in me, and lead me in the way everlasting." He seems moved and takes his seat.

Then Harold rises from the third row and walks to the lectern.

"Good morning. A reading from Paul's Epistle to the Romans, chapter 8, verses 12 to 28." He reads about corporeal indebtedness and flesh and what the body's deeds can lead to. When he gets to the twenty-eighth verse, Harold pauses for a long beat and resumes, "We know that all things work together for good for those who love God, who are called according to his purpose." Harold stares a second at verse 28 before he leaves the lectern and returns to his seat in the third row.

Pastor Wilson rises to approach the lectern, and the congregation rises for the Gospel reading. He is in his middle fifties, wispy haired, and sees the world through round-rimmed glasses. At the lectern, he looks at his congregation for a moment. In him is the beaming quality of someone who has spent much time considering mortality, forgiveness, the theology of letting go.

"A reading from the Gospel According to Matthew, chapter 13, verses 24 to 30 and 36 to 43."

When he has read these verses, Pastor Wilson looks up from the Bible and recites from memory verse 24: "The kingdom of Heaven may be compared to someone who sowed seed in his field." He smiles at his congregation. "This seems pretty simple. Heaven is a farmer. One who tills, who plants, who cultivates, who brings forth new life. When the disciples ask Jesus to explain the meaning of the parable, Jesus says, 'The one who sows the good seed is the Son of Man; the field is the world; and the good seed are the children of the kingdom.'"

Pastor Wilson lets this verse sink in. When he is certain it has reached a certain depth, he says, "'And the good seed are the children of the kingdom.' Let's assume we are the good seed. Each of us was planted in this field for a specific purpose. Each of us was planted in this world for a specific purpose. Here is where I think the metaphor gets trickier. What is the purpose of the good seed? What's our purpose? Are we to remain where we were planted and grow into wheat? What kind of wheat are we? What beings do we feed? Are we to blame for gluten allergies?"

The congregation chuckles.

"On the one hand, such questions aren't really what these parables are about. But, on the other hand, they are. I am reminded of the koan in which the Buddhist monk goes to the master and asks, 'What is the way?' The master answers, 'An open-eyed man falling into a well.'"

The congregation chuckles.

"Who of us has not asked God some version of that question? Did you get an answer? Or some version of 'An open-eyed man falling into a well'?"

Pastor Wilson lets his congregation sit a minute with the questions.

"These two parables are mostly focused on the planting and the harvest. What, however, do they say about the way? What is the good seed supposed to do between the planting and the harvest?"

Pastor Wilson lets these questions dangle.

"When I was a boy and asked my mother questions that she couldn't answer, she would say, 'God knows.' In one sense, this is simply a deflection, right? Another way of saying, 'I have no idea.' In another, it is the expression of the greatest truth. We cannot know what God knows, but we trust God's infinite wisdom. Though we trust, how often don't we see what God has given us to know, what God has given us to help answer that perplexing question: 'What is the way?'

"In the Genesis reading, we heard about the ladder, this divine connection, this amazing link between earth and Heaven. God showed this to Jacob in a dream. Why Jacob? Was he special? Was he any different than the rest of us?" He pauses. "Do you know what Jacob was? A pastoralist. A nomadic livestock farmer. God considered Jacob, a nomadic livestock farmer, to be worthy of this vision. Jacob could have blown this vision off as a delusion, just a dream. Jacob could have written off the whole thing as the consequence of having eaten bad bread or a psychedelic legume. But he doesn't do that. What he does is make a choice. A little later in the chapter, Jacob vows, 'If God will be with me, and will keep me in this way that I go, and will give me bread to eat and clothing to wear, so that I come again to my father's house in peace, then the Lord shall be my God.' God spoke through Jacob to us all.

"In Psalm 139, the psalmist says to God, 'You search out my path and my lying down, and are acquainted with all my ways.' With all our ways is God acquainted. God knows. Have you ever wondered if your life was heading in the right direction? Have you ever wondered what the right direction is? Have you felt lost? Who oriented you? Who reassured you? If there was no orientation, if there was no reassurance, did you just assume you were on your own? Did you assume that navigation was a one-person job? Did you move on?"

Pastor Wilson knows the answers to these questions may not be immediately accessible. He takes his glasses off and cleans the lenses with a tissue he has taken from his pocket. When he puts his glasses back on and adjusts them, the congregational assumption is that Pastor Wilson sees the world more clearly and has given them sufficient time to do the same.

"The psalmist says, 'Search me, O God, and know my heart; test me and know my thoughts. See if there is any wicked in me, and lead me in the way everlasting.' The psalmist may not know the way, but he is sure that God knows. Search me. Test me. Lead me. Does this mean the psalmist gives up human agency? Gives up free will? The psalmist makes a choice here. The psalmist chooses to trust God. He chooses to have faith that God knows the way.

"So what is this thing that keeps coming up? The way? What is the way? For us, the answer should be easy. We already know that Thomas says to Jesus, 'How can we know the way?' and Jesus says, 'I am the way, and the truth, and the life.' So there is one way, but there are many ways to the one way. Sounds like a koan, doesn't it? But think of the many ways as tributaries flowing toward one river, which itself is flowing toward the ocean."

Pastor Wilson gives them leave to think.

"Recall what Paul says in his letter to the Romans: 'We know that all things work together for those who love God, who are called according to His purpose.' That is an important clause: 'Who are called according to His purpose.' 'Called' is an important word.

"As I was working on this sermon, I began to think about this notion of a calling, this belief that somewhere out there is this work that we are meant to do, our life's work. For days I thought about this, but I didn't feel like I was making progress with the sermon. I had in the sermon what the lectionary indicates I should have, but I felt that there was something more to say about the nature of a calling. I was puzzled. In my puzzlement, however, after several days, God handed me the puzzle piece that made the bigger picture clear. Max Weber was the clarifying piece. Max Weber was a nineteenth- and early twentieth-century political economist and sociologist who wrote *The Protestant Ethic and the Spirit of Capitalism*. I had read this book in college, but since then I haven't really thought about it much until this week."

He reaches into the middle of the lectern and takes out the book. He slides the Bible slightly to the left and lays Max Weber's book beside it.

"So I looked around the house, and I found this. What God had given me to know was on a bookshelf in my basement," says Pastor Wilson, opening the book. "If you'll permit me to depart from Scripture for a while, I will try to bring the sermon back around to what we heard today in Scripture."

Pastor Wilson pauses to confirm permission.

"Weber writes the following in Chapter 3, entitled 'Luther's Conception of the Calling': 'Now it is unmistakable that even in the German word *Beruf*, and perhaps still more clearly in the English *calling*, a religious conception, that of a task set by God, is at least suggested. The more emphasis is put upon the word in a concrete case, the more evident is the connotation. And if we trace the history of the word through the civilized languages, it appears that neither the predominantly Catholic peoples nor those of classical antiquity have possessed any expression of similar connotation for what we know as a calling (in the sense of a life-task, a definite field in which to work), while one has existed for all predominantly Protestant peoples.'

"We could sometimes use reminding that a calling doesn't necessarily imply a calling to religious vocation. Paul says we are called according to God's purpose. We forget at times that carpentry or farming or custodianship or aviation or whatever is your occupation is as much a calling as the ministry. And we could sometimes use reminding that a calling doesn't necessarily imply withdrawal from the world and giving up the wide community, society, in favor of monastic or hermitic life, in favor of religious purification via abnegation, via solitude. In fact, Max Weber says the higher calling is the opposite. The higher calling is engagement with the world, says Weber: 'The conception of the calling thus brings out that central dogma of all Protestant denominations which the Catholic division of ethical precepts into *praecepta* and *consilia* discards.' *Praecepta*, a Latin word meaning, obviously enough, *precepts*, are moral dictates one must follow to attain eternal happiness. *Consilia*, a Latin word meaning *counsels*, though not required, are supposed to expedite the process, mainly through monasticism, which, I learned, as I composed this sermon, is a word whose roots are in the Greek *monastikos*, whose roots in turn are in the Greek *monazein*, which means *to be alone, to live alone*. For Protestants, however, Weber says, 'The only way of living acceptably to God was not to surpass worldly morality in monastic asceticism, but solely through the fulfillment of the obligations imposed upon the individual by his position in the world. That was his calling.'

"We believe as Protestants, as Methodists, that we are called to be our best selves in this world, to be among each other, and to work for one another. Wasn't Jesus in this world, among us, giving of Himself to us? And even when He went into the wilderness, away from us, He went into the wilderness for us. We do not work in one world and worship in another. Worship should be evident in what we do from day to day. What good is coming here each Sunday for an hour if, in your position in the world, you do not work according to God's purpose? What good is coming here each Sunday for an hour if we don't remember we are called according to God's purpose not for only sixty minutes on the seventh day but for each second of the seven days. 86,400 seconds every day.

604,800 seconds every week. How many of those seconds do we honestly devote to God?"

Pastor Wilson scans the congregation, peers into the face of private calculation. He is conscious of the line between productive moral inventory and unhealthy self-recrimination, so, a minute passing, he returns his focus to the German's book and reads a little more.

"'The monastic life is not only quite devoid of value as a means of justification before God, but Luther also looks upon its renunciation of the duties of this world as the product of selfishness, withdrawing from temporal obligations. In contrast, labor in a calling appears to him as the outward expression of brotherly love. This he proves by the observation that the division of labor forces every individual to work for others...The fulfillment of worldly duties is under all circumstances the only way to live acceptably for God. It and it alone is the will of God, and hence every legitimate calling has exactly the same worth in the sight of God.'"

Pastor Wilson closes *The Protestant Ethic and the Spirit of Capitalism.*

"We are intricately bound in what we have been called to do in this world. We are intricately dependent on each other. Our community, society, the world at large, is but an ecosystem. If a cornerstone relationship is ruined, if a cornerstone component is withdrawn, if an invasive species comes, the balance of the ecosystem is disrupted, this discrete upheaval radiates, and in it are the seeds of chaos sown.

"In the second parable we heard this morning, Jesus says, 'The kingdom of Heaven may be compared to someone who sowed good seed in his field; but while everyone was asleep, an enemy came and sowed weeds among the wheat, and then went away.' But the Master doesn't want the weeds uprooted. Why? 'For in gathering the weeds you would uproot the wheat along with them.' What does this suggest about our temporal existence? Does the good seed presuppose the bad? Are good and bad essential to the field, the world, our ecosystem? If so, what then is the wheat supposed to do? How does the good seed not get overrun?

"Let's think about this for a attinute. Even in the balanced ecosystem, there are forces that exist in opposition to each other's interests. In that conflict is the ecosystem's balance, its stability. We must remember that this balance is a temporary state, a transient condition. It is not the everlasting.

"In the parable, the Master says, 'Let both of them grow together until the harvest; and at the harvest time I will tell the reaper, *Collect the weeds first and bind them in bundles to be burned, but gather the wheat in my barn.*' The wheat must bide among the weeds and do what it is called to do, secure that in the end will be fruition. We must do the same.

"Of course, our callings are more various than the wheat's. Our powers somewhat larger. Think about your calling. Who depends on you? Be generous to them. Be sheltering. On whom do you depend? Be grateful and, if possible, reciprocate. Cooperate and work for one another. 'Labor in a calling appears to Luther as the outward expression of brotherly love.' Beyond that we are not too different than the wheat, the good seed. We must trust the Master who has sown us in this field. We must accept what we cannot control. We must have faith and bide, content with our positions, certain of them. We must know that when the cycle runs its natural course and it is harvest time we will be gathered in the Master's barn."

At the conclusion of the service, Harold and Klara file out of the pew and up the center aisle toward the exit, where they compliment the pastor on his sermon and exchange departure pleasantries. They leave the spired tower arm in arm and walk up Church Street to their Forester.

Harold drives south on Church and north on Main to Berry's, where they sit in a familiar booth and have the usual: two coffees, regular, two sausage-egg-and-cheese croissants, two apple-spice-cake slices. They discuss the sermon and consider whether Pastor Wilson's use of Weber in the homily may have transgressed a theological and lectionary line, relying too much on the secular to do the work of Scripture.

"My initial inclination was to think that Weber's writing overshadowed Scripture," Klara says. "But then I thought the pastor's point must be that Weber had been called to write that book and in that calling he was not attempting to surpass God but to serve Him. Serve us. The pastor said we need to be reminded that the secular, the earthly, is not separate from the sacred. Isn't that the point of Jacob's ladder? Wasn't that the pastor's point in saying that a calling doesn't mean you have to be a minister?"

"I think it was," says Harold.

"I appreciated that he ended with the image of the barn," says Klara.

"Yes, the way he brought it back to Matthew at the end was nice."

When the last crumb of the apple spice cake is no more and neither wants more coffee, Harold pays the check and waits for Klara, who excused herself to use the bathroom. As he browses the preserves shelves, Harold thinks of something worth imprinting. He returns a Mason jar of pickled carrots to its shelf. He takes a pen and notepad from his shirt pocket, flips the notepad to a blank page, and writes ten words and two numbers. Harold slides the pen and notepad in his pocket, nears the register, and holds his left arm out to Klara as they merge and say kind words about the food and service to the hostess, whom they've known for many years in several contexts.

The drive home is quiet. They digest. They limit their remarks to features that the drive north has invested with an observational priority the drive south, due to variables directional or temporal, had not.

"That silver maple was too harshly limbed," says Harold.

"It's a shame," says Klara. "Such a beautiful tree."

They do not comment further on this topic. Harold's speed does not exceed the limit.

Klara says, a little farther on, "The McIntyres made some progress with their siding."

"Yes," says Harold, "I can hardly see the Typar."

They remark on nothing else, not even on the distant picketers they see as they approach their house. Their Forester is a quarter mile from their driveway when the picketers, aligned on both sides of the road, are certain it is Harold's car. They've turned en masse, their signs and phones now facing Harold and Klara.

Harold slows.

He knows the point of no return is near. The final meeting is tomorrow. It is clear to everyone on both sides that the project will get underway. The project will get done. He looks at signs and faces, lawfully indignant, peaceful, orderly. But Harold also knows that imminent defeat, the looming sense of loss, of being causeless, can inspire a believer to devalue wellness, and desire nothing more than to relinquish it as evidence of willingness to go down with the cause.

Harold scans the picketers on both sides of the road and tries to estimate which one, at odds with the inevitable, might sacrifice the body in commiseration with the cause and hurl it in the Forester's path.

A parody of martyrdom, thinks Harold. A ploy to sue.

He slows and scans.

But no one sacrifices. No one hurls.

As he turns up the driveway, he sees Chris Atwater on his left. He stops and opens his window the remainder of the way.

"Hello there, Mr. Brown," says Chris. She lowers her *No E/W Corridor* sign, bends at the waist, and looks at Klara. "Hello there, Mrs. Brown."

"Quite a turnout, Miss Atwater," Harold says.

"The people don't want the East-West Corridor," says Chris.

"Some people. This is not a referendum, Miss Atwater," Harold says.

"That's true. It's not a referendum. You made sure we didn't get the referendum. But the turnout doesn't lie."

"We will agree to disagree on the significance of sample size," says Harold, reaching for his shirt pocket. "Which reminds me." Harold flips his notepad open and tears out a sheet, which he holds out the window. "Since we have developed something of a one-sided correspondence, I thought I would share this with you." Harold looks up at the sky. "It's getting cloudy, Miss Atwater. Be safe. I trust I'll see you at the meeting tomorrow night."

He is about to continue up the driveway when a woman steps forth from the ranks. She holds no sign, but in her hands she cups a small paper bag waist high.

"Excuse me, Mr. Brown."

"Yes, ma'am." He looks at her, and in his face is registered a partial recognition. "Mrs.?"

"Lesiak."

"We've met," he says, his intonation indicating half a question.

"In Garland. On the H.C. Haynes property. On the former H.C. Haynes property."

"Of course, Mrs. Lesiak. Good morning. I apologize. The context threw me off." He looks from Mary to the picketers and back to Mary. "Am I to assume that your participation here is a rejection of our offer?"

"Oh, I'm not participating here. I'm friends with Chris, but on the subject of the Corridor we disagree."

"I take it then that you've accepted."

"We're close to a decision."

"You're aware that time is running out."

"We are."

They look at one another for a moment.

"May I ask why you're still holding out?"

"Oh, we're not holding out. My husband's sentimental. He has an attachment to the land. He bought it twenty years ago with money that the government paid out to settle in the matter of his father's death. The issue isn't that we're holding out. It's that my husband's holding on. He's having difficulty letting go."

"The offer is as high as it will go," says Harold.

"We're not haggling. We agree the offer's fair. The issue isn't monetary. It's emotional."

The nearest picketers, who overhear the conversation, seem dissatisfied with Mary, and they look to Chris, who seems composed.

"But you are close to a decision," Harold says.

"I brought you this," says Mary, handing him the small paper bag in which is firmly packed a pound of ground chaga. "In the interview you did with *Bangor Daily News*, you said that you like chaga tea in the afternoon."

"I do."

"I harvest chaga. That's my company," says Mary, pointing to the label on the bag. "Bog Chaga. This is something new. It's summer chaga. High in melanin, which boosts acuity and vision. Anyway, I wanted to deliver this to you and let you know we're close to a decision."

"Thank you. I appreciate the kindness," Harold says.

He is about to drive away when Mary says, "Would you reach out to Albert?"

"Mrs. Lesiak, we have reached out to him."

"You personally, I mean. Can you sit down with him? Explain the situation? Whether we accept or not, the Corridor will happen, won't it?"

"It would make things easier if you accepted, but the Corridor will happen one way or another, yes."

"Can you explain that to him? Can you look him in the eye and tell him that?"

"Mrs. Lesiak, he knows."

"The truth is we don't need the land, but we could use the money. I don't know if you remember, but we have two boys."

"I do remember," Harold says. "Our grandson is autistic."

"Then you understand."

"I'll see what I can do," says Harold. "Thank you for the chaga. Miss Atwater."

Up the driveway Harold goes.

Chris turns to the picketers nearby and says, "She isn't really selling out. We're doing what we can to buy more time."

They seem relieved.

"Well, Operation Third-Eye Activation is now underway," says Mary.

"Harold Brown will need a lot more than a pound of summer chaga to decalcify his third eye," says Chris.

"Small steps," Mary says.

"We're running out of time."

"But there are measures that can still be taken."

"Legally we're limited."

"But there are measures."

"Monkeywrenching."

"'The offenders are always vulnerable somewhere.'"

"From the monkeywrenching manual?"

"*Ecodefense: A Field Guide to Monkeywrenching*. Albert's been reciting passages."

"It doesn't work," says Chris.

"It rarely works," says Mary.

"Maybe the melanin will be enough and Harold Brown will see the light."

"Remember when you said that you would kill the baby Leo Henrik Baekeland if it meant that plastic died with him?" asks Mary.

"I'm not killing Harold Brown."

Light rain begins to sprinkle.

"What was in the note he gave you anyway?"

Chris reads, "Let both of them grow together until the harvest. Matthew 13:30."

"Weird."

Chapter Six: Katahdin

Hours before the first birds welcome morning, Cosme Esperanza takes his hammock and mosquito netting down. He flaps them so they lie flat on the ground. He flaps his pocket blanket, lays it on the hammock and mosquito netting, rolls the three together, smoothing as he goes, and stows the compact bundle in his backpack.

It is dark, but Cosme does not use a light. The morning coolness chills him, but he does not build a fire.

Cosme takes his pack and walks down the streambank near his campsite. He sets it on a dry rock and removes from it a tin cup. Everywhere the soothing, ceaseless mumble roar of water come down from the mountain. Cosme faces upstream, listening.

He squats and dips his tin cup in Katahdin Stream. He drinks, examining the granite rocks, the faintest outline of the downstream footbridge, the divinity of darkened evergreens.

He has not carried water on the Trail nor has he purified or filtered any. From Springer Mountain to Katahdin Stream, his lightness has elicited concern from certain hikers, curiosity from certain others, and reverence from the ultralights, who travel heavier than Cosme.

"Does the black bear carry water? Does the black bear purify or filter?" he has asked them. "Does the porcupine? The moose? The raven? The coyote? I am not more special than the animals. I travel in their spirit. If I come to water, then I come. If water comes to me, then water comes."

His legend spread along the Trail.

He dips his cup again and drinks. The vision of the thousands trampling alpine flowers comes to him. He takes a Nalgene bottle from the cool stream and unties the large rock that had weighed it down. He rises, wraps the bottle, and then puts it and the tin cup in his backpack.

He walks up the streambank, scans the campground in the darkness, and sees no one. Cosme waits to urinate. He leaves before the others wake.

He signs in at the trailhead kiosk, falsifies the time so that the register reflects he left at sunrise, and becomes the steady crunch of footsteps unassisted by a hiking pole or headlamp on the Hunt Trail up the west side of Katahdin.

About a mile up the mountain, Cosme pauses on the footbridge at Katahdin Stream Falls. This is the last reliable source of water when the weather has been dry. He crosses, slides his backpack to his front, and takes his tin cup out. It rained two days ago, but Cosme steps down to the pool below the Falls and dips his cup. He stands to drink and feels the weather of the Falls. The trees envelop even here and huddle out the sky. He wants to linger, but he wants more to move on, to leave the campers down below behind. He packs his tin cup and resituates his backpack.

Past the Falls, the forest quiets. Cosme steps and scrambles, slips and steadies, rising, and the sound of flowing water fades. The forest presses on the trail. The lower, broken limbs of balsam fir and white pine jut like skeans and dirks, unmoving, pointing here and there at Cosme.

A mile from the Falls a small brook trickles across the trail, and Cosme stops to skim his tin cup just above the silt. The water is too low to truly skim. He drinks his quarter cup of water and his thimble's worth of silt. He feels the grit go down. He eats a little of the mountain, which he thanks the mountain for. He has not eaten anything since yesterday, mid-morning. Cosme crossed the Abol Bridge and bought a single orange at the campground store. He sat below the bridge, his bare feet cooling in the West Branch of the Penobscot River. Cosme peeled and ate his orange, savoring each segment as he idolized Katahdin in the distance.

Cosme tips his tin cup, finishing his water, finishing his silt, and stows it, repositioning his backpack.

It is dark still. What he can and cannot see is less than certain. Shapes shift. Cosme feels a presence parallel to him. He cannot say if it is left or right, above him or below. He thought he sensed it half a mile back, but while he was in motion he could not be sure. While Cosme moved, he told himself that it was natural, moving at his rapid pace through darkness he had never traveled through, to feel pursued.

But in the darkness, standing by the shallow brook, a little of the mountain in him, Cosme does not feel pursued. He feels accompanied, assisted upward, spirited by his protectors, by the beings whom his father gave him when the only thing that Cosme wanted after crippling sickness was to move. But maybe by the beings of the mountain also, maybe by the spirits of the trees and plants and animals and rocks and water, maybe by the spirits of the People of the Dawnland, maybe by what spirits he cannot imagine here, four-thousand miles from the Ucayali and the forest that he knows.

He crosses. All is crossing.

White pine, red pine, balsam fir, black spruce give way as Cosme climbs. One-tenth of a mile, two-tenths, three-tenths, four, five, six—the forest's range recedes, its density relents, the canopy becoming dark gray sky, the greater eastern lightening not far behind. He pushes, drawn by dawning sky, and does not see the slab cave to his side. The presence parallel to Cosme whispers, "Treeline." Cosme whispers, "Treeline." Point-one farther on, the treeline, the transition zone, the obstinate arboreal goodbye, the new scope, the granitic, the sublime.

The trail zags toward the treeline, switchback after switchback, an approximation of an upward spiral, tightening until the treeline, tightening until the center seems to hold no longer, until the center seems to have collapsed into a scramble of Devonian boulders, gray and pink and lichen-hued and weathered mega-annum after mega-annum, recently blazed white at intervals to argue there is still a way, an organizing principle, a spur to lead the elevated human on.

Beyond the treeline, Cosme looks up at a Hunt-Spur boulder, slab-like, twice his height, and sheer, a monolith of feldspar, mica, hornblende, quartz.

The sky is lightening. The wind is here.

A white blaze beckons from the face of the adjacent boulder, rounder, portly, roughly Cosme's height. At ease with apertures, he slips between the boulders, finds a small protrusion, shin-high, plants his toes and phalanges on it, leverages, his hand on the boulder top in search of purchase, settling for flatness, for the gift of friction, and uplifts himself, his right foot upswung, heel down on the boulder, and stands, surveying.

Many who have stood where Cosme stands were certain their surmounting was a conquering of something somehow in defiance of them: distance, altitude, inertia, mineral insensitivity. But Cosme, on this rock, is certain he has gotten here by fitting in, by yielding to each aperture and blaze and smooth protrusion, by accepting the provisional as well as what will ever last, by abdicating to the logic of water, land, and sky, by abdicating to what detours, what obstructions, what epiphanies, what harms, what deprivations that beings he has had but glimmers of positioned to facilitate he still knows not what end.

The eastern sky has pinkened. Daylight is less shy. How far he is from Ucayali.

"You are like the black spruce," says the presence parallel to Cosme. "You are out here."

Cosme sees a black spruce growing from the last extremity of granite, unprotected, past the treeline, far above sea level, beyond the soil of the lower world, a disciple of the sun and wind, of always looking upward, outward, holding on, an adamant progenitor, the needled vanguard.

"I am out here," Cosme says, approaching the extremity, admiring the black spruce. "I am like the black spruce that way. But, when I was young, for months I could not move for illness. All I wanted was to move. I am more restless in my nature than the black spruce."

"How far from the treeline is the black spruce?" asks the presence parallel to Cosme.

Cosme looks down at the treeline.

"Yes," says Cosme, seeing now with clarity the correspondence. "There are many ways to move."

He holds out one palm to the needles and communes before withdrawing, moving onward, upward, to maintain his distance from the people who are coming his way from below.

He fits in gaps and plants and grips and presses torso, back, posterior, and parts of his anatomy not otherwise conscripted in the normal human course of moving on. He is led by cairns and blazes, led by the appearance of no other way to go, past scrub and over sediment, an ant whose colony is nowhere to be found. Past boulders, for a while, seconds, Cosme sees a mile on the spine of granite, vertebral and undulant, an ancient stairway to the eastern sky, the Gateway to the Tableland. It seems both far and near, illusory and tangible, a stark place and a gauzy one, and then it disappears again, obscured by yet another slab, by yet another boulder.

Cosme stops and chuckles, pats the backpack to his rear. Before him is a boulder of no scalable dimension, offering no small protrusion, no approachable adjacency, no aperture, no natural invitation.

"I have heard of you," says Cosme, chuckling.

Embedded in the boulder are six iron rungs. A ladder.

"Ayahuasca is a ladder," says the presence parallel to Cosme.

Cosme smiles as he climbs each rung. Above the final rung, embedded in the boulder's top is a vertical iron bar, six inches high and forged so that its tip is curved, presenting dullness. Cosme grabs the handhold, pulls himself toward it, and rises.

Cosme pats his backpack.

"Ayahuasca is not one thing, but one thing that ayahuasca is," says Cosme, "is a ladder, that is true."

He looks down at the boulder rungs and thanks the being who embedded them.

He climbs and scrambles toward the Gateway rising toward the lightened east and feels the pressure of western thunderheads before he sees the clouds themselves. He does not speed his progress. Many forces cannot be outrun, and trying to outrun sometimes just accelerates pursuit. He knows behind whatever storm comes will be light. And yet, thinks Cosme, as he climbs another boulder ladder, each rung a conductor, that which tends to not abide—his being at this height, a lightning strike—cannot be held as nothing.

Cosme pauses at the Gateway's base. No scrub trees here. No cover. Cosme follows with his eyes the rise of the granitic spine. The dragon's. Wings unevenly serrated, roughly scaled, at rest to either side. He peers up at the top but sees no head, no indication of transition. Cosme sees just spine and past it only daylight. Eastern sky.

He knows the Tableland is up there, flat and floral, dogged, delicate. But from where Cosme stands it seems unlikely all of a sudden that it all goes on, that up there is the Tableland and Baxter Peak a mile more beyond it. He wonders if he has misread the map or maybe misjudged distance and topography and missed the alpine flowers. Cosme wonders if what he is looking at is Baxter Peak, the terminus, the end.

He has been warned about electrolyte deficiency and dehydration and confusion. Cosme shuts his eyes and tries to diagnose if anything disorienting is internally unfolding.

"Maybe," says the presence parallel to Cosme, "all you want is not to move."

It is true that Cosme, after traveling from Ucayali, after hiking ultra-ultralight for more than two-thousand miles on the Trail, appreciates not moving on a level unattained by beings who have not moved as he has, who have not gone as far as Cosme, for as long. And it is true that Cosme longs each evening to become a fixed point in the landscape, to sit back against a tree or cedar log, to lie on ground, to feel enduring points of contact, to be earthbound, heavy with exhaustion, sunken, grateful to be still. But such is not the motionlessness of invalidity, and such is not the stillness that prepares one for the astral transformation.

Cosme, eyes closed, shakes his head. He feels electrolyte sufficient, watered well enough. He feels a drenching coming. He is clear. He tells the presence parallel to him, "I don't think that all I want is not to move."

Yesterday, when Cosme saw ahead the light of clearing, he experienced the jubilation of discrete completion. When he reached that light and left the dense woods of The Hundred-Mile Wilderness, which he had been a being in for seven days, he felt the jubilation dim despite the light of clearing. He had heard the rumbles for a mile, but he had not seen their makers. When he walked east on the Golden Road and passenger conveyances and logging trucks and RVs passed him on the dirt road, kicking dust and gravel up, he was reminded that the world he had been walking in for seven days was always next to this one, motorized, imperious, dependent, always wanting something from the world he just left, from the animals, the plants, the earth, the water, and the sky. He was assailed by the illusion of division on the Golden Road. He told himself division wasn't true. But where was evidence of unity, of reciprocity, of mutuality beyond the reservation ethos? Who acknowledged in the animals, the plants, the earth, the water, and the sky their brother spirits, sister spirits, father spirits, mother spirits, father of the father spirits, mother of the mother spirits? These are things he's tried since Springer Mountain to convey to people, but in general he has found their interest to be superficial, vaguely anthropological, polite, or mostly focused on procuring ayahuasca. On the north side of the Golden Road walked Cosme, jubilant no longer, wanting nothing more than to get back into the woods, the sentient forest, where he understood the true economy to be, the higher consciousness. He hoped to meet whom he was meant to meet, to say what he was meant to say.

It is true that first he sat below Abol Bridge and peeled a single orange he had purchased at the campground store and ate each segment by the West Branch of the Penobscot River as he eyed Katahdin. Cosme sat, his bare feet cooling in the river and the orange peel unraveled near him on the sand. He focused on Katahdin in the distance, miles past the river, an immense form seeming halfway risen, a leviathan whose ancient breaching had apparently been petrified midway, a mass apparently unmoving but whose infinitesimal dynamics are invisible in toto, whose erosions and accretions and mysterious exchanges, constant, infinite, cannot be grasped by a pedestrian at rest beside the river, savoring a fruit that had been trucked in from afar, conferring on his beaten feet relief, imagining himself up there, cannot be fathomed by a seated form whose being is not similarly scaled and does not seem to similarly be of underworld, water, earth, and sky at once.

Cosme did not sit beside the river long. He did not dry his feet before he put his socks and boots back on. He did not leave his orange peel unraveled on the sand. He did not feel defensive or inadequate about relating to Katahdin as a tourist whose interior was elevated by the main attraction of a stunning vista but could not intuit the transcendent interactions that he somehow felt Katahdin truly was, could not unravel, could not parse, its physical and spiritual particulars. He walked back to the Golden Road and headed east. Cosme saw the white blaze on the north side of the road and turned left, a being of the woods again.

He crossed the footbridge over Abol Stream, the boundary. He was now in Baxter State Park. Cosme hiked the trail northwest and paralleled for several miles the West Branch of the Penobscot River, which paralleled the Golden Road and flowed southeast toward the Atlantic Ocean. The trail turned north, away from the river, away from the road, and paralleled Nesowadnehunk Stream, which flowed south to the West Branch of the Penobscot River. Cosme forded the lower branch of the stream and then the upper branch a mile later. Fords reminded Cosme of our tributary nature, of how we are always intersecting, passing, of how we are always being drawn toward something overwhelming, of how in the overwhelming we are lost, combined, subsumed, transmuted into egoless particulars of an immensity.

The trail turned northeast, still paralleled the stream, curved east and pulled away, no longer parallel, no more a close relation to the stream, passed Daicey Pond and Elbow Pond and Tracy Pond, became one with the Tote Road for three quarters of a mile, and then became one with the Campground Road for a tenth before the trail became just the trail again, a footpath past his campsite near Katahdin Stream, a narrow way that step by step became the mountain.

"Yes," says Cosme, opening his eyes and looking at the Gateway, "I want more than not to move."

"Do you know what the flora up there know?" the presence parallel to Cosme asks.

Cosme pats his backpack and looks up to where the dragon's spine appears to join the sky. He thinks about the alpine flowers in his vision and their trampling.

"Is it true to say you are not Percival?" asks Cosme, starting up the Gateway.

"How will you communicate to others what the flora up there know? How many will you tell?" the presence parallel to Cosme asks.

He climbs and pats his backpack at whose center is the buffered ayahuasca.

Thunder rolls behind him and explodes above. Wind-blown raindrops, countless tiny hands, push Cosme up the Gateway.

"Is it true to say you are a spirit of the People of the Dawnland?" Cosme asks.

No answer but the storm.

Cosme climbs. The lightened east is light no more. Large rain falls, envelops Cosme as if elevation and horizon are irrelevant, as if what had been ancient orientation staples do not have the agency to orient in this. He cannot see what he'd seen before. The precipice on either side is cloud. The Gateway must be apprehended piecemeal. What had been its panoramic grandeur must be patched together now by inches.

"Is it true to say you are Pamola?" Cosme asks the presence parallel to him.

No answer.

Thunder rolls above him and explodes, an auditory version of the mountain. Stark and jagged, lightning warns him to take cover, to not be the path it's drawn to. But there is no cover. Just the rain. The clouds. He knows he should get low and crouch to minimize himself. Instead, he climbs and thinks of how the notification of his death by lightning on this mountain would begin up here, a hiker finding Cosme's body not long after the weather cleared, and travel down ahead of Cosme's body as it's carried down by alternating groups of stretcher bearers who try hard to reconcile the mountain's beauty with the hard fact that already grief heads toward the body's relatives and friends, accruing on its way the force of terrible inevitability as it gets closer to the body's hometown and its parents who, thinks Cosme now, are likely dry in Ucayali.

Cosme carries little metal. No hiking poles. No cook stove. No tent, no stakes. But the tin cup in his backpack. And the hammock rings. The pot. The pair of carabiners. These things made of ores, transformed by metallurgy and hellacious heat, have power to draw lightning, to invite it to seek ground through Cosme.

Rain-soaked, leaning uphill, Cosme powers up the Gateway with the metal objects in his backpack and is certain that it is irrational to move on under these conditions. To not set the tin cup down, the rings, the pot, the carabiners, to not crouch and try to balance on the balls of his feet a hundred yards away from them, his gaze averted from the lightning, is irrational. It is irrational to not heed lessons from the hardships of the stricken and the nearly so.

Rationality alone, however, is a blinkered guide, too certain of its way.

Cosme looks down at the granite spine, the rain a sheet to either side, the clouds impenetrable beyond the rain.

Rationality alone could not have gotten Cosme here from Ucayali.

He replays his vision. He remembers how the orchid petals fell, the heliconia petals. He remembers San Martín, the Biblioteca Municipal, the painting of the screaming man, the web quest.

"False division," Cosme tells himself. He slips. He rights himself. "But also not false."

He pauses as if waiting for the presence parallel to him to temper his conclusion.

"Then okay. That is enough of that," he says, saturated, as he nears the Gateway's end.

The Tableland is shrouded, a geography of clouds and rain. The angle of this upper world has flattened. Cosme does not strain. He sees no alpine flowers. How, then, not to trample? Cosme is not certain of the way. He slows, a grounded being on this plain that seems afloat. A cairn materializes. Cosme heeds. A white blaze on a rock forms from the ether. Cosme follows. No sky. No horizon. No void to fall into. Nothing adamantine rising in the distance. Nothing in relief. No foretaste of the trail's progression. The effect is of a bodily compression, an enfolding into something elemental, nebulous, amorphous. Cosme is aware in theory of what lies beyond him, but the fickle weather of perspective whispers, *Maybe not.* It is like being in the forest, Cosme thinks, the jungle.

Cosme sees, chest high, a form take shape, rectangular, a sign.

THE PLANT GROWTH ON
KATAHDIN'S TABLELAND
IS EASILY DAMAGED
BY FOOTSTEPS.

PLEASE HELP US PRESERVE
THIS AREA BY STAYING
ON THE TRAIL.

THANK YOU
BAXTER STATE PARK

Lightning strikes the ground ahead, and thunder shakes the Tableland. Cosme sits an arm's length from the signpost and arcs his torso, sheltering his backpack.

As the rain pours, heavy, necessary, Cosme whistles a song as if trying to assuage his backpack's fears and lull it to untroubled sleep. He feels the alpine flowers' consciousness, the water in their veins. He whistles the song, now a bird's lilt, now the shifting babble of a forest brook.

Still whistling, Cosme takes the Nalgene bottle from his backpack and unwraps it. He unscrews the bottle cap and drinks the quart of ayahuasca in the storm. When Cosme finishes, he screws the cap back on and nests the bottle in his backpack with a doubtless cleric's tenderness.

Cosme sings to call the wise ones.

Even when ayahuasca is prepared correctly under normal circumstances and conventional conditions in the Ucayali forest, Cosme does not know if they will come. Sometimes the vine does not comply with his desires. On Katahdin in this weather, as he sings, he struggles not to wonder if the wise ones hear him, struggles not to wonder, if they hear him, will they come.

A year ago, when Cosme left the Biblioteca Municipal and thought about what seemed to be the insurmountable logistics of leaving Ucayali, making it to Springer Mountain, and continuing on foot 2,190 miles to Katahdin, he primarily was mystified by how he could bring ayahuasca, which would teach him what the flora know and whom to tell. Even if he could get past the borders with the ayahuasca vine and the chacruna leaves, he could not simply take them and expect them to retain their properties and potency so far away from Ucayali so long after they were cut. And even if their properties and potency were durable, how could he bear the four large clay pots he would need for ayahuasca preparations along the way? How could he hike 2,190 miles with such pots? He did not think it could be done.

And even if he could brew ayahuasca in the Ucayali forest, bottle it securely, and then somehow get it past the borders, Cosme knew that ayahuasca in its unrefrigerated liquid form would not retain its properties and potency, would not be ayahuasca so far away from Ucayali so long after the vine and leaves had been correctly severed from the forest and prepared. The mother of tobacco is not like an orange that one plucks and ships to some clime inhospitable to orange cultivation.

One day soon thereafter, Cosme sat beneath his favorite cumaceba tree and thought about the implications of inaction, of ignoring Percival, of not telling people what the flora know, of not believing that his web quest had been clear on how he should proceed. As Cosme leaned against his favorite cumaceba tree, he thought about imagination and coincidence and how they had the power to appear to place a person at the center of a vast space that in truth was centerless and nothing. Cosme shook his head. What he had seen and learned because of ayahuasca, everything that flowed from ayahuasca, could not be imaginary, could not be explained away as products of coincidence. He felt the ingrate's shame for even briefly thinking so. His favorite cumaceba tree conveyed to him that he should go, that it would be there for him to sit under and to lean on when he found his way back home. But still the problem of transporting ayahuasca and protecting its integrity and spirit nettled him. He dozed against his favorite cumaceba tree, his dreams a zone of unrest.

When he awoke, an ethnobotanist from Furman University stood near him. She was in her middle thirties and wore sandals, lightweight shorts, a t-shirt that said *Yajé*.

"Oh, I'm sorry," said the ethnobotanist. "I didn't mean to wake you. I just came to see your favorite cumaceba tree."

"It is okay. My dreams were of no comfort."

"May they be tonight," she said.

"Please sit."

"Thank you," she said, accepting Cosme's offer. "We sat here the day you told me of your vision of the lupuna tree. A stairway in its trunk led to the canopy."

"Yes," said Cosme. "You may say that we are bound by memory."

"She's very healthy," said the ethnobotantist, "the cumaceba. Each white flower is so beautiful."

"She has a healthy spirit," Cosme said, admiring the flowers and the leaves. He brought his eyes down to the ethnobotanist and said, "So you are back to study."

"I am," she said.

"Ah," said Cosme, "you are studying a negative development."

"Commodification has made naturally occurring ayahuasca unsustainable. It's being sold more rapidly than it can grow. So I've been studying communities along the Ucayali River, interviewing healers, shamans, learning how they're adapting to commodification, if they are adapting."

"Ayahuasca has gone deeper in the forest," Cosme said. "The only thing the healer can do is go deeper."

"Everyone is going deeper."

"You may say," said Cosme, "I have seen that is the way of capital."

They sat in silence for a while in the shade of Cosme's favorite cumaceba tree.

At last the ethnobotanist declared, "I didn't bring my notebook."

"Yes, I see."

"You said your dreams were of no comfort. Even underneath this tree."

"The tree is not to blame," said Cosme, who then told the ethnobotanist about his visions, Percival, the mountain and the alpine flowers, the directions he divined from fallen orchid petals, fallen heliconia petals, Pucallpa, San Martín, the Biblioteca Municipal, his web quest, and his mystifying inability to see how ayahuasca could go with him.

As Cosme spoke, the ethnobotanist looked at the cumaceba tree's white blossoms as though they were stars. She listened. She considered his dilemma.

Looking at the blossoms still, she said, "I know an agronomic engineer upriver near Iquitos. He can help us."

Cosme perked up, but he did not press for details.

She looked at Cosme.

"I have worked with him before. Eduardo can dehydrate ten liters of liquid ayahuasca so that all that volume is condensed into a brick," she said, her hands approximating the dimensions of a common burnt clay brick. "The dehydration process doesn't change the nature of the ayahuasca, and in brick form ayahuasca travels much more easily."

"You have experience with ayahuasca in this form?" asked Cosme. "You have tried it?"

"Yes. Eduardo placed the brick into the water pot and stirred. He slowly brought the water to a boil. It was ayahuasca, Cosme. I am telling you. Its spirit was preserved."

Cosme did not seem entirely persuaded.

"This Eduardo," Cosme asked, "he is a healer?"

"No, but..."

"Ah," said Cosme, "he is not a healer."

"No, but a Shipibo healer first prepares the ayahuasca in the forest."

"A Shipibo healer?"

"Yes."

"What is his name?"

"Sixto."

"Sixto," Cosme said. "And you were present at his preparation?"

"No."

"You met this Sixto?"

"When he brought the ayahuasca to Eduardo."

"Then the dehydration?"

"Then the dehydration."

Cosme thought about departing in this manner from tradition.

"He sells to this Eduardo," Cosme asked, "this Sixto?"

"Yes, but we can bring your ayahuasca to Eduardo. We can make arrangements to refrigerate it on the boat."

Cosme looked up at the cumaceba blossoms.

"So no Sixto," Cosme said.

"No Sixto."

"Somehow," Cosme said, "this does not feel like my decision."

"Well, I know it isn't mine."

"No," said Cosme. "No, it is not yours."

A dog ran past them from the village.

"Someone's on a mission to get somewhere," said the ethnobotanist.

They watched the dog until he disappeared, the forest closing in on him, enfolding him.

"How does it come with me?" asked Cosme.

"Ayahuasca?"

"Yes."

"We mix the ayahuasca in with hiking gear and other stuff and ship the package to a town near Springer Mountain. Every Trail town has a business that holds packages for hikers. We fly to Atlanta on the same day that we ship, we get an airport rental car, and we are in the Springer Mountain town before the package."

Cosme smiled.

"You have experience in shipment," Cosme said.

Three months later, in the middle of a mild March, the ethnobotanist drove Cosme to the Springer Mountain trailhead in the Chattahoochee National Forest where they said goodbye. For seven miles Cosme hiked the trail to Springer Mountain. Then he left the clarity of trail and fit himself through spaces it did not seem probable the human form was meant to go. Deeper in the forest, farther from the beaten path, through vine and thorn he moved, a spirit of reticulation, an intimate of density. A mile. Two. The bustling hush of trickling water led him to an arching grove of rhododendron, broadleafed, insulated, evergreen.

He built a tripod out of three stout branches he found lying on the ground. He bound the tripod's nexus with a piece of thin-gauge wire he had taken from his backpack. From the nexus, Cosme hung a longer wire, which extended to a foot above the ground. He gathered kindling, firewood. Underneath the wire, he arranged what he had gathered. Cosme took a stainless steel pot from his backpack and attached its bail handle to the hanging wire, testing to confirm the pot was level, the wire plumb. Then Cosme slept beside the tripod, not far from the stream, until the sun set.

When he woke he lit the fire, tending it until it could continue for a while on its own. The grove glowed, a cocoon of light. He used his tin cup to scoop water from the trickling stream and filled the hanging pot. He sat before the waxing fire, his backpack prostrate on his lap. He slid the brick of ayahuasca out, unwrapped it, severed one tenth with his clean knife, gently introduced this ayahuasca portion to the pot, and shook the severance remnants on the wrapper in. He wrapped the shortened brick of ayahuasca and returned it to his backpack. Cosme stirred and sang. He kept the fire.

The water boiled. For another hour, Cosme sang and stirred but did not further feed the fire. The boil became a simmer, which gave way to thick placidity. The firelight became just ember glow. In that diminishing intrusion on the darkness, Cosme held the bail handle and detached the tripod wire. He set the pot for final cooling in the stream.

He sat beside the stream and sang. Two hours later Cosme drank the ayahuasca from the pot directly.

In the darkness, Cosme sang.

Each rhododendron leaf began to radiate magnetic waves, and Cosme saw the mother of the forest woven through the rhododendrons so that plant and mother at many points seemed one. Behind her head, a sorcerer sat, and from the sorcerer's head shot flames of red and yellow.

Cosme sang.

Behind the sorcerer, a healer sat and tended to the rhododendron leaves. Celestial fire, blue and red and yellow, emanated upward from the healer's head, and Cosme knew by this the healer's substance.

A tended rhododendron leaf became a hummingbird that flew to Cosme, and he knew that dehydration and reconstitution had not harmed the ayahuasca.

But when Cosme got to Harper's Ferry, West Virginia, he went deeper in the forest, built a tripod, hung his pot, woke up to light the fire, scooped water, filled the pot, put in some ayahuasca, brought the water and the ayahuasca to a boil, set the pot for cooling in a stream, sang beautifully, and drank the ayahuasca from the pot directly. This time, though, no mother of the forest and no hummingbird. No visions. Cosme knew this happened sometimes. If the spirits did not want to come, they did not come.

But Cosme wondered. Maybe time had harmed the ayahuasca. Maybe distance had.

Three months and 1,164 miles later, sitting in a thunderstorm and singing the song to call the wise ones, Cosme feels the shaken Tableland beneath him and himself inside the wind, inside the water and the charged air, unified, until the self seems unbelievable, a recent fiction, and what room there was in him to fear that time had sapped the ayahuasca, or that distance had, is gone. What Cosme thinks is what he sings, and what he sings are not like words and rhythm voluntarily arranged but universal particles, remote at first, aswirl, then orchestrated suddenly, aligned like that by happenstance, by gravitational attraction, the mysterious galactic draw, possessed of credibility no troll can gainsay, elemental credibility, the credibility of wind and water, the inexorable sincerity of thunder and the fact of lightning, coalescences not personal but cosmic, not hermitic but unbound, beyond the tendency and pull of human circumscription.

Thunder shakes the Tableland, and lightning strikes the ground near eight-petal mountain avens.

Rain comes down so densely its intensity feels consciously directed.

A female scream flies by him on the wind.

The great steamboat of the wind has come.

In front of Cosme, the countless indecipherable relationships of raindrops simplify and suddenly become two strands of rainfall, twining from the bottom where sits Cosme up to where the steamboat hovers, disappearing in the clouds above the steamboat. Cosme rises, puts his backpack on, and climbs the rope of rainfall. Halfway up, his hands no longer feel the coolness or the wetness of the braided rain. They feel the epidermal smoothness and the bonelessness illusion of two serpents. Cosme's cheek is close to them. He sees that one strand is the giant anaconda, one the rainbow boa. Cosme climbs, illuminated now by the fluorescent snakes, and does not question transformation or entwinement. Cosme's arm veins bulge, their blueness radiating like the colors of the serpents. In his arm veins, Cosme hears his beating heart and what it says about the sinuous and circular and bringing something of his inner self to hinterlands, extremities, and going home, possessed of powers to resist and to revive.

He climbs up to the steamboat's gunnel, and an angel's hand helps him aboard. The angel stands beside him but does not impart instruction. Cosme walks back to the gunnel and looks over it. He sees himself below, beside the signpost, sitting in the rain, his backpack prostrate on his lap. The lower Cosme looks up at the steamboat Cosme and then points beyond the signpost to the Tableland. The steamboat Cosme looks beyond the signpost. One by one, the alpine plants and flowers—diapensia, dwarf rhododendron, Bigelow sedge, star saxifrage, eight-petal mountain avens, Labrador tea—begin to glow like beacons, white and yellow, green and purple, red and blue. Above each glow the rain recedes, and each glow brightens in the space of each recession. Luminous and earthy, radiant and rooted, blossom after blossom sends to steamboat Cosme waves that tell him to be open, ancient and just born, extinguished and becoming, like the river in which is contained the point of its beginning and the convolutions of the way and its expansive end, its spilling into all the rivers of the world.

A wise one in a long-sleeved shirt and jeans stands next to steamboat Cosme, who looks down to where the wise one, barefoot, set his shoes. The wise one holds a white snake out to Cosme and confers on him new healing powers. Cosme feels these powers in him now.

"What do the flora down there know?" he asks the wise one.

The wise one does not answer but looks past the steamboat's gunnel.

Cosme likewise looks and sees the blossoms glowing on the Tableland.

"What do you know?" he asks, his hands upon the gunnel.

Vibrations from the plants and flowers do not fly to him in answer.

Steamboat Cosme looks to signpost Cosme, who then points beyond the signpost.

Steamboat Cosme opens, and again he looks beyond the signpost.

Through the rain the glowing blossoms send him waves that wiggle to him and express the wisdom of the Tableland's 400 million years. He understands that what the flora know is not convertible to language.

Steamboat Cosme tugs his left ear. Signpost Cosme tugs his right. One stares at the other as a man whose age has one day caught him by surprise stares at the temporary stranger in the mirror.

Steamboat Cosme turns back to the wise one, who no longer holds the white snake. Cosme glances at the angel, who has not relieved the wise one of the white snake. Cosme flexes his interior and feels in there the healing powers recently conferred. He sees the wise one's shoes are still beside him on the deck.

The storm ends. No rain. No thunder. No charged particles. No wind.

The silence does not register immediately with Cosme. As an anxious mind still tenses after the discernible disturbance has elapsed and, calming, comes to the conclusion that perhaps the mind was the disturbance all along, so Cosme's mind eventually acknowledges the spacious silence. Even to the east the sky is still dark, but at lower altitudes the phosphorescent blossom glow gains on the darkness.

Cosme looks down at the Tableland, and where the blossoms were aglow before they are aglow now. But their relationship, perhaps distorted by the storm, is clear to Cosme now. The eastern blossom lights are ranged so that the end effect of their arrangement is a tapering, which thickens as the lights move west. The thickening eventually arrests, but near the signpost blossom lights curve briefly out and then curve back again, the outline of an arrowhead that has been softened by millennia in contact with the earth. What Cosme sees in the arrangement of the blossom lights is a reversal of his course, the mother of the mother of tobacco telling him to go back down the mountain.

Signpost Cosme rustles. He unwinds and rises. To the west he sees the light of day unveiled. He puts his backpack on, leans slightly forward like a stemmed thing, and walks toward the light, in the direction from which he had come. Each step he takes extinguishes a blossom light behind him.

Steamboat Cosme blinks.

The wise one stands beside his shoes and says, "In missing also may be meaning."

As darkness closes on each afterimage, a Katahdin arctic butterfly emerges, fluttering a moment in the zone where shined the blossom light, and follows Cosme toward the western light.

The final blossom light goes out.

As Cosme nears the Gateway, a butterfly kaleidoscope enshrouds him. Wingbeats, puffed air, lift him over talus, past slick slides.

A woman's scream, now stark without the din of storm, flies up to him and past him.

Steamboat Cosme climbs the gunnel, reaching for the twined snakes, gripping, but the angel holds him by an ankle. Cosme is a short bridge from the steamboat to the snakes. The wise one takes off Cosme's boots and sets them on the deck, beside the shoes that he now puts on Cosme's feet. The angel lets the ankle go, and Cosme's body swings down to the twined snakes. He holds tightly as if he would be entwined, as if the giant anaconda and the rainbow boa, as if twoness, twinning, twining could through his addition be perfected.

A woman's scream flies up to him.

He loosens and descends, obscuring stretches of fluorescence on his way.

His backpack jangles as he touches down and hurries toward the western light and signpost Cosme, whom he has lost sight of, and the butterfly kaleidoscope, which likewise he no longer sees. He hurries, steady, toward the woman's scream, which suddenly he sees as strings flung forth from dual guitars. The scream, expression of a brutal need, perturbs the stormless air.

The strings reach Cosme and, like tendrils, gracefully ensnare twelve parts of him. They pull him down the mountain. Guidelines from the darkness to the light.

Before he sees the woman, Cosme sees a vision of her mouth, contorted, strained, a shape for which geometry does not account, the shape of the primordial desire for attraction and correction, for the hand of God to lay a finger on distortion and reshape it into lineal tranquility. He flies, just barely levitating on descent, the wise one's skimming shoes an inch above the talus slides and boulders. Then the twelve strings unfurl and let him go. He flies into the form and flutter of the butterfly kaleidoscope and into signpost Cosme, who becomes this Cosme who has flown. In each Cosme is the other now. The two once more are one.

The butterfly kaleidoscope rises, basking in the full bore of the western light, which is now everywhere the day's light. Cosme stands atop the boulder he had stood before below, the boulder of no scalable dimension whose six iron rungs he climbed to reach the iron handhold, vertical, six inches high, and forged so that its curved tip does not offer sharp protrusion.

From this handhold hangs a woman, upside down, her right thigh run through midway by the handhold, from the bottom to the top, so that the curved tip just peeks through the punctured skin, a dull barb, merciless, that cannot think of letting go. There's not much blood. Her back does not lie flat against the rock. The top two rungs press on it horizontally. Her hands press on the third rung, pushing down with greater force at intervals to raise her body just a half inch toward the boulder top to even for a second slightly ease the kneeward pressure that the handhold, even with her faith in isometrics and alleviation, will not stop exerting on her stuck thigh. She's exhausted.

Cosme takes his backpack off and sits down near her right foot. He unties the brown lace of her hiking shoe.

The woman screams.

"Is someone there?" she yells. "Is someone there?"

"I am a healer," Cosme says as he removes her hiking shoe and sock.

"Please get me down from here," she yells.

"I am a small man," Cosme says as he inspects her foot. "You may say I am not strong. My forearms, they are strong, and yet I cannot say if they are strong enough to get you down from here."

"But you're a doctor?"

"I am a healer," Cosme says as he massages with his thumbs her sole.

"Please call the ranger station. Tell them I need rescue."

"Ah, I do not have a telephone," says Cosme.

"Look," she yells. "Look down. My cell phone fell. It's just below. Climb down and call the ranger."

Cosme puts her foot down, gets up, and peers over.

"I do not see a telephone."

"It's in my pack. You see my pack down there?"

"I see your pack," says Cosme. "Yes, I see your pack."

"Climb down there, please, and call."

"This does not seem so easy."

Cosme looks down at this woman, upside down, her thigh impaled.

"You do not have a spirit animal," he says with clinical concern.

She looks at him but does not seem to comprehend.

"You have no guardian."

She seems to know that this is true.

"What do you see when you look up at me?" asks Cosme.

"I see you. I see the sky."

A Katahdin arctic butterfly returns and flutters next to Cosme as he peers down at the woman. Then another butterfly returns and flutters. And another. Soon, around him, the kaleidoscope again. He sees each fuzzy face and pair of compound eyes, the miracle of many lenses. Cosme sees the paradox of each wing and how gamely each one beats against endangerment. Through each wing he sees sunlight, and in sunlight he sees each wing's heavenly design, the substance and the nothingness, the close resemblance to the membrane of existence. Cosme sees with other than his eyes the butterflies above him and behind him and beside him and below.

"So me and sky," calls Cosme down, "is all you see?"

"Yes, you and sky. What difference does it make? I told you," she yells up, perplexed by his question. "Climb down and call for help already!"

Cosme stands up straight and steps back from the edge. The butterflies move with him. Cosme kneels beside his pack and takes from it a long pipe and a pouch. He packs tobacco in the bowl and lights it. He draws deeply three times on the pipe. He holds the third draw in his lungs and leans in toward the woman's wound until his mouth is inches from the iron bar. He blows smoke on the center of her wound and sings in one unhurried exhalation. Wingbeats waft the smoke, which moves in ways that speak to Cosme.

"What is going on up there?" the woman yells. "Please leave my leg alone! Climb down and call!"

"Your spirit," Cosme says directly to her wound, "is strong but also, you may say, inflexible and unassisted."

Three more times he blows smoke on the center of her wound and sings and listens to the motions of the smoke.

"Please call!" the woman yells. "Just call!"

He knocks the ashes from the pipe and sets it on the granite near his backpack.

"I am calling," Cosme says as he gets up and steps back toward her right foot. Cosme kneels and holds her foot without uplifting it. With both hands, he massages it. He sings. For half an hour Cosme does this, and the woman does not yell.

He rises with the butterflies, who flutter with him as he steps back to the edge.

"Is what you see when you look up at me the same?" asks Cosme.

She says nothing for a while. Her eyes are wide.

"I don't see you," she says at last, still looking wide-eyed up in his direction.

"I am here," says Cosme.

"I'm hallucinating. I must be hallucinating. My electrolytes are low."

The butterflies detach from Cosme and descend en masse. They flit around her head and torso, fanning her. They float around her trembling arms and hands, which press down on the third rung to relieve the pressure on her punctured thigh.

"You see they are not in your mind," says Cosme as he steps back from the edge and kneels beside her right thigh. From his pack he takes a t-shirt, which he tears along a seam and ties around her upper thigh above the wound.

She does not yell or writhe.

He puts back in his pack the long pipe and the pouch. He zips and stands. He slides his pack on, steps back to the edge, and readies to descend. He crouches so his weight rests on his right leg. With his thumb and first two fingers of his right hand, Cosme grips the dull barb of the iron bar, still slick with blood. His fingers feel the heat of her wound. His left leg dangles down the boulder face and finds the short projection of the sixth rung, then the fifth. The butterflies make way. His left hand finds the short projection of the sixth rung, and his thumb and first two fingers of his right hand let go of the iron bar's dull barb. He climbs down to the boulder's base.

"Your telephone," he says.

"It's in the pocket on the back. The butterflies," she says. "There must be thousands. Tens of thousands."

Cosme asks, "What do I call?"

"Call 911," she says, still studying the butterflies.

He calls.

"No answer," Cosme says.

"No answer or no service?"

"Nothing," Cosme says.

"Please climb and see if you can get a signal where you were," she says, her tone now not imperative, her volume conversational.

"We go," says Cosme. "Maybe down below we call again, but now we go."

He takes his backpack off and zips her phone inside an upper pocket. He then rolls her daypack, minimizing its dimensions, and inserts it in his pack. He shifts the ayahuasca so her daypack is positioned as an added buffer, and he slides his pack back on.

"You said we go?" she asks, still focused on the butterflies.

"You are in pain?" asks Cosme.

Silence. Wingbeats. Breeze.

"I was." She pauses, searching. "I don't feel it now."

He sets his right foot on the first rung. Cosme sees he is no longer in the wise one's shoes, and yet he does not feel the wise one or his healing powers have abandoned him.

"You said your forearms weren't strong enough to get me down from here," she says.

"Ah, no. I said I was not sure if they were strong enough," says Cosme, his left foot on the second rung.

"And now you're sure?" she asks, the butterflies extending the perimeter in order to envelop Cosme.

"No," says Cosme. "I am only human."

Cosme studies where to step.

He says, "Between your hands is where I will step next," and sets his right foot on the middle of the third rung. Next to it he sets his left. He grips the sixth rung with his left hand, and he lays his right arm lengthwise underneath her from her lower back to where the iron bar went in her thigh. He splays the ring and middle fingers of his right hand, and he slides the splay until the fleshy base between the fingers hits the iron bar. His palm and fingers press against the backside of her thigh and feel its wounded heat.

"I will push up from underneath your thigh. When you are free," says Cosme, "I will bend you at the waist and bear you down."

Two butterfly detachments separate from the kaleidoscope. One flutters in alignment to the right side of her wounded thigh. One flutters in alignment to the left. As Cosme's palm and fingers ease her thigh up off the iron bar, each line of butterflies, in parallel formation, rises with her ragged thigh until her ragged thigh is free. Each line returns to the kaleidoscope, assimilating seamlessly as Cosme bears her on his shoulders and climbs down.

"You are okay?" asks Cosme as he touches down and turns around, engulfed in the kaleidoscope.

"I think so."

"No pain?"

She considers, searches. "No."

"We go."

"No bandaging?" she asks.

"The butterflies," he says, "have healing powers."

"They'll be with us?"

"For some way, I think. Remember them."

"And you can bear me?"

Cosme starts down toward the treeline.

"We will see."

Chapter Seven: Restructure Him

"Insertion," Albert says, "is critical."

He sits with AJ in the Shaw's Tacoma.

AJ scans the campground's pebbly parking lot and says, "Insertion helps the world go round, no doubt."

Albert looks down at his dog-eared copy of *Ecodefense: A Field Guide to Monkeywrenching.*

"Says here this guy Howie Wolke got six months for pulling survey stakes."

"Six months for that? Fucked up," says AJ. "Insertion error?"

"Just says he was careless. Target-selection error maybe. Planning error." Albert looks at his side of the parking lot as though in stationary observation of the wider world he will discover resolution. "Still, it seems to me an operation hinges on insertion."

"Man, I hear you, but on this one I'm with Gandalf."

"Gandalf?" Albert asks.

"How many Gandalfs do you know?"

"So you're with Gandalf on the issue of insertion?"

"I'm with Gandalf on the issue of preparedness *before* insertion."

Albert laughs.

"No joke," says AJ.

A hiker heading toward Katahdin Stream spots the *Shaw's Shuttle* magnet sign on Albert's door and holds an upraised thumb in their direction. They respond in kind.

"You see the calves on that guy?" Albert asks.

"Very well-developed. Almost gauche."

"So you're with Gandalf?"

"Gandalf's wisdom is applicable."

"Like how?"

"Like 'It does not do to leave a live dragon out of your calculations, if you live near him.'"

"That's Gandalf talking?"

AJ nods.

"Okay, I'll give you that one. That's applicable to planning."

"And to target selection."

"And to target selection."

"Gandalf, baby."

"What does Gandalf say about determining just where the dragons are?"

"You don't need Gandalf telling you where one of them will be tonight."

"The Dover meeting."

"Harold Brown's a dragon, man," says AJ.

"He's already in my calculations."

"Eva Desjardins's a dragon, man."

"And she is out there somewhere, but I don't know where."

"Due diligence," says AJ, pointing at the book. "Due diligence. Unless you want to be like what's his name."

"Like Howie Wolke," says Albert.

"Be prepared."

"I can't say I aspire to imprisonment," says Albert, looking once more at the chapter on Security. He reads, "'Most operations worth monkeywrenching consist of a long chain of events ranging from the corporate boardroom or government office to actual field activities. Before selecting a target for monkeywrenching, gather as much information as possible on this *chain of command*.'"

"Like I said. Due diligence," says AJ. "Smoke before we go?"

"I can't hike Katahdin high."

"You underestimate yourself," says AJ, opening the ashtray.

Albert notices a man, a distant agent of officialdom, dressed sharply in a khaki shirt and drab-green pants, walking double time in their direction.

"Put that shit away," grits Albert. "Ranger's coming." Albert smiles out the window as the man approaches. "Morning, Ron."

The ranger stops at Albert's window.

"You guys picking up right now?"

"Not till three or so," says Albert. "Thought we'd hike Katahdin in the meantime."

"Well, we sure could use your help. A female hiker got impaled just past the treeline. We just got the call."

"Holy shit," says AJ, getting out and gearing up. He does not shut the windows.

"Impaled on what?" asks Albert, putting on his daypack. "How?"

The three of them assume a brisk pace toward the Hunt Trail trailhead.

"Fell back somehow on a handhold, and it went clear through her thigh."

"Holy shit," says AJ. "Grievous."

"Who's your pickups?" asks the ranger.

"Cosme Esperanza," Albert says.

"Yep, he's the one who found her hanging."

"Bill McIntyre is the other," Albert says.

"We'll leave a message for him at the ranger station."

"So she's hanging up there past the treeline by her thigh," says AJ to himself but out loud, trying to accommodate this new reality.

The ranger shakes his head.

"He somehow got her off the handhold. This guy's carrying the woman down the mountain. Otherwise we would have called in for a helicopter rescue."

"By himself?" asks Albert.

"By himself. Two hikers saw them just below the treeline. Got what information they could get and called it in once they were able to get service. The caller said this Cosme wouldn't stop to talk. Just kept descending."

"No way he can carry her the whole way down," says AJ.

"The caller said the way he moved was unreal."

"How so?" asks Albert.

The ranger throws his hands out as if to commune with all that goes unanswered in the world.

"Who's the female?" Albert asks.

"A day hiker. Eva Desjardins."

"Holy shit," says AJ.

"Eva Desjardins," says Albert.

"You know her?"

"No, not really. I know *of* her," Albert says.

They see ahead another ranger with a group of rescue volunteers in different attitudes of restlessness around the trailhead kiosk.

"Eva Desjardins. No way he can carry her all the way down," says AJ.

"We're more worried that she might be bleeding out," the ranger says.

When AJ, Albert, and the ranger reach the group, the other ranger, younger and more finely tuned than Ron, says, "Thank you all for stepping up on such short notice. As by now you all know, the report is that a good Samaritan was seen below the treeline, carrying the injured hiker on his shoulder down the mountain. Yesterday I met this good Samaritan. He's not a big man. How far he can get is anybody's guess. But, based on when the call came in, they can't be far below the treeline. So no more than three miles up for us and three miles down. Once we get the injured hiker stabilized, we'll split up into three teams of four. Each team will bear the stretcher, slow and steady, half a mile. Each team at most will take two turns, assuming that the good Samaritan has not been injured while descending, which is why we have the second stretcher," says the ranger, pointing to the second stretcher folded in its orange carrier exactly as the first is folded in its own. "Concerns?"

The ranger scans the group to gauge its physical condition and its will. He nods, affirming that what he has seen will do.

"Okay, then. Thank you. Let's not waste more time. We'll switch off carrying the gear on the ascent. Be careful," says the ranger, picking up a folded stretcher by its carrier handles and extending it without additional instruction to a passing volunteer. He picks the other folded stretcher up and carries it himself.

The ranger waves to Ron and says, "I'm guessing eight to ten hours up and down, assuming Cosme hasn't gotten hurt."

"The med kit's in your pack?" asks Ron, returning the departure wave.

The ranger reaches back and pats his pack.

"The radio is on," says Ron. "Good luck. Stay safe. An ambo will be here when you get back. Keep in touch and let me know if we'll need more than one."

"Ten four," says the ranger, searching the terrain around him and departing like someone who has headed up this mountain on this sort of mission many times. His pace is steady, workmanlike.

He does not rush to catch up to the hikers, who initially cohere as they move up the mountain, chatting, basking in the camaraderie that naturally attends the early stage of an endeavor in which each participant is bound to minimize the self and share with the contingent others in the sacred purpose of assisting injured life.

They do not jettison this purpose as they climb, but higher on the mountain they compartmentalize it and regard it for a while as existing in abeyance as increasingly they separate from one another and grow quiet. They attend to exigencies. They hike their own hikes.

For some, this means acceleration, leaving the inferiors behind. For some, this means becoming conscious of their breathing, picturing the basic bellows action of the lungs or trying to remember what the Anapanasati Sutta says about the breath. For some, this means imagining their feet and friction points and wondering why duct tape and why not the supple moccasin. For some, this means not stepping on the toads who hop out for a better look at the commotion coming or who hunker as though blending in is good enough to ward disaster off. For some, this means obsessing over water, over calories or slippage, and considering *what if*. For some, this means the world is open, means not being so prescriptive.

Some lose sight of others in the group.

"Gauche Calves is on a mission," Albert says, becoming silent again.

"He's hauling ass, no doubt," says AJ from not far behind.

To keep the general sense of group cohesion and to keep the faster hikers somewhat fresher for the stress of the descent, the ranger, consciously positioned in the middle of the pack now, calls out at intervals of half a mile for two hikers who have not yet borne the folded stretchers to assume that obligation.

For the first exchange, the ranger calls up to Gauche Calves and another vanguard hiker to inform them that their turn has come to bear the folded stretchers. So they pause and watch as from below the ranger and the other hikers rise. The ranger does not want the folded stretcher to appear to be a burden he is glad to be relieved of. He continues holding his until the other stretcher bearer reaches them. The transfer happens casually, without the air of onus shifting, as the stragglers are subsumed. The group, coherent, moves on, separating, distancing, each member hiking his or her own hike for half a mile more.

The ranger calls out at the bridge across Katahdin Stream. Another transfer of the folded stretchers, coalescence, motion and ascent, dispersion, atomizing into the particular devotions.

Past Katahdin Falls, the woods hush. Pole tips clink, find purchase, sink. Synthetic fabrics whoosh and rustle, hinting at the intimacies of friction. Breath percusses. Here and there a carabiner tolls. Two siskins float around the center of the mule train for a moment and decide a moment is enough. From time to time, a trickle whispers how much water is below. From time to time, a breeze rubs through the needles, heading east, and sounds at first like uprush, water springing somewhere in the woods. However one may hike one's own hike, commonalities abound. The separated hikers have these sounds in common. Habit does not ask much time to form. These sounds, for half a mile, are their aural background, sensed, internalized, accepted as the soundtrack of this stretch of their reality. What sounds there are beyond these sounds must be experienced in stark relief and as remarkable projections from the plane of auditory normalcy, requiring an unanticipated interruption in the rhythm of this half a mile.

The highest hikers, hearing song above, stop first. The stopping ripples quickly through the group and to the hiker who brings up the rear. They all look up toward a phenomenon that they at present trust but cannot see.

A lovely male voice sings a line, and then a lovely female voice repeats it in a way that makes the line sound new. The song proceeds with each line subject to such alternation.

> "From the alpine flowers on the mountains fly
> the butterflies who heal us and descend with us,
> delivering an urgent message from the flowers
> and the mountain to the humans down below
> in whom the spirit, glowing still, says, 'Listen.'"

The members of the rescue team, dispersed at intervals allowing one to hike one's hike, look with tilted heads and raised eyes toward the trail bend where no more about the way can be discerned without ascending. Some are slackjawed. All look upward at the risen forest. They unite in being mesmerized.

When Cosme, bearing Eva on his shoulder in a firefighter carry, comes around the high bend, singing still with Eva as though strolling with her by an almost level stream, the members of the rescue team—the high, the median, the low—do not yet move. They marvel at the footwork and the form. They marvel at the seeming lightness and the pace. They gaze to really press upon their memories this singularity, the music and the movement, how this woman with the ghastly thigh wound and her rescuer do not seem fazed.

At last the ranger breaks the spell and heads up, yelling, "Cosme!"

The singing and the upper movement stop.

"Hallo," says Cosme, looking at the rescue team stretched out below and on the move now. "You are help?"

"We are," the ranger says, accelerating up the trail. "Stay put. We're coming up."

"We are not far, yes?" asks Cosme.

"No, not far," the ranger says. "About another mile and a half is all."

"Ah," says Cosme, "not far. Thank you."

Cosme squats, then kneels, unfolding Eva from his shoulder as he does so, and lays her gently on the ground in a position that allows her to observe the rescue team ascending. Eva does not look below, however. She looks up and side to side and twists to see behind her where the trail bends, disappearing.

"Yes, a mile and a half is not far," Cosme says to Eva.

"The butterflies are leaving," Eva says to Cosme.

Cosme turns and watches as the butterflies, kaleidoscopic, flutter round the bend.

"Yes, they are going up the mountain," Cosme says, "returning to the alpine flowers. They have told us what the flowers know." He sits down next to Eva. "They have given you a spirit guardian. Two spirit guardians."

"I feel them," Eva says.

They watch the rescuers ascend.

"You are okay?" asks Cosme.

"Yes. I'm just amazed," says Eva.

When the highest hikers and the ranger get to them, the ranger says to no one in particular, "Let's get a stretcher out." He takes his pack off and removes the med kit. As he kneels by Eva's injured thigh, he says,

"Let's get you stabilized."

"I'm stable," Eva says. "More stable than I've ever been."

"Let's see," the ranger says, examining. "You tied a tourniquet?"

"It is not very tight," says Cosme. "There is blood but not much." Cosme stands and steps aside to make room for the stretcher.

"Yeah," the ranger says, "you couldn't elevate her thigh the way you had to bring her down. A tourniquet lightly tied was probably the way to go to slow whatever bleeding."

"And the butterflies," says Eva.

"What?" the ranger says as he takes Eva's pulse.

"The healing powers of the butterflies slowed down the bleeding also," Eva says.

The ranger looks at Cosme.

Cosme shrugs and says, "Well, yes, you may say there were butterflies."

"And Cosme's healing powers. Cosme's healing powers slowed the bleeding down."

The ranger nods.

"Your pulse is good," the ranger says, observing Eva's rate of respiration. He then feels her forehead, cheeks, and hands. "Do you feel nauseous? Dizzy?"

"No," says Eva.

"I'm not seeing signs of shock."

"I'm not in shock."

"Have you had any fluids?"

"My position wasn't optimal for fluid intake," Eva says.

"Okay, let's get you some electrolytes."

He takes from his pack a well-known electrolyte replenisher. He opens it and passes it to Eva.

As she drinks, the ranger says to Cosme, "Have you administered any drugs or healing agents? Anything I need to know about?"

"I blew tobacco smoke," says Cosme.

"Where?"

"Directly on the wound. It is traditional. And I massaged her sole."

"Her soul?" the ranger asks.

"Her right sole, yes. It is traditional," says Cosme.

"Nothing else?"

"As she has said, the butterflies."

"The butterflies."

"But I did not administer the butterflies."

"Who did?"

"That is a question for the butterflies."

"And where are they?"

"They near the Tableland."

The ranger reaches into his pack and takes out another bottle of the well-known electrolyte replenisher, which he then hands to Cosme.

"Thank you, no," says Cosme.

The ranger slips the bottle back into his pack and says, "Let's see here. Eva, we are going to get you set up on this stretcher here, if that's okay with you, and then we'll clean your wound and take a look."

"Okay," says Eva, looking at the rescuers assembled. When she gets to Albert's face, she studies it with interest but says nothing.

"Here we go," the ranger says as he and two others transfer Eva to the orange stretcher. "Very good."

The ranger studies the substance of the wound, the dried and drying blood, the ragged skin.

"I'm going to spray a little saline solution on the upper wound. Sterile saline water. This might sting a little."

Eva looks at Albert as the ranger sprays.

"Okay?" the ranger says.

Returning her attention to her right thigh, Eva says, "I'm fine."

"And one more time," the ranger says as he gently lifts her leg and sprays the lower wound. "So let's see what we have here." He inspects the wound from different angles, and his face seems pleasantly compressed. "You're right," he says to Cosme. "There's remarkably little bleeding for this type of wound, and I don't think how the tourniquet is tied accounts for it."

"The butterflies," says Eva.

"Maybe, maybe," says the ranger, indulging her. "Did you get enough electrolytes?"

She holds the empty bottle up.

"Not that the fall was lucky," says the ranger, "but it may just be that how you fell was good enough to keep this manageable. It could have been much worse."

"The butterflies," says Eva. "Cosme. The songs."

"The songs?"

"We sang some songs," says Cosme.

"Well, whatever forces were at work, they kept this wound from being catastrophic," says the ranger. "Eva, what I'd like to do is spray a little sterile saline water on the top and bottom of the wound again to clean it out a little more, if that's all right with you, and wrap the whole thing in a sterile gauze bandage. Then I think we're good to go."

"Okay," says Eva, looking once again at Albert.

When the wound is cleaned and freshly bandaged, the ranger says, "I must say it's incredible you're not in more pain."

"The butterflies," says Eva, gazing on the clean white bandage. "Cosme. The songs."

"It's incredible," the ranger says, securing stretcher straps across her chest and waist. "You're sure you didn't give her anything."

"Tobacco smoke," says Cosme. "Sole massage. No more."

"And butterflies," the ranger says.

"They came. I sang," says Cosme. "I did not administer."

The ranger stands.

"Okay," he says. "Four people on the stretcher for the first half mile."

AJ, Albert, and two others take the first shift.

"Let's rotate," says the ranger to the stretcher bearers, "so her head is facing downhill and her wound is elevated. Slow and steady."

They descend.

The stretcher bearers feel their way and try to find the groove of method, of the one mind in the four. What each experienced in going up is atmospherically applicable in going down, is even spatially applicable. Same air, same rocks, same trees, same lateral expanse. The bump of the familiar.

But the texture of descent, the gravity of bearance, and the tricky choreography of the collective feel at times like a conspiratorial arrangement, nudging them to question, fleetingly and privately, despite their memories' fidelity and the disinterested proofs of landscape, whether they had been this way before.

It does not help that Eva's eyes keep closing for twenty, thirty seconds at a time as though she has gone under and then opening as though she has brought back from the beyond an insight she cannot contain.

The ranger is out front, downhill, navigating, calling uphill, warning of uncertain footing, warning of restrictive passages through which the stretcher must be carefully maneuvered. Twice he pauses when he's told about her eyes and twice walks uphill to the stretcher and examines Eva. Neither time does he observe dilation trouble. Neither time does he see signs of physical or cognitive decline.

"I'm fine," says Eva each time. "I'm picturing the butterflies we floated down with."

Each time the ranger looks to Cosme.

Cosme shrugs the first time.

The descent resumes.

He shrugs the second time and says, "There was flotation, yes."

The ranger's lips compress. He nods and starts downhill again. The rescue team moves on.

Though Eva's eyes keep closing and reopening and though a stretcher bearer calls down once more to the ranger and communicates this fact, the ranger in this stretch of half a mile does not go uphill to her a third time.

The last time Eva's eyes reopen, beaming, faraway at first, the afterimage of the butterfly-flotation reverie still lingering, they take some seconds to reorient and fix on Albert, who upholds the stretcher handle near her right foot. Albert is preoccupied with footwork for a while but eventually looks up and notices her stare. He meets it for a moment, looks away, and meets it once again.

"I know you," Eva says. "I saw you in Garland when I flew the drone."

"That's true," Albert says.

The Falls' roar gradually intensifies from their perspective as they near. Eva stares at Albert still, but Albert must attend to the necessities of gravity and carriage and terrain.

When he picks up her stare again, she says, "Don't sell."

"You hearing this?" asks Albert, looking to his right at AJ, who upholds the stretcher handle near her left foot.

"Strange shit," says AJ, who, like Albert, knows that Eva's signature is on the papers that transferred ownership of properties, from Costigan in the east to Coburn Gore in the west, to Harold Brown and Chinco.

The ranger calls out, "At the Falls, let's switch up stretcher teams."

Albert stares at Eva.

Albert struggles to make sense of what she said. *Don't sell.* He struggles to explain why Eva Desjardins formed shell companies with regionally endearing names—Penobscot Forest, Black Bear Forest, Kennebec West—and bought all the land she could along the Corridor route and came from Boston to endorse the paperwork and sold it all to Harold Brown and Chinco and now looks a holdout and an owner of a dog-eared copy of *Ecodefense: A Field Guide to Monkeywrenching* squarely in the eye and says, "Don't sell." It makes no sense.

He studies her, and she looks back, serene, assured.

He cannot understand, the way her thigh has been run through, how she can be so.

At the Falls, the trail for some feet levels.

"Here is good," the ranger shouts, his voice against the tumult of the Falls.

"I've been restructured," Eva says to Albert.

The sound of water leaping from the ledge, particularizing, falling, crashing, spraying, atomizing, flying off into the woods or coalescing in the downstream rush is an enormous sonic cushion into which the sounds discrete, the sounds not unionized, are drawn, subsumed and muffled, humbled by the scale and scope of hydrological eruption.

Albert, near her, hears.

"The water we began with," Eva says, "is all the water there will be."

Gauche Calves approaches Albert for the handle transfer. Albert feels the ache and the relief of the impending letting go.

"Restructure him," she says as he releases.

Gauche Calves assumes control of Albert's handle, and the other members of the second team assume control of AJ's and the forward bearers' handles.

"Very good," the ranger says. "Let's take it slow and steady. Steep descent ahead."

The ranger scouts the way. The stretcher follows him downhill.

"Strange shit, man," says AJ.

"Maybe she just needs electrolytes," says Albert, stopping for a drink of water.

AJ drinks from his hydration pack and shakes his head.

"I doubt it, man. She got electrolytes. That shit was mystical."

They head downhill.

"So," says Albert, catching up to Cosme, "you know wound care."

"I have learned some things from teachers, yes."

"Did you hear what she said to me back there?" asks Albert.

"Yes," says Cosme.

"What was that about?" asks Albert.

"She is healing."

They are silent for a while and negotiate the way.

"You met my wife the other day," says Albert. "Mary. In the ferns."

"Yes, Mary," Cosme says. "She found the summer chaga."

"Right."

"She did not harvest."

"No, not this time."

"Yes, she listens to the chaga, to the tree. That is important," Cosme says. "Too many now are not receptive."

They attend to the necessities of footwork.

"You are Albert," Cosme says.

"I am, and this is AJ."

"I am Cosme, but you know. Hallo," he says to them. "You're my ride."

The three of them discuss accommodations and amenities at Shaw's.

When they get near the campground, Albert asks, "So you don't think she needs electrolytes?"

"The ranger gave to her electrolytes," says Cosme.

"Told you, man," says AJ.

"And this person that she told me to restructure."

"Yes," says Cosme.

"How do I restructure him?"

"Well, psychological analysis is one way. Meditation, as your wife knows, is another. Both take time."

"And you think that's what she was telling me?" asks Albert.

"No. What she was telling you was to restructure him with ayahuasca."

"Right on," AJ says.

"This comes with complications. It is faster, but it takes its own time. Ayahuasca is not to be fooled with."

"What she said then. It was mystical?" asks AJ.

"Everything is mystical. Of course. It all is mystical," says Cosme.

AJ says to Albert, "Told you, man."

"To see it truly so," says Cosme, "that is the rub in these times, no?"

Chapter Eight: Cosme Shrugs

The monkeywrenching manual does not say anything about shamanic practice; it does not say anything about the mother of the mother of tobacco; it does not declare that ayahuasca is the eldest teacher and as such, if she so chooses, can transform the consciousness of even an industrialist; the monkeywrenching manual, revised in 1993, does not suggest abduction as the first step in the process of restoring elasticity and clarity and openness to even an industrialist's long-calcified third eye; but, after Albert drops off the second fare, Bill McIntyre, at the AT Lodge in Millinocket, Cosme Esperanza does.

"I hear you, man, but I don't know," says AJ in the shotgun seat of the Shaw's Tacoma. He flips through the dogeared copy of *Ecodefense: A Field Guide to Monkeywrenching*. "Get caught kidnapping and that's it, man."

Cosme rests his left arm on his pack beside him on the back seat and looks out an open window as they pass through Millinocket's outskirts.

"Yes, I understand," says Cosme. "I have had my troubles with the law. I cannot have such troubles here."

"Well, there you go," says AJ.

"Yes, but you may say we are protected. I do not propose or not propose. My spirits tell me we are guarded. I tell what they tell."

They pass the Millinocket Regional Hospital, where Eva's equanimity and talk of butterflies have made a deep impression on the medical professionals.

Taking Route 11 south toward Milo, Albert says, accelerating, "She may be restructured, but she can't undo what she's already done. She can't unsell the properties she sold to Harold Brown."

"Yes, this is true, but she has given the undoing key to you," says Cosme.

Albert thinks about this key.

"And it is also true," says Cosme, "that her company is in negotiations with Peru, my country, to, you may say, *privatize* the public water system. This, you may know, does not help the common people. But she will not do that deal now. She will change the terms so that the water quality improves and yet the water stays Peru's. She is restructured. I am telling you."

"She told you all this on Katahdin?" Albert asks.

"Yes, coming down Katahdin."

"You believe her?"

"Yes."

"But how do you know she's not delusional?" asks Albert. "How do you know that what she said is true?"

"What she experienced was not delusion. What she said is true," says Cosme.

AJ packs a bowl, lights it, ceremoniously inhales, and passes it to Cosme, who declines, and then to Albert, who declines. He takes another hit and holds it with the other in his lungs.

"We're dealing with the mystical," says AJ, billowy, oracular.

"Of course. You see. When you are open, this is clear," says Cosme. "You are open." He taps AJ on the shoulder. "You are open." He taps Albert.

"Right on, right on," says AJ, slightly rocking in the shotgun seat. He thumbs through the field guide.

Albert opens to the possibilities of Eva's key. *Don't sell. Restructure him.* What would be lost if they change tactics, shift perspective?

What if Chris Atwater just stops advocating rationally against the Corridor? What if she stops depending on the legal system to right environmental wrongs? The Corridor will happen either way. The long game almost always favors industry. But what if Chris gets mystical?

What if Albert stops his monthly contribution to the rehabilitation project that reintroduces traumatized orangutans to forests that are not long for this world? With Albert's money or without, the project will not change the consciousness of the deforesters. It will not change the consciousness of those who sell the oil of the palm. It will not elevate the consciousness of those who eat the oil of the palm. What if the project, mission-wise, gets mystical?

What if Mary stops her grass-roots vigilance and does not guard against particulates and PFAs and phthalates and bisphenol A and fluoride and the rest? The grand scheme does not change. Yes, Mary's summer chaga may one day help calcified third eyes to open slit-wise, but the threshold consciousness of the particulate producers and the others, the polluters, will remain as sealed as it has ever been. But Mary is at least conversant with the mystical.

What if Jake and Ryan set aside their tin cans for the hose? Does one hose more or less, employed in garden irrigation, make a difference in a world awash in hoses? If the hose executives get mystical, however, if their consciousness goes through the wringer, then, thinks Albert, hallelujah.

What if AJ stops removing every survey stake and tape he sees? What difference has removal ever made except to further calcify the rival consciousness?

What is the point of monkeywrenching? What enduring good has it accomplished other than allowing monkeywrenchers to believe they occupy the higher moral ground?

What if Albert spikes trees? What if Albert pours sand in the lubrication system of a forest harvester or excavator? What if Albert undermines the roadbed underneath the whole length of the Corridor? What good would any of it do? What is the point of fighting back against such forces? Confrontation only strengthens their resolve, inspires their redoubled efforts. They regroup, retool, relitigate, get cagier, develop obviation capabilities they never had before the troublemakers on the higher moral ground looked down on them.

Maybe Albert, Mary, Jake and Ryan, Chris, and AJ, in their own ways, have expected too much of conventional resistance. Maybe confrontation, surface tinkering, have never been the answer. Maybe vigilance, omission, outrage, pressure, and donation never had much chance against deforesters, developers, particulate producers, and the others. Maybe all along restructuring has been the answer. Maybe all along the answer has been ayahuasca.

Albert looks at Cosme in the rearview.

"You think this will work?"

Cosme shrugs.

"Your spirits said we're guarded."

"One who knows the forest cannot always keep one who does not know from the hidden panther. One who knows the mountain cannot always keep one who does not know from the path of lightning or the falling rock," says Cosme.

"How to kidnap isn't in here," AJ says. He lays the field guide on the center console.

Cosme reads the title out loud and then says, "You have a guide."

"In theory," Albert says. "In practice, sometimes."

"It anticipates, your guide, but it does not predict, yes?"

"Sounds about right," says Albert.

"What is *Ecodefense*?" asks Cosme, studying the cover.

Albert summarizes the philosophy and practice.

"You are monkeywrenchers."

"Well, we like to think so."

"Man, we're monkeywrenchers," AJ says with the conviction of a soul not sorely tested.

"We do little things," says Albert. "Pull up survey stakes. Take down survey tapes."

"What does this do?"

"It's the first rule of monkeywrenching," AJ says.

"Not much. It's aspirational."

"What does this mean?"

"I guess it means that we've been waiting."

"What for?"

"If you'd asked me that this morning, I would probably have said that we've been waiting," Albert says, "for greatness to be thrust upon us."

"Right on," says AJ.

"But I'm starting to believe what we've been waiting for is you."

"And Eva," Cosme says.

"And Eva, yes."

For miles, they don't discuss the metaphysics of their intersection.

They cross the Brownville Junction Bridge, the Pleasant River flowing, perpendicular, beneath them. From the middle of the bridge, they see the junction's southern curvature, concave, a long arc that recalls the way the world goes round. Six lines of freight cars curve into the distance. Three appear to have no end. Abandonment and confluence make up in equal parts the junction's atmosphere.

"May we explore this junction?" Cosme asks.

"The railyard?" Albert asks.

"The railyard, yes. The Brownville Junction."

"Why?" asks Albert, slowing down and veering onto the dirt road.

"It is just to see."

No one is around. They get out and cross the empty tracks.

"The Pleasant River we crossed over. It is a relation of the West Branch of the Pleasant River that I drank from after Chairback?"

AJ says, "It is for sure."

"And it is a relation of the East Branch of the Pleasant River that I drank from after White Cap?"

"All connected."

These relationships please Cosme.

Stepping on and over one coupler, then another, they pass through two lines of boxcars. They approach another coupler and step on and over it. They walk between two lines of empty centerbeam railcars, open, skeletal, reminders of what will be left in the collapse's wake before the vegetation closes in and keeps the secrets of what reigned once to itself. In each line arcing west-northwest, each railcar alternates, one green, one red, one green, one red, as far as they can see.

"Where do they go?" asks Cosme.

"I don't think they run right now," says Albert.

"No?"

"An oil train that these guys operated," Albert says, knocking on the *MMA* emblazoned on one railcar, "came down from the tar sands into Lac Megantic and exploded. Killed what, forty, fifty people. Wrecked who knows how many buildings. Total clusterfuck. The Montreal, Maine and Atlantic Railway didn't last long after that. Went bankrupt."

"Where did all the oil on the train go?" asks Cosme.

"Where it always goes. The ground. The lake. The river. What burned up went in the air and came down somewhere." Albert sits down on a green centerbeam railcar. "Harold Brown keeps saying there are no plans for an oil pipeline through the Corridor. But there will be. You'll see. A water pipeline on the one side and an oil pipeline on the other."

"Not if we restructure him," says AJ.

Cosme looks at Albert's centerbeam railcar for a while and then at the two lines arcing west-northwest beyond where he can see.

"The oil trains would travel this way to the tar sands," Cosme says.

AJ and Albert nod.

"You know where else this goes?" asks AJ. "You remember where you left the woods past Big Wilson Stream? These tracks are those."

"Yes, I remember," Cosme says. "These tracks are those." He turns and looks to where the tracks arc east-northeast. "Where goes this way?"

"To Saint John. New Brunswick. Canada. An oil refinery. The ocean ultimately."

"And that?" asks Cosme, pointing to a tributary track, beyond the boxcars, that runs south-southeast.

"To Searsport. To the ocean."

"Like the river," Cosme says.

"Except the railroad ties are soaked in creosote," says Albert, "and the metal for the rails was mined from somewhere."

They inspect the rails and ties beneath the railcar on which Albert sits.

"Just think," says AJ, lighting up a bowl and savoring a relatively shallow puff, "about the human effort that went into all of this, and this is what it comes to."

AJ extends the pipe to Albert, who accepts and takes a shallow puff. He passes it to Cosme, who declines, and hands it back to AJ, who examines its interior and takes a terminal hit.

"For now," says Albert.

"What?"

"It's come to this for now, but nothing says tomorrow it won't come to something else. Consider this from Harold Brown's perspective. What's he always going on about? A hub. An intermodal paradise. The Corridor will only be like twenty miles south of here, if that, and it'll roughly parallel the tracks from Saint John in the east to not quite Lac Megantic in the west. The Searsport tracks will intersect it. He's always said that rail is crucial to his infrastructure vision. Look what's here. This is exactly what he needs to tie together all the pieces. Everything connects. The port in Eastport, the container ships, the tandem tractor trailers on his private road, a right of way that's wide enough for an oil pipeline on the one side and a water pipeline on the other, and the intermodal freight lines. All that's missing is connection to the airport. He's connecting all the pieces."

"Moot," says AJ.

"Moot."

"Yeah, man, moot. Restructure him, and what you said is moot."

A red fox trots beneath a centerbeam railcar coupler, freezes for some seconds to assess the three of them, unfreezes, and continues trotting, underneath another coupler, tending toward the Pleasant River.

"Healthy-looking fox," says AJ.

"Beautiful. A good sign," says Cosme, nodding.

"Is it?" Albert asks.

"You are determining a course. A healthy fox appears and puts a feeling in you here," says Cosme, indicating with four fingertips his center. "You are at a junction. Yes, the fox is good."

"I still don't know what I should do."

"Let go of energy that traps you when you think of Harold Brown."

"In my relationship with you," says Albert, pausing, summoning the words of Ram Dass, "who I think I am affects who I see you to be."

AJ breathes and says, "Right on."

"The feeling in you here," says Cosme, indicating with four fingertips his center, "do you think a man who wishes to pave over so much and believes so in extraction feels it as you do? As AJ does? As you are able, help him. Ask the fox for her assistance."

Albert bows his head and asks the fox.

"The feeling in you here," says Cosme, fingertips upon the existential center, "when you see a forest cut down or a river dying. He must feel such loss."

"Right on," says AJ. "Ruin something dear to him."

"This is not what I mean," says Cosme. "You're not a vandal, are you?"

"No."

"Are you a man of violence?"

"No."

"Coercion does not teach a way beyond coercion," Cosme says. "Such energies must be let go."

"To kidnap, you know, without coercion, I don't know," says Albert.

"Do not kidnap with coercion in your heart."

"I don't see how that's possible," says Albert.

Cosme sits beside him on the railcar and is on the verge of saying something when a Boeing Stratotanker flying west from Bangor draws their gazes skyward. They withhold their speculations on its destination and intentions. When it disappears and its reverberations do not reach them any longer, they continue gazing for a while as though to be put back together as it was the sky requires witness.

"You say this place is a hub," says Cosme.

"It is, or was."

"This man we are discussing, in him is the vision of a great hub. In him is the spirit of the hub."

Albert and AJ cross their arms and bow their heads, affiliating.

"In him is the spirit of control."

"And in him is the spirit of the asshole," AJ says, his head still bowed.

"Would you control him in whom is the spirit of control? The spirit of the asshole?" Cosme asks.

"I would," says AJ.

Albert says, "I would. What choice is there?"

"You said before that who you think you are."

"Affects who I see you to be."

"Who do you think you are? A spirit of the hub? A spirit of control?"

Albert and AJ, arms crossed, heads bowed, think what they are the spirits of.

"Of course you do not think you are such spirits. See him as you think you are and help him to become not under the illusion of control. This cannot be coercion."

Cosme hops down from the railcar.

"It is said that ayahuasca is a ladder to the sky, the heavens, everything. This track," says Cosme, squatting, pointing to the rails and crossties, "it looks like a ladder, yes? But it is flat. Held fast. The track is limited in how far it can take you. Limited in what it can reveal." He stands. "It is, you may say, like the consciousness of Harold Brown. We cannot make the track a ladder to the sky. We cannot make his consciousness what it is not. We are a bridge," says Cosme, pointing toward the Brownville Junction Bridge. "We offer him a way."

"And if he doesn't take it?" Albert asks, his arms still crossed, his head still bowed.

"Be open."

Chapter Nine: The Greater Good

A bearded man of plaid and denim limps down the center aisle of Central Hall in Dover-Foxcroft. Stage left is an easel on which rests a sign that says in simple terms why almost every hall seat has been taken: *East-West Transportation, Utility, and Communications Corridor.*

The man is in the middle of the aisle when he sees three vacant seats in one row to his left. He limps a little farther, stopping by the occupant of that row's center-aisle seat. He indicates the vacancies and asks if he could bother her to get by.

"I'm sorry," says the occupant, her tone commiserative, expressing an awareness of the random nature of predicament. "They're saved."

The man surveys the seats on both sides of the aisle and does not see other vacancies. He looks up to the single row of balcony seats that horseshoe ring the hall and sees no hope up there.

"It's almost seven," says the man, returning his attention to the woman in the aisle seat. "The meeting starts at seven."

Chris Atwater, who has occupied this aisle seat for half an hour, looks six seats to her left—beyond the three vacancies, past Mary Lesiak's two sons—and holds her hands out, asking in this manner for some guidance on what she should do.

Mary turns in her seat and elevates a little, peering at the population of the standing room. Not seeing Albert, AJ, or Cosme, Mary turns around, comes down, and gestures that perhaps the time for saving seats is over. Jake and Ryan play computer games and do not register a tension.

"Hang on," Chris says to the man of plaid and denim, who has turned and limped a few steps toward the standing room. "Sit here."

"Obliged," the man says, limping back.

Sidling three seats to her left, Chris says, "The people we were saving for, I don't know why they're still not here. I'm sorry."

"Don't be," says the man, now in the aisle seat. "We're territorial by nature. Ain't that why we're all here?"

A couple who observed with interest the succession of the aisle seat detaches from the population of the standing room and claims the last two vacancies.

Enter Harold Brown stage left. He walks directly to the lectern as if not observed unfavorably by hundreds, turns the lectern laptop on, and glances at the route map on the screen beside him.

A vibration startles Mary. She takes out her phone and reads a text from AJ: "Change of plans. We're taking him tonight. I'm in position now. A and C are on their way to you. 15-20 min."

Harold Brown begins.

"Good evening. Thank you all for coming to the final public meeting. Getting to this point has taken all of us a long time. Almost ten years, if you're counting. But we're here."

Mary leans and hands her phone to Chris, who reads the text. The reading raises Chris's eyebrows. They stay risen as she hands the phone to Mary, who in answer raises hers and nods.

"The purpose of this meeting is to let you know about developments regarding the East-West Corridor since we last met in February. These developments you may have heard reported from the meetings that I did last week, but I prefer to personally report them. What I couldn't tell you in February that I can tell you now is that the route is set. We have in all but one or two cases, which themselves are being finalized, reached equitable agreements with the owners of the Corridor-abutting properties."

Some members of the audience, both on the floor and in the balcony, begin to boo.

Jake and Ryan tense and then continue playing their computer games.

"As I have said from the beginning, not a single property would be acquired via eminent domain. And not a single property has. I've kept my word on that. On this entire route, not once was eminent domain invoked."

Someone coughs and in the cough says, "Bullshit."

Harold Brown cannot detect the person, but he tries to reason with him.

"Tell me once when eminent domain was used."

The hall is silent.

"This is what you do," says Chris, not rising for the declaration.

"Excuse me?" Harold asks. He squints and tries to locate the speaker.

"I said, 'This is what you do,'" says Chris, who rises.

"Ah, Miss Atwater. By which you mean what?"

"By which I mean you're right. You don't use eminent domain. You engineer and enter into mutually profitable arrangements with such companies as Waterloo and Kirk, which spin off shell companies like Black Bear Forest, companies on paper, to buy up the properties along the route without informing sellers that these properties will then be sold to you to put the route together, cover up your tracks, and tell us all how noble you and Chinco are for standing back and letting an organic process play out free of eminent domain. By 'This is what you do,' I mean you play a shell game."

By grumbles and by variable cheers, attendees high and low voice solidarity with Chris.

Jake and Ryan tense again, continue playing their computer games.

"Miss Atwater, all these acquisitions are recorded in the Registry of Deeds. There is no shell game here. There is no secrecy. Shell companies provide investors liability and tax protections. That is all."

"We aren't stupid," Chris says, sitting down. "We know what they provide."

The audience assents by cheer and grumble.

Jake and Ryan tense.

Mary leans toward Chris and says, "It's getting kind of triggery in here. The boys and I are going to take a walk along the river. Don't worry about saving seats."

Mary, Jake, and Ryan exit by the side aisle.

Things settle down, and Harold says to everyone, "Well, let me ask you. When have I or Chinco ever steered you wrong? When have we not been totally transparent with the citizens of Maine?"

Chris stands again and asks, "Was Chinco not successfully sued and ordered by the court to remediate a Superfund site that still affects the citizens of Brewer? Didn't Chinco recently circumvent the public-notice and permitting process in an aquaculture venture, leaving Searsport citizens no way to dewater pipeline dredge spoils?"

"Miss Atwater…"

"My apologies. I thought you were seriously asking if you've ever steered us wrong or not been totally transparent with the citizens of Maine." She sits.

Uproar.

Harold Brown does not try to acknowledge Chris's charges and declared apologies again. His thumbs rest on the lectern, and his fingers drape down either side. His digits do not grip. Excessive knuckle whiteness is not evident. This is not unfamiliar territory for his digits or his visage, but his facial equanimity seems forced. Too much composure means that he desires some support. He waits for the collective passions to subside. The uproar drifts down to a murmur. Quiet comes. The audience awaits.

"I guarantee you there has been no circumvention of the public-notice and permitting process, or of any other process, in developing the East-West Corridor. There will be nothing to remediate. How many times have I been here in the past ten years to keep you in the loop on project updates? Six? Seven? I assure you we have dotted every i and crossed every t, and I assure you we have done much more than that. I'm sure you've heard me say before that the construction of the highway will be ISO-14001 compliant, meaning that it will adhere to strict environmental standards that will minimize environmental impact. Almost every facet of this project goes beyond what's federally required."

Chris stands, her hand raised. Harold Brown addresses her immediately.

"Miss Atwater, please just hear me out. I'll answer any questions in conclusion."

Chris resumes her seat without objection.

"You may not believe this," Harold Brown continues, first addressing Chris and then expanding his expression to address each person in attendance, "but I understand emotions running high because of land-use conflicts. I was born and raised in Livermore Falls. I've lived there all my life. When Route 4 came through in 1931, I wasn't yet alive, so I have no aversion to its being there. It's always sort of been there in my consciousness, you understand. Route 17, however, which came through in 1949 when I was five years old, was a catastrophe that I remember clearly to this day. My family was forced to move because of 17. Our home was razed to let it through. Our trees were chopped down and uprooted. Every toad and frog I knew was gone. No natural thing I loved was left. A lot of what defined me as a person at that time was overrun, just disappeared, and was replaced by what I did not love. To this day, I resent Route 17 as deeply as an old man can resent a road. I use it. I appreciate its benefits, but what it took from me when I was five I still feel taken. So believe me when I tell you that I understand emotions running high."

He takes a sip of water and returns the clear glass to the lectern.

"But you know what? To my children, 17 is just a road that owes them nothing. To my grandchildren, it is just a road that owes them nothing. And to every generation after, that is what it will be."

The audience does not object to what appears to really be sincerity, and Harold Brown does not appear to be self-satisfied with his part in the atmospheric alteration.

The unobtrusive whirring of the ceiling fan puts in relief the silence of the ruminating souls who sit below.

"So why would I put others through what I went through at five years old, you may be wondering. I've asked myself this very question many times. I think we all agree there is a common good, a greater good. What it consists of we may differ on, and that's important, but I think we all agree there is a common good, a greater good, whatever you prefer to call it. I've thought a lot about this good, what we rely on, what we need and use collectively. I've thought about the damming of the Dead River in 1949. You've heard me talk of this before. To generate electric power for a population that did not yet have it, an entire valley, twenty-two miles, and two villages were flooded. Sunk. I've thought about the construction of the Maine Turnpike in the forties and fifties. 303.2 miles of destruction and displacement and upheaval. Landscapes were transformed, and ecosystems were upended. Farms were lost, and ways of life were altered. People sacrificed and suffered for those projects. Many voluntarily, and many not. Many not. I've asked myself did power generation and did such a transportation upgrade justify the costs, the asking of so much, the sacrifice and suffering of thousands. I believe they did. I do believe they did. Does anyone believe the people out near Flagstaff would give up electric power if we could undam the Dead River and remake the valley as it was? Does anyone believe that people would give up the ease of movement that the Turnpike offers if we could demolish it and reconfigure those 303.2 miles as they used to be? I've asked myself who had to make those hard decisions to move forward. They were people who could not indulge the luxury of personal morality. They set aside their personal morality to shepherd projects for the greater good. I know that future generations will look back on what we are about to do and will conclude that it was for the greater good."

"And you're the one who sets aside his personal morality and takes this noble burden on?" asks Chris, who this time does not rise.

"I'm one of them. I'm not the only one by any means, but, yes, I'm one, which I'm aware may sound a little grandiose. But is it grandiose to recognize this region's problems and do something to alleviate them?"

A woman from the balcony calls down, "You mean the region that you called the hollow middle of Maine?"

The memory of civic insult riles the audience again.

"A poor choice of words I have apologized for using," Harold Brown admits, appearing chastened, "but my indiscretion does not change the fact that this region has been hollowed economically."

He turns stage right and trains a red dot on the route map's eastern terminus.

"Do you know what percentage of the Calais population lives below the poverty line? 16.5%."

He moves the red dot west to Dover.

"20.5% below the poverty line in Dover."

He moves it south.

"26.4% in Garland."

Harold Brown turns toward the audience and lays the pointer on the lectern.

"This is nothing new. The story is the same throughout the region. I'm not telling you what you don't already know. You may not know the numbers, but you know the signs. We all know what the signs are. Dilapidated properties and houses. Shuttered businesses where once they thrived. Persistent unemployment. Will the Corridor solve every problem right away? Of course not. But it will bring jobs."

"Those jobs," starts Chris.

"Those jobs," says Harold Brown, forestalling her objection, "some dismiss as temporary, in the case of the construction jobs, or low wage, in the case of certain service jobs. But all construction jobs are temporary. When the project's done, you move on to another project elsewhere. And with the service jobs, remember that the minimum hourly wage in Maine is twelve dollars. That is not too bad to start."

"You can't reduce this just to economics," Chris says, staying seated. "What about the problems that the Corridor creates? You've sort of taken care of those who sold. You'll take good care of who cuts down the trees and drains the bogs and moves the earth. You'll take good care of who provides the asphalt, and you'll take good care of who provides the concrete and the fencing for the walls. But what about the rights of the Penobscot through whose sovereign land the Corridor is routed? What about the people who depend on what the Corridor destroys, pollutes, obstructs, and marginalizes? What about the rights of nature?"

"Miss Atwater."

"What about the watershed? The air? The animals? Migration patterns? Fractured landscapes and communities? Will you take care of them?"

"As I have said before," says Harold Brown, "we will have vegetated overpasses and underpasses for the animals."

"Magnanimous," says Chris.

A grandma in the third row stands and says, "Your private toll road is a border wall across the center of our state. It's shameful."

"Ma'am, to clarify, it's public-private."

"Going back to what the lady said about you've taken care of those who sold," a bent-backed farmer in the last row says, "I wouldn't have agreed to sell three years ago to Black Bear Forest if I'd known who I was really selling to. To my neighbors who are here, I'm sorry."

The hall feels like a Quaker meetinghouse in which the silence has been stunned and one by one the Friends, inspired to express what inwardly they've heard from the divine, arise and have their say.

Chris sits quietly and thinks about the note that Harold Brown passed through the window of his Forester as she stood near his driveway with the others yesterday. *Let both of them grow together until the harvest. Matthew 13:30.* She went home that afternoon, took down her Bible from her bookshelf, ran her index finger down the page, and read. *Let both of them grow together until the harvest; and at harvest time I will tell the reaper, "Collect the weeds first and bind them in bundles to be burned, but gather the wheat in my barn."* She did not understand at first how this applied to her, why Harold Brown had only passed the passage fragment through the window of his Forester.

But as she listens to the discontent aboil, as she watches Harold Brown, a pressed but stoic figure in its midst, she thinks she understands. To him the wheat are those good souls who sold, attained a little something for their troubles, and contributed a little to the grand scheme, and the wheat are those good souls who will fulfill their functions in the project and collect their fees. The others, the Penobscot, nature, air, the watershed, the animals, the people testifying in the hall, herself, are weeds. They will be burned. She understands that Harold Brown is right and has been all along. The Corridor is happening.

It doesn't matter what she says tonight. When things calm down and Harold Brown officially announces to the Dover audience the expedited permit approval for the water pipeline in the right of way along the Corridor, it will not matter if she says that it amounts to water mining or that water exportation is a crime against the people and the ecosystem or that water is a natural right or that the absolute-dominion rule whereby the owner of the land above the groundwater is the water's overlord and may exploit it at his will must be abandoned for the American rule, which would forbid the water's exportation, or that Harold Brown's oft-stated claim that Nestlé Waters North America's extraction of 900,000,000 gallons from Maine's aquifers each year is only .0000357% of Maine's annual rainfall is a smoke-and-mirrors claim that she can easily rebut with figures of her own. It doesn't matter now. The Corridor is happening. She understands it always was.

The hall lights flicker. Off-on, off-on, off-on.

This intermittent deprivation of a baseline quantity of light distracts the audience's attention, draws the gazes ceiling-ward, then stage-ward, and occasions a transition from a mode of criticality to one of *What is going on?* Until this question is resolved, the Corridor feels distant somehow, ancillary, not as stirring as it just was. Settled, quiet now, the audience appeals without a word to Harold Brown for resolution.

"Ladies and gentlemen, I understand emotions running high tonight. But if we all speak out at once, then no one will be heard. I'm here, like you, to listen and be heard. But talking over one another, we accomplish nothing. So let's listen to each other. Let's be heard."

He pauses as if to recall the old ideal of civil discourse to this general body in the hall, to clarify, materialize, the shadowy collective memory of politic communication, to revivify what once may have been held more certainly in common.

"I propose we take a short break. Decompress. Refresh. Let's reconvene in fifteen minutes."

Harold Brown does not slot time to entertain alternatives to his proposal. Exiting stage left, he speaks a moment with a man whom Chinco hired for security and finds the backstage bathroom.

"Excuse me," Chris says, sidling past the couple to her right. "Excuse me. Sorry."

They slide sideways and politely try to minimize themselves.

The bearded man of plaid and denim has already stood and in the standing stretches, but he does not leave the area.

"Excuse me," Chris says. "Sorry to dislodge you."

"No need for apology." He steps into the center aisle to allow her passage. "No, my doctor says I need to move more." He observes that she has left behind no clothing article to signal that her seat is saved. He indicates her empty chair and says, "You coming back?"

Chris sighs.

"This meeting's sort of pointless."

"If you'd like to think it over, in the meantime I can save your seat," he says.

"I doubt I'm coming back, but thank you."

"So you're giving up?"

"It's over."

"Is it?"

"You don't think so?"

"I don't know."

"It's over."

"Sounds to me like you don't think there's nothing you can do."

"If you know something I can do, I'd love to hear it."

The man's beard in the region of his mouth begins to move as though he's repositioning tobacco.

"If you leave, there's one less voice. There's that, right? Strength in numbers."

"One voice more or less means nothing now." She scans the hall.

"Three-hundred voices more or less mean nothing now."

"But your voice is the strongest. He refers to you by name."

"I've raised my voice against this thing for seven years. The evidence will show my voice is not that strong. But thank you."

Chris navigates the center aisle to the exit. Outside, in the waning daylight, people mill about and chat and smoke.

"The meeting's done already?" Albert asks, approaching on the sidewalk.

"Fifteen-minute recess," Chris says. "Nice to see you again, Cosme. Congratulations on your thru-hike."

"Thank you, yes, so nice to see you too."

"The end, I heard, was quite eventful," Chris says.

"Yes, no summit but eventful," Cosme says.

"You must be so tired."

"I do not carry anything. I do not have to climb or watch out for the steep decline. I do not feel so tired now," says Cosme.

"Mary and the boys are inside?" Albert asks.

"She took them to the river when the meeting got a little triggery. They're fine."

The three of them are silent for a while and, as if by prearranged accordance, they withdraw some steps from those who mill and chat and smoke. When distance seems to offer them sufficient auditory insulation, Chris says, "So you're doing it tonight?"

"We are," says Albert.

"Good."

"Good?" asks Albert.

"I still think it's stupid and you'll probably get caught, but I don't know what else there is to do. Where's AJ?"

"In the woods off Route 6 in Sangerville."

"Why there?"

"The shortest route from Dover to Livermore Falls goes through Route 6 in Sangerville. When Harold Brown leaves here tonight, Cosme and I'll follow him. When we get near the Route 6 woods, we'll call ahead to AJ, who will lie as though dead in the road. When Harold stops..."

"What if he doesn't stop?" asks Chris.

"He has to stop," says Albert.

"What if someone else stops?"

"It's all coordinated," Albert says. "When Harold stops, we snatch him up and AJ takes his car."

"Then what?"

"We restructure him in Garland."

"With ayahuasca."

"Yes."

"You are an entity of light. You are encouraged to attend the ceremony," Cosme says.

"I need to think this over," Chris says. "How long will this take?"

"It will take time," says Cosme.

"Hours? Days?"

"It may take days. It may take weeks. I have not met this man."

"I'm going to the river," Chris says. "You guys take the meeting."

Chapter Ten: He Is Sick

When Cosme got to Shaw's, he was not ravenous. He did not seek a calorie. He did not eat a drop of grease the day his thru-hike ended.

In his room, he found a compact paper bag in which was summer chaga, ground for tea. It was a gift from Mary, who had gone back to the river birch with Jake and Ryan three days after she and Chris had stumbled onto Cosme in the ferns. She sat beneath the tree and meditated with the boys. The river birch communicated willingness to let a little of the summer chaga go. Mary cut two modest nodules from the black mass and sat back down with the boys among the long beech ferns to thank the river birch and say goodbye.

In his room, Cosme held the open bag up to his nose, inhaling deeply, smelling earth and bark. He did not make a cup of chaga tea. The morning ayahuasca was still working in him. He did not wish to risk a regional mycelium precluding the completion of the lesson.

In the grand confinement of the hall, the people pack back in for part two, unified by something just above the register of murmur. Cosme— used to smells arboreal, smells fungal, used to Trail air, air not agitated by so many people breathing and a ceiling fan—is certain the majority of people whom he stands among are bacon eaters. Just beneath that something just above the register of murmur, he detects a sizzle, which may be electrical, the bane of finer sensibilities, or which may be sclerosis slowly hardening the larded arteries of the majority.

Albert stands beside him in the hall and mentally goes over the abduction plan, but scenes from *Fargo* keep occurring to him, interrupting his review. Jean Lundegaard's abduction in that movie did not go as Jerry Lundegaard had planned. So Albert asks himself why his plan won't cascade into catastrophe like Jerry Lundegaard's.

For one, the aim of Jerry Lundegaard's abduction plan was money, pure and simple. Avarice directed it. But Albert thinks nobility of cause, which in itself may not mean much to forces charged with orchestrating such cascades, still has to count for something. For another, the success of Jerry Lundegaard's abduction plan depended on two seedy criminals whose interest in his plan was likewise purely mercenary. But if idiomatic wisdom passed down from the forebears is to keep on keeping on, thinks Albert, practical and vital, then the company one keeps must count for something. Albert thinks of AJ in the Route 6 woods, of Chris and Mary by the river with the boys, of Cosme standing next to him and Eva in the hospital. He trusts the company he keeps as Jerry Lundegaard could not have trusted Steve Buscemi and the other guy. He tells himself that cause and company and trust should be enough to prove that his plan isn't Jerry Lundegaard's.

But still he wonders, really, who is Eva Desjardins? Was she ecstatic on the mountain or electrolyte deficient? Mystical or chemically imbalanced? He asks Hamlet if there really are more things in heaven and earth than are dreamt of in Horatio's philosophy. Hamlet assures him that there are. There really are. And if he hadn't thought this to be true already, Albert would have been converted to the faith when Cosme told him that his vision on the Tableland, above the Tableland, made Cosme two and led the lower Cosme, then the higher, from the Tableland to Eva hanging from the iron handhold where the twinned became a singularity again. And if he hadn't been already a believer, Albert would have been converted to the faith when Cosme told him that he saw the butterflies that Eva saw and heard what Eva heard and that they both learned on the mountain what the flora know.

But still, no mention in the monkeywrenching manual of planned abduction as a method to resist environmental wrongs is an omission Albert cannot easily make peace with.

Harold Brown reenters stage left and adjusts his glasses as he squares up at the lectern. To his right, the route map is projected on the screen as it has been throughout the intermission. He brings up a closed fist to his mouth and clears his throat without a proper cough. Without additional preamble, he begins.

"I'd like to ask you all, respectfully, to see the world we live in as it is, not as we wish it was."

He pauses to allow some time for the perception shift.

"I hated those men who decided for a region where Route 17 would go. But what I didn't understand when I was young was that the desires of the time, the time's needs, the economy, and so forth had already determined that the road would be constructed somewhere, if not by those men I hated, then by others, and wherever it was going there would have to be some sacrifice. Some folks would have to suffer. The environment would have to suffer some. I wish the world we live in operated otherwise, but wishing doesn't do us any favors.

"Whether it is roads or dams or powerlines or real-estate development or mineral extraction or what have you, we have all, implicitly or otherwise, bought into the agreement that some people and some natural places have to pay the price for our desires, needs, economy, and so forth. Our desires, needs, economy, and so forth, they are natural forces in and of themselves and must be served by someone. And it doesn't matter much by whom."

Harold Brown attempts to locate Chris Atwater, but, since no objection rises from where he believed she was, he slackens somewhat and resumes.

"If those men I hated had withdrawn, then other men would have stepped in and built that road. Before it ever was, that road was as assuredly a fact as anything you could have laid your hands on. Those men did not so much construct that road as it constructed them. The regional desires, needs, economy, and so forth constructed them. And if those men had not been there, then others would have come the same way people in the old days headed west. Such folks are not the natural forces. What such folks are drawn by are. Such folks are simply servants of those forces. Look at me," says Harold Brown, sidestepping stage left from behind the lectern, arms extended as in invitation to appraisal. "Do I look like a natural force?"

The audience in general chuckles. Albert does not crack a smile. Cosme deepens his observance.

"I am not," says Harold Brown, his arms resuming their positions at his sides. He sidles stage right, very much unlike a natural force, and stands behind the lectern.

"I am interchangeable. Dispensable. And so is Chinco. If it isn't me, it will be someone else. And if it isn't Chinco, it will be some other company that serves these forces that will make the Corridor reality. Let's talk about what this reality will look like."

Harold Brown taps his computer, and the image now projected on the screen is of a trench in which an orange stripe of fiber-optic conduit lies waiting for the workman at the trench's lip to finalize the burial.

"When I was first drawn to this project, I envisioned fiber-optic cables in the rights of way for high-speed internet, but 5G made that vision obsolete."

He taps his laptop, and the image now projected on the screen is of a wasteland as seen from the vantage of a satellite: a drilling rig, two gas flares, storage tanks, a fleet of trucks and hauling trailers, and a smaller fleet of RV trailers, unattached and scattered. Tan, tan, tan the land is in this snapshot of a land unloved.

"So with the boom in Bakken crude and the Alberta tar sands and with the explosion of the Lac-Megantic train, I started thinking that the project drew me for a different reason. I envisioned oil pipelines in the rights of way. With all the accidents and risks, why ship by rail instead of pipeline? But politically, environmentally, operationally, and so forth, oil pipelines come with heavy baggage. Look where we seem headed. Green technologies. Electric cars. So, no, the project did not draw me for the purpose of constructing oil pipelines. I have said I cannot rule them out because I cannot say what may develop ten, twenty, fifty years from now. But, frankly, I don't see a future in which oil pipelines figure. This should put some minds at ease."

He taps his laptop, and the image on the screen is of a clutch of desiccated trees, their branches dagger-like, denuded, and of sand that stretches to a cloudy mountain in the background.

"This is only several miles outside Cape Town, South Africa. The population of the metro area is just about five million. These trees used to be submerged when this, which looks like desert but is actually supposed to be a major reservoir, was full. This same scenario is playing out everywhere. There is a global water crisis, and it will be catastrophic if the steps to mitigate it aren't taken now. Imagine how unstable things become if a metropolis like Cape Town runs out of water."

Harold Brown allows his audience some time with their imaginations.

"This is not an isolated crisis. Mexico City, with a metro-area population of over twenty million, is at risk of running out of water.

Cairo, Egypt, also with a metro-area population of over twenty million, is at risk of running out of water. Countries in the Middle East, which has a population of over four-hundred million, are at risk of running out of water. This is why Rajendra Singh, known as the water man of India, declared, 'The third world war is at our gate, and it will be about water, if we don't do something about this crisis.'"

Now the image on the screen is of connection side by side with disconnection, an expanse of mudcracks, jigsaw gaps between close puzzle pieces, integration and disintegration coexisting as competing concepts, each force tugging at the other as though settlement is still an open question. In the middle of the image rests a weathered dinghy, half sunk, beached, a creature of the mudcracks. In the distance is a water body, hugged by mountains, of dimensions difficult to limn.

"This isn't in South Africa or Mexico or Egypt or the Middle East or India," says Harold Brown, directing everyone's attention to the mudcracks and the shrinking water body. "This is Lake Mead in Nevada. Twenty-five-million people depend on it for drinking water. Since 2000, Lake Mead's water level has decreased a hundred-thirty feet and shows no signs of rebound. And Lake Powell, which is second to Lake Mead in reservoir capacity, is in a state of similar decline in Arizona. Things are getting dire. The Colorado River watershed is drying up. The water source for forty-million people, one in eight Americans, is drying up. This trend is not sustainable. It goes beyond the Colorado River watershed.

"Los Angeles, Phoenix, El Paso, Miami, and Atlanta are on the growing list of US cities that are running out of water. This will not resolve itself. Exactly how long it will take for worst-case scenarios to play out is uncertain, but they will play out if something isn't done."

Now on the screen is just a number.

24,000,000,000,000

Harold Brown allows his audience to take in all those zeros.

"Average annual rainfall in our state is twenty-four-trillion gallons. Maine is not at risk of running out of water. We are blessed in that regard, and in this blessing is the project's draw. The transportation part of it has gotten all the press, but water's really what this project is about. It took me years to see this, but it's clear now that this project will position Maine as a preeminent provider of what no life can do without."

Cosme's eyebrows rise.

"This is a nascent market," Harold Brown continues, "and an opportunity for Maine to do the right thing. Though we will be partnering with Nestlé Waters North America on this part of the project, this is not about more bottled water. This is not about more plastic. This is about two pipelines, in the rights of way, efficiently transporting water down to Eastport, where it will be loaded onto water tankers and then shipped to the distressed."

.004% appears now on the screen.

"We believe that we initially can ship in excess of a billion gallons of water, .004% of annual rainfall, out of Eastport every day."

1.5% appears now on the screen.

"365 billion gallons annually amounts to 1.5% of annual rainfall. Imagine the good that this can do for Mexico City. For Los Angeles. This is capitalism as it is supposed to be. We serve the most important human need, we do our part to keep the peace, and we bring billions each year into Maine's economy because we have been blessed with a renewable and absolutely necessary natural resource. We project that we can export ten percent of annual rainfall without significant environmental implications."

The hum of discontent swells through the hall and then subsides.

"With this number, we would meet the water needs of somewhere on the order of 150 million people. So, you may be asking, why is no one doing this right now? The obstacles are several. One is that at present tanker shipping costs are high, eighteen times the cost of desalination. One is that the infrastructure needs to be developed to accommodate such shipments. Logistically, it's daunting. And another is the risk of undertaking an endeavor that's ahead of its time but dearly needed now.

"So what do we have in the works to make these obstacles not obstacles? We're currently in talks with companies transitioning to diesel-fuel alternatives, which will dramatically reduce the tanker shipping costs. We're currently in talks with several US states and several countries about creating water hubs, which may involve pipelines, highways, rail lines, or what have you to facilitate delivery from hub sites to their satellites. Domestically, at four cents per liter, it makes economic sense to ship by rail smaller quantities to towns and cities suffering from drought or source contamination.

"Will this project solve the water crisis? No. There is no silver bullet. But this project will be an important part of the solution. Shipments via tanker, rail, and pipeline, conservation efforts, wastewater reclamation and recycling projects, and who knows what other opportunities will present themselves will make Maine a leader in the effort to avert the third world war that's at our gate. In fact, the wastewater reclamation and recycling projects we're developing will actually negate our exportation water loss. Our net loss will be zero."

"I wish Chris were here," says Albert. "She'd know how much of this is real and how much is bullshit."

"He is sick," says Cosme.

Albert nods and looks back up at Harold Brown, who taps his laptop. *~$1,000-$1,600* shows up on the screen now.

"This will not be your average infrastructure project. We believe Maine's water is the people's water, and that's why we'll be doing something similar to what they do up in Alaska with the Permanent Fund, which pays a dividend to each Alaskan, sort of like a share of the profits that the oil business generates. This dividend has ranged from about $1,000 to $1,600 over the past decade. Once our project is complete, each Mainer can expect the same."

The hall explodes with shouts of affirmation and disorganized applause that suddenly becomes as synchronous and mesmerizing as a starling murmuration.

"He is sick," says Cosme.

"Yeah, there's no way what he's saying adds up."

"No," says Cosme, circling his right hand counterclockwise around his abdomen and groin. "Cancer maybe. Maybe something in the blood."

"How do you know?"

"I could be wrong," says Cosme, lowering his voice as the applause and shouts of affirmation ebb.

An atmospheric alteration has transpired in the hall.

"This project offers something for us all," says Harold Brown. A voice in him decides against expostulation. In a lower register, he says, "The project offers something for us all. Thank you. I will answer questions."

Here and there a citizen gets up and asks for clarification on one aspect of the project or another, but the general feeling, inarticulate, communicated through the shoulders and the mandibles of the majority, is that the robber-baron ethos is not operational in Harold Brown.

"I do not think tonight," says Cosme confidentially.

The audience begins to file out.

Albert waits until the zone around the two of them is clear.

"Abduction-wise?"

"I do not think tonight."

"But what about restructuring?"

Cosme gestures toward the stage where Harold Brown is gathering his presentation implements.

"Be open with him."

"Have you healed this sort of thing before?"

"Of course. I am a healer. But," says Cosme, "I am just a healer."

Albert tells himself, "Be open with him," and approaches Harold Brown. He climbs the riser, but, before he steps foot on the stage, he asks, "You got a minute?"

The man in charge of Harold Brown's security steps forth.

"It's all right," says Harold Brown. "Come up. I have the documents for you to sign."

"I love my land," says Albert.

"It will never be worth more than what it's worth right now."

"Would you be willing," Albert asks, "to walk it with me? Say tomorrow morning?"

"Then you'll sign."

"You're sick," says Albert, lowering his right hand and beginning counterclockwise circulation.

Harold Brown does not immediately respond. He stows a power cord inside a case.

"Who told you that?"

"My friend," says Albert. "You have cancer. Or an issue in the blood."

"He told you that?"

"He told me maybe."

"Who told him?"

"Whoever's out there," Albert says, expansively positioning his arms as though to emphasize how insufficient is his reach to get a handle on the multitudinous unknowns.

"Whoever's out there."

"He's a healer. From Peru. His medicine's indigenous."

"A healer from Peru."
"You do have cancer, don't you? Or an issue in the blood."
Is honesty a violation of one's sovereignty, one's natural boundaries?
Harold Brown says, "Yes, I do."
"Then what is there to lose?"

Chapter Eleven: A Class B Waterway

Burnham Brook, according to the relevant department, is a Class B waterway. The oxygen dissolved in it should be in concentrations more inviting to the benthic macroinvertebrates and algae. This condition and the nonpoint source pollution that created it caused lip compression in the relevant department that included Burnham Brook on the impairment list. No evidence suggests the brook lacks moxie or desire for reclassification as a Class A waterway, or even double A. A thorough study has been done.

Upstream are four-hundred dairy cows and an impoundment pond, and west, beyond the pine and hemlock woods, are hayfields, row crops, mostly corn, a dirt road. Somewhere downstream, chawing sideways, paying nitrogen no mind, ten horses graze, and somewhere downstream, chawing sideways, paying phosphorous no mind, ten beef cows do the same.

Above the brook, the pine and hemlock branches stretch like the appendages of ancient long-limbed athletes. Some trees slouch like silent-movie stars and lean with no discernible momentum toward the brook, betraying no impatience, nothing mortal, no desire to just fall and let it out. *A span*, they say without a sound, *an era of abridgement in its own time comes.*

The brook flows, clear, a natural babble, sounding now and then as though a breakthrough into human language is at hand. The atmosphere above the brook and laterally some length beyond its banks is water-laden, cool, the rising and expansion of the brook, its ministration and its misting. Outreach. All is outreach. In a bend below, the water pools and fingerlings oppose the flow. They wiggle, ripple, in suspension, motile, watching what is in the water and without. A layman, watching them, would see such life, such presence, and conclude that all is well. A layman would not miss what is not on the bottom, would not notice vacancies where life forms used to be.

The fingerlings do not disperse as they watch two terrestrial behemoths ford the rocky shallows upstream from the bend.

The first behemoth says, "This brook's on the impairment list."

"Impairment was considered," says the second, "when the Corridor was routed through here. People tend to not get so worked up about a waterway that's not pristine."

The behemoths climb a pebbly knoll whose root exposure is extensive, and they take a narrow duff path leading deeper into woods, through ferns and lichen, distancing themselves from the observant fingerling formation in the dappled brook light.

"DEP made recommendations to restore the water quality," the lead behemoth, Albert, says. "This brook can be pristine again."

Theirs is a humid, shaded way. The brook bends with them deeper into woods.

"Two miles upstream is a dairy farm," says Harold Brown. "Eight-hundred acres. Corn and hay fields less than half a mile through the woods here. And a mile downstream is another farm. Six-hundred acres. Soil erosion. Runoff. Cow manure. Fertilizer. Pesticides. This watershed is compromised."

"Impaired," says Albert, circumventing an illuminated web that vibrates slightly and subsides. A zig-zag line of silk is centered, oriented vertically, and in the center of the zig-zag line a black and yellow garden spider, oriented likewise, luminous, aligned, abides.

"Impaired," says Harold Brown, who likewise circumvents.

"It doesn't have to be."

"It is what it is," says Harold Brown. He wipes his brow. "A watershed within an agricultural community. Do you think anyone's abandoning their land and livelihood to make a brook pristine?"

"The DEP doesn't recommend abandonment. They recommend rotational grazing, conservation tillage, cover crops, and contour farming."

"Recommendation isn't implementation. What compels the farmers to comply? You underestimate the implementation obstacles."

"So your solution to impairment is development. A four-lane toll road through the woods. Just fuck it all."

"Development's the course we've always taken. And by *we* I mean the species. Ours is not entirely a voluntary course. It's evolutionary. Biological. Divine. I think you see this, which is why I still believe you understand your only option is to sell."

"Rewild."

"What?"

"Rewild. Give the wild back its wildness. No domestication. Let it be," says Albert.

"So reverse the course of history, in other words."

"Just let it be."

"And how do you incentivize rewilding?"

"How do I incentivize it?"

"What is the incentive for a person who owns land to let it go and let it be? It isn't economic, is it, the incentive?"

"No."

"Then what? You'd give your land up here for what?"

"My land?"

"Your eighteen acres and your cabin and your outhouse."

"I'd give them up for nothing."

"You'd give them up for nothing."

"If you mean as part of a coordinated effort to rewild, I would give them up for free."

"It's counter to the course we've taken as a species. It's unnatural."

"You don't want to be rewilded?"

"Me? Rewilded?" chuckles Harold Brown. "I'm almost seventy."

"You're telling me that if it's possible you wouldn't want to be removed from the impairment list."

"I'm a human being, not a Class B waterway."

"You're just a human being. Put yourself in your impairment's place."

The light of clearing is ahead.

"What is its incentive," Albert asks, "to let you be?"

"My point exactly."

In the clearing, which is roughly circular and whose diameter is roughly twenty feet, stands Cosme, who extends his hand to Harold Brown and says, "I dreamed last night of what is in you."

Across the clearing is a dome tent. In the middle of the clearing is a tripod made of pine boughs, and within the tripod's boundary is a ring of brook stones. Near the tripod is a camp chair. Three more are arranged beside a fallen hemlock, whose trunk has a six-foot segment shorn of branches lying in the clearing.

Cosme motions toward a camp chair.

"Sit please. You are sweating. It is warm."

"Forgive my skepticism, but what is it that you think you dreamed?" asks Harold Brown as he sits down, adjusting to the chair.

"Your cancer," Cosme says.

"You dreamed that I have cancer in me where?"

"In your urethra." Repositioning the tripod camp chair, Cosme sits and leans toward Harold Brown. "The dream was very clear."

This information causes Harold Brown to shift.

"The cancer is advancing," Cosme says respectfully.

"And you don't think I know that?"

"May I say you feel no longer in control?"

"It's humbling, I'll tell you," Harold Brown confides. "The chemoradiation starts next month." He runs a hand across his brow.

"You want some water, Harold?" Albert asks.

"Yes, thank you."

Albert walks across the clearing to the dome tent's vestibule. He stoops and enters, pops a jug lid, pours. He hands the cup to Harold Brown and sits beside him.

"Thanks."

"It's from the brook," says Albert, causing Harold Brown to hesitate. "Don't worry. It's been filtered."

"You said last night that you are not a natural force," says Cosme.

Harold Brown does not deny it.

"I have said before to others that to live in this dimension, in this form," says Cosme, holding out his arms, then touching several of his torso parts, "control and no control must coexist. I say this to you now."

"The paradox of free will and divine omniscience."

"It is not a paradox," says Cosme.

"No."

"They coexist."

"They do," says Harold Brown.

A large bird flaps its wings nearby, abandoning its perch, and threads its way through forest.

"You may say there is control in letting go," says Cosme.

Harold Brown does not respond. He bides his time and drinks his water, dries his lips.

"In here," says Cosme, pointing to his lower torso, "who controls?"

"In where?"

"In your urethra. In your cancer."

Harold Brown considers how oncologists are prone to hedge. At last he says, "God has a plan."

"You know this?"

"Yes."

"You do not know that plan?"

"That's right."

Cosme leans back in his camp chair, straining the synthetic fabric. He observes a hemlock crown, a masterpiece of tapering.

"This tree," says Cosme. "You may cut it down or let it be. This is in your control."

"It is."

"How do you know which course to choose?"

"According to God's purpose we are called."

"How do you hear this calling? How does God communicate with you?"

"The Bible. Through the Bible, through my pastor." Harold Brown adjusts his glasses. "Through what I suppose you could call intimations."

"Visions?"

"Signs."

"Signs are important," Cosme says. "Clear vision is important."

Harold Brown does not dispute these declarations.

"Do you ever feel that sometimes God takes pleasure in outwitting you?" asks Cosme.

"This examination, is it standard for a healer to proceed this way?"

"The healing process can be very rigorous," says Cosme.

Harold Brown does not prefer to contemplate these rigors now.

"I don't think God takes pleasure in outwitting me," says Harold Brown, who looks up at the hemlock crown. "But if you're asking me if I think God withholds from me what I should see or grasp, I think it isn't God withholding but my being human, a deficient creature whose prescription, in a sense," says Harold Brown as he adjusts his glasses once again and looks down from the crown, "has lost its power to correct for my deficiencies, which I've discovered are resourceful sons of bitches."

"May I ask," says Cosme, "what you do in such a case?"

"I pray."

"And when you pray, what do you see? What do you grasp?"

"It's variable."

"But you are open."

"Yes."

"So you may say there is control in letting go."

"I may."

The world as presently configured—roughly circular and tree rung, offering a portion of the sky as if seen from the bottom of a dry well, making room for seated company, society of no great sample size—appears less vulnerable to impasse.

Carrying an inchworm corpse across the duff plain, unconcerned with the enormous risks the three behemoths pose, an ant heads for an unseen nest without delay, without considering reserving on the way a little something for himself.

"Doesn't matter where you go," says Albert, watching with the others from their seated heights the ant's progression, "ants are always there."

As individuals they think of possible exceptions, but they do not voice them.

When the ant leaves the clearing, crossing into woods again, the three men in their torsos feel the passing as a lesson on the universal application of disinterested action.

"What's the tripod for?" asks Harold Brown.

"Suspension," Cosme says.

A faint commotion from the north approaches, a phenomenon of sociability and friction. Voices clarify and rise. The pace is leisurely bipedal. Twigs snap. Earth is scuffed. The rustle of material, the sheer dependence on imported fabric and remote extraction, transport Albert to consider what must run through the gorilla minds when deferential tourists or their brethren, poachers, come with such commotion to the mountains or the lowlands. Albert turns. A locomotive abnormality is fast approaching, audible, a quickening, a bounding. Charlie Watts flies from the forest, landing lithely on the fallen hemlock, wagging, nuzzling, running point for this reunion of the living.

Chris Atwater is the first to follow Watts into the clearing. She wears a blue bandana folded ten times, yielding more or less two inches of exposed bandana circling her head, except where it is knotted at the back. The Amish egg basket hanging from her right hand swings in front of her one time past her left leg's stopping near the camp chair from which Harold Brown has risen.

"Miss Atwater."

"Mr. Brown," says Chris, her basket filled with fiddleheads.

Next in is AJ, also carrying an Amish basket filled with fiddleheads. His eyes are clear. He eyeballs Harold Brown and says, "I'm AJ."

"You look familiar."

AJ lifts the basket from his side. "The fiddleheads are here."

When Mary enters emptyhanded and when Jake and Ryan follow, bearing not a single fiddlehead, they have the aura of the inhospitable, although the fiddleheads already harvested are ample for the eight of them. She sits and separates the Velcro of a cargo pocket. With liturgical precision, she removes from it a beeswax wrap whose shape geometry has yet to classify. She holds the beeswax wrap as though it were a heavy-lidded bird and lays it on her lap, her hands becoming shields on either side, her fingers curling like unfinished fiddleheads.

"I found a river birch," says Mary.

"On our property?" asks Albert.

"With a beautiful mycelium," says Mary, nodding.

She unfolds the beeswax wrap. Within it lies what seems to be an igneous formation, pockmarked, black. A golden seam along one ridge is like a filament of lava flow. She lifts the chaga from its wrap and shows its inner goldenness to Harold Brown, whose lips purse as he nods. She lays it on the beeswax wrap and is not as protective with her hands.

"I'll take you to the river birch," she says. "I'll show you how to meditate and harvest."

Harold Brown does not scoff at the mental image of him meditating in the shadow of a river birch.

"We'll show you where to find the fiddleheads," says Chris.

"The rigors of the healing process," Cosme says, "you may say we will undergo with you."

"What rigors in particular?" asks Harold Brown.

"The diet," says Cosme.

"The diet."

"It is more than diet, you may say."

"In terms of rigors it is more than diet?"

"Let me ask you, does your family know that you are here?"

"My wife does."

"Does she know why," asks Cosme, "you are here?"

"She knows I'm here to buy this property."

"She does not know you also came here to be healed?" asks Cosme.

"No."

"She must know you will be here for eleven days and why."

"Eleven days," says Harold Brown. He rubs his chin.

"A rigor of the healing process."

"In eleven days you're saying I'll be healed?"

"You are not entering a contract," Cosme says.

"But you have healed this sort of thing before?"

"What you may say are miracles," says Cosme, "I have witnessed. But before the miracles came rigors."

"Harold, what is there to lose? The chemoradiation," Albert says, "will still be there when this is over."

Harold Brown observes the twins as they run fingers over hemlock needles. The humidity is rising. The mosquitoes buzz in it like indecisive motorboats.

"You carry your fears in your pack," says AJ.

"I've brought nothing with me," Harold Brown replies. His buttoned shirt, his khakis, and his shoes say nothing.

"You need no materials," says Cosme.

Jake and Ryan leave the clearing for the darkness of the woods. The hemlock branch is a vibration for a while after their departure.

"I suppose the chemoradiation isn't going anywhere," says Harold Brown. He dials by the dome tent's vestibule.

He speaks to Klara in a tone that is more tender, telling her why he has come and how long he will be here. He admits there will be rigors, which she wants to know the nature of. He tells her they are mostly dietary, possibly involving certain mystical components. No, he cannot say what these components are. They may not even factor in, but his tradition is indigenous. He's from Peru. The Amazon. She says the pharmaceutical concerns have interests in the Amazon. She wants to know what's in it for the healer. Harold Brown does not believe the healer feels material temptation. He appears devoted to his calling. What is there to lose? The chemoradiation isn't going anywhere. She asks once more about the rigors. What could happen? They will see each other in eleven days. She will tell work it is a medical emergency that he prefers to not disclose. Reciprocal expressions of commitment and romantic love. The call ends.

Harold Brown looks at the vestibule, considering the mystery of his urethra.

"Well," he says, returning to the clearing's other side, "what now?"

Chapter Twelve: The Diet

Gray smoke rises past the pot suspended from the tripod's nexus. Harold stirs the fiddleheads and focuses. As if experimenting with an incantation cadence, he intones three times, "No salt, no meat, no alcohol, no drugs, no intercourse, no sweets"—six prohibitions Cosme stipulated as essential rigors. Harold lifts his fork. A dripping fiddlehead droops from its tines. The clockwise current in the pendulous pot makes six more revolutions, each one a diminished imitation of its predecessor. He expels two long, unhurried breaths upon the fiddlehead, as if to gently wake it or impart to it some respiratory intimation of his Methodist soul, and raises it so that its tips are at the level of his barely parted lips. He bites the furl, considers, and consumes the rest. He doesn't seriously consider prohibition violation. He will do what he can do for his urethra, but the fiddlehead could use a little salt.

Harold holds a cloth around the handle of the pot and lifts the handle from the tripod wire. In the process of detachment, something illustrative flashes. What the illustration may be of he cannot limn, and in this inability lies doubt, admission of ridiculousness, retraction of the glimmer of reception.

"You may say it is okay to be a rationalist," said Cosme, "but to only be a rationalist is not why you are here."

Harold sets the pot down on a flat rock in the center of a sturdy plastic table.

He untucks his shirt, unbuttons it from top to bottom, and removes it. Like an antiquated cavalier, he drapes it on the camp chair's shoulders and sits back down as though the code he's lived by has expired. As the pot cools, Harold thinks about what Cosme said before he left him in the clearing on his own: "The plants will speak to you if you will listen. If you are receptive, they will teach you."

Cosme said this to them all because they all agreed to undergo the diet with Harold. But, since solitude, per the tradition Cosme works within, is necessary for attunement, Cosme had examined Albert's property map and situated Harold in the northwest, Albert slightly north of center, Chris in the southwest, AJ in the southeast—each within a short walk of the brook, connected by the Class B waterway and consciousness of its impairment, present and potential. Mary is not situated in the woods. She went home with the boys and Charlie Watts because the boys do better with routine and Watts around. She will subsist on fiddleheads and chaga as the others will, and, if the boys are okay with subsisting likewise, they will so subsist. She will refrain from salt, from meat, from alcohol, from drugs, from intercourse, from sweets as will the others. But, because of her remove, she will not feel the same depth of seclusion or receive botanical communiques of similar immediacy, and she will not rejoin the others to drink Cosme's ayahuasca when the sun sets on the tenth day. Everyone but Cosme said that Cosme, after traveling so far, should have the honor of residing in the cabin. Cosme thanked them but was adamant that the invoking process would be more sensational if he were closer to the plants, in contact with the earth. He laid his hammock on the duff about a hundred yards across the brook from Albert's cabin. When he turned and looked in the direction from which he had come, he could see nothing but the forest's layered genius.

Harold eats the fiddleheads directly from the pot. He twirls them now and then like pasta strands, but mostly he impales each one and eats it in three ruminative bites. As he progresses toward the bottom of the pot, he pauses several times to see if he feels any different, if the cumulative effect of fiddlehead consumption has unlocked in him a latent faculty, regenerated a vestigial capacity for mutual intelligibility across the special lines as was the norm, says Genesis, before the balkanization of it all. But Harold feels no different, no expansion of his reach, no more receptive than he was pre-fiddleheads, no radiating sense of a pristine urethra. When he eats the final fiddlehead, he drinks the water from the pot because the water, Cosme told them all, is rich with essence. Harold tries again to catch some alteration in his being, but he only thinks ill thoughts of vegetarians and wonders how an omnivore such as himself could have invested in a fern such hopes.

"How?" he asks aloud. He rises, sighs. "Urethra cancer's how."

He takes the pot and parts two hemlock branches as he leaves the clearing for the woods. He hears the brook, but sometimes when he thinks he hears the brook he really hears its relative, the breeze. The way the brook winds in this region makes it sound as though it lies in more than one direction, which it does. In the direction Harold chooses for approach, the forest's duff floor yields to root exposure, which itself gives in to lichen-covered ledge on either side of the contracted vein of water flowing like a stoic serpent, coiling into shallow pools in some depressions and unspooling, drawn by gravitation, gliding past the chance-piled rocks as if to slough the old skin and show off the new.

He steps onto the ledge in search of footing and proceeds as someone who has fallen in his time, though he sees purchase ridges in the ledge and dryness on the surfaces where water used to be. He crouches, a position he is rarely in the habit of adopting at this stage of life, and from this humble elevation he looks up and down the brook, from his side to the other, and observes that he is crouching in a river valley of no grandiose dimensions but dynamically no different from the venerated watersheds.

He dips the pot into the brook, and in the brown aquatic fuzz that coats the rocks below he sees a crayfish lying as if waiting for predation to play out on either of the spectrum's ends. He sets the pot down and inserts a stick into the brook. The crayfish does not move, except in subtle undulations with the water. When the stick makes contact, nudging once, the crayfish levitates, then rotates, settling without intention on its side into the brown aquatic fuzz.

He takes a knee, experiencing in segments of his viscera sensations universally ascribed to limbic-system activation on encountering the intact body of what the encounterer would formerly have termed a lower-order form of life, whose claim, now as self-evident to the encounterer as sunlit condensation, to exist here and live out its full allotment was as unassailable as the equivalent claim of the encounterer now stricken. Harold wonders why restorative priority should be conferred on his urethra, and he wonders as he rises with the water if the fiddleheads are somehow kicking in.

In the clearing, Harold hangs the pot again and feeds the dying fire underneath it. Though the fire pit is lined with sand and gravel Albert gathered by the bucketful and mounded, Harold cannot shake the fear of root fire. He takes the bucket Albert left and fills it from the brook. Back in the clearing, Harold bends and douses the fire pit's perimeter, extending outward, circular, concentric, a brigade of one at last left with the bucket, upside down, the last drop coalescing on the bucket lip and letting go, descending, landing on five browning needles whose potential for combustion is not by this piddling volume much diminished. Harold looks up at the sky. The clouds move in as evening comes.

He puts his share of Mary's chaga in the pot, stirs clockwise twice, and sits, a creature of appointment and projection, imposition and activity, accumulation and accomplishment, attempting to approximate the selflessness of steeping. Harold sweats but does not move back from the fire's heat. The perspiration freshets feel like necessary purification elements, but the desire for American chop suey suddenly becomes quite powerful in him. His stomach grunts despite the fiddleheads. He tries to will this hunger elsewhere. Harold tries to let it go. Though Cosme did not call this process the beginning of enlightenment, he muses, what else could it be?

He crawls into the vestibule, retrieves an empty notebook and a pen that Cosme left for him, and crawls out backward. Sometimes, Cosme said, recording powerful impressions is an excellent elicitor.

Harold sits and writes down the particulars of his desire for American chop suey. As he does so, he remembers vividly when he was ten and went against his natural tendencies, convinced that he could switch and make it as a lefty in his Little League. He writes down details of his prototypical humiliation and looks up, the notebook open still on Harold's thigh.

A hermit thrush who has been singing at a distance sings now from a near perch. Harold, pierced, tries hard to pinpoint the performance. Seeing nothing but a watchful phoebe and concealing trees, he shuts his eyes as though to bathe in the cascade. Time's passage seems to slow. He opens them again like someone who has been washed clean. He does not lick his primary fingerprint when he looks down and flips the notebook page. He draws a bar graph whose y-axis, hashmarked 1 to 10, enumerates the stages of Enlightenment/Healing and whose x-axis plots the three predictor variables that come to mind: Days in Seclusion, Pots of Fiddleheads Consumed, and Pots of Chaga Drunk. Immediately he sees the bar graph's limitations and illogic in the face of the unquantifiable. He nonetheless delineates a squat bar on the line above the Pots of Fiddleheads Consumed predictor variable. The squat bar rises to the height of hashmark number 1, but Harold does not feel the satisfaction of authentic correlation. He prepares to rip the bar graph out and lay it on the fire. As the upper paper presses on the wire binding, Harold wonders if what he's recorded in the bar graph has elicitation powers he may need some days to fathom. He lets go and listens to the hermit thrush. He tends the chaga for about two hours, stirring on occasion, questioning his faith in data analytics and predictive modeling. He drinks the chaga from the pot as night falls. The mosquito sorties harry him. The hermit thrush goes silent, but the silence doesn't register with Harold right away. He thinks its absence into being and remarks on it internally as he extinguishes the fire. He crawls into the vestibule, unzips the entry to the main compartment, and retires, nagged by the awareness that he did not do the simple thing that capitalism asked of him today.

It does not rain this night.

He harvests fiddleheads and chaga in the morning and does not cross paths with any of the others.

Days meld. Time slows. Harold does not sense a third eye opening as Mary said it might begin to. Harold listens but hears nothing from the plants. With a psychiatrist's exactitude, a naturalist's finesse, he many times records impressions, memories, but he does not perceive how they relate to healing his urethra. Harold's phone, surrendered on the first day with the others, sometimes still feels present in his pocket. Solitude oppresses him at intervals that are irregular, and when these stretches come he doubts the others are experiencing the rigors with him. But he does not call for them. He does not wander. When he feels oppressively alone, he takes his clothes off, leaves his glasses on, lies down like someone undergoing diagnosis in the brook, and lets the Class B water rustle him and lets the canopy, whose majesty is magnified from this perspective, tell him no one is alone. So he hears something. Harold has no soap to rub a layer of himself off, but he floats to some degree downstream and into the Kenduskeag, into the Penobscot, into who knows. He has never been a river Baptist, but the draw of transformational immersion is not lost on him.

On the fourth day, Harold wakes in predawn darkness. He hears nothing that would have awakened him and slackens. In the tent with him, however, is a faint unpleasant odor. Skunk musk, he assumes at first. His nostrils flare as if patagial, as if to bear him like a flying squirrel on an updraft through the lofty darkness to a tree he intimately knows. Instead, his nostrils see the odor in, invite it to invade him as it strengthens into a sensation whose existence has become material to him. He feels it in his nose, now on his tongue, now in his lungs. He feels a strong desire to ascribe but only conjures partialities. He pictures ancient liverwurst, prescription-medication compounds, burning tires, rancid bacon, chemicals known to the state of California to cause cancer, the releases of some forest creature's pores, some forest creature's glands. A unifying origin does not emerge. He does not wish to breathe in and holds his breath and crawls out of the overwhelmed enclosure with the spastic quickness of a refugee who has been outmaneuvered by a force that does not countenance the sanctity of havens.

Outside the tent, the air is cool and unconfined, yet Harold, in his underwear, perspires. He takes a deep breath, and the odor, undiminished, enters him and dives as deeply as he breathes. He coughs and squints in the direction of the vestibule. He half expects to see the unleashed odor flowing from it like the northern lights, but he sees nothing clearly in the darkness. Harold puts a hand up to his mouth and asks, "What *is* this?" Something suddenly perturbs the air and rasps on bark and swoops down shrieking over Harold's head. He shields himself and shrieks as loudly, realizing as he does so that an owl has just buzzed him and departed. Harold stands erect again, regaining his composure, which, in solitude and darkness even, seems essential to get back. His heart, which has no troubling history, does not regain its customary beat until the sun comes up. He finds the camp chair, sits, and alternates between imagining whose death the owl may have signed to him to ready for and wondering how the odor, worsening, defies the physics of diffusion.

Now and then, as Harold waits for sunrise, he remembers Arthur Dimmesdale shrieking on the scaffold in the night. The governor appeared, a lit form in a distant doorway, waiting for a repeat. When it didn't come, he closed the door. The house went dark. It was the night the first John Winthrop died.

Before the sun comes up, the birds begin, the hermit thrush among them. Harold is encouraged and enlivened. Once the sky is lit, he crawls inside the tent to get his khakis, shirt, and socks. He takes his Rockports from the vestibule. The odor in the tent compartments has ballooned despite the ventilation. Harold leaves his shoes beside the tripod, wrings his clothes and underclothes in the brook, and lies down naked, but for his glasses, in the water. Harold holds his glasses up, submerging backward his entire head, and even underwater he is hounded.

In the clearing, in anticipation of the sun's appearance overhead, he drapes his wrung belongings on the tripod and the camp chair to be sun-dried. Harold cleans the specks of loam and needles from his feet and slips his stinking Rockports on. He takes a small knife from the plastic table, takes the tripod pot, and, clouded by the odor, walks into the forest. After gathering the fiddleheads, he finds the river birch and even at a distance sees by the mycelium that others have been here since he came yesterday. He pulls up short and drops the knife when he sees Eva Desjardins against the river birch's trunk and on its roots, reclining naked, with a freshly punctured thigh, not even wearing shoes.

"Can this be you?" he asks. "You're in the hospital."

"You smell," says Eva.

Harold looks down at his shoes and says, "I should have rinsed them in the brook and left them in the clearing for the sun to dry."

When he looks up, she's gone. He takes his glasses off and rubs around his eyes.

"Four days," says Harold. "Is this all it takes for me to lose my mind?"

He puts his glasses back on and reclines against the river birch where Eva was. His brown shoes do not do his pale legs any favors. Harold slips the shoes off.

"If I'm losing it," he says, "there has to be a cause. There has to be a cause."

He runs through possibilities, conventional and otherwise. Inadequate nutrition. Fiddlehead infusion. Something in the water. Third-eye activation. Heat stroke. Hypothermia. Circadian arrhythmia. Electrolyte deficiency. Metastasis. Metastasis. Can it have spread this quickly to his brain? He lays a palm upon the fuzzy alabaster plain beneath which his urethra is. That could explain this unrelenting smell, he thinks. That could explain the vision.

"Shit, shit, shit," he says.

He leans his head back on the trunk and sees a gold seam in the underside of the mycelium. He is inclined to take this as a sign that he is free to harvest, but he meditates for confirmation.

Deer flies land on him. He lets them twitch and bite.

He shuts his eyes and tries to be as nondenominational in his appeal as he can be.

"Dear river birch, dear chaga, I'm unclothed today and humbled. Though I claim no worthiness to ask, I pray this morning for permission once again. I pray you help me be receptive. If it is to be, please help me heal."

He breathes as Mary showed him.

"Be here now," said Mary. "Be receptive. There is more to life than language."

Harold breathes, a project manager accepted into the community of trees. He does not fear metastasis as much, and then he does not fear at all.

He falls asleep and dreams of being gently handled. Crow calls wake him. Harold blinks and sees a monarch butterfly on each of his big toes. Their wingbeats, synchronized and leisurely, make him feel faintly fanned, less viscous somehow, slowly drifting from the gospel of demystification.

Harold's backside shining like a bifurcated mushroom cap, he picks the knife up when the butterflies depart and holds it as he listens for the way the chaga would be cut. His thumb guides the incision like a boatman. Harold slowly parts a shallow depth, proceeding from the trunk side of the gold seam toward his eyes which almost press against the underside of the mycelium and move back in proportional reaction as his wrinkled thumb approaches. When the chaga emissary falls two inches to his palm, he sits against the river birch in silence, giving telepathic thanks.

The smell continues to assail him on the way back to the clearing. Harold enters his impressions in the notebook. He records what Eva said, inspects the sweaty cold-cut sheen upon his skin, inhales himself, and suddenly it hits him that, as Eva said, he smells. He is the odor's source and essence. It is clear to him that no deodorant, no soap, no powder made of talc, no toothpaste, no detergent can refresh him. His is no condition for surfactants. Harold's discharge goes much deeper.

As he writes these new impressions on the notebook page, a shadow dims his words. The sky goes dark. It soon begins to rain. He crawls into the vestibule, which fills with Harold's reek, to keep his notebook dry and finish his recording.

For the next four days it rains.

His clothes and underclothes, which have not dried, he does not put back on. He leaves the tent each day to harvest early in the morning, but the fire has gone out. For half the day, twelve hours, he steeps the fiddleheads and chaga in the single pot with water from the brook and hopes the long duration compensates for the subtraction of the heat. He also leaves the tent at unappointed times each day to lie down in the rising brook for reasons he cannot articulate now that he knows the odor emanates from deep within himself, secure from even rising water's powers of dilution and renewal.

Time slows down the first night. Raindrops strafe the tent on end. He cannot see. He cannot sleep. He wiggles fingers, wiggles toes, to prove he still has agency. He probes his odor. Condensation forms on the interior as Harold breathes. The droplets fall according to no system that he knows. At first he flinches at each droplet and experiences the civilized indignity of someone who cannot believe the manufacturer did not foresee and obviate all unacceptable contingencies. Past midnight Harold tells himself that such indignity is probably unnatural, probably a construct that entrapped him at a time he probably could not have formulated what free markets meant to him. He pictures all the trees he's ringed by. Harold listens to them softening the raindrops' landing. No indignity. No unreal expectations placed upon the efforts of their kind. Apparently unsystematic droplets spatter on his lenses, on the tent floor, on the skin above where his urethra is. They spatter where they may. He does not let or not let. Opting, Harold tells himself, is losing under such conditions its traditional effectiveness. A brief flash, and his sudden fear is retinal detachment. Thunder follows.

Only lightning, he assures himself. Just lightning.

Harold struggles less the second night.

He finds some peace the third.

He dreams he's almost weightless, perched atop a hemlock spire. He gazes up and left, and up and right. His neck stays craned some time. His neck and chest are white, not pallid white, not wan, but white like the beginning of the afterlife. He iridesces, red and green, a beauty of such range. He lifts off skyward like a Jetson, up and up, reverses, diving, curving, parabolic, zooming skyward once again, a mirror image, perfectly reversible, and traces this course down and up, down and up. Then suddenly he deviates and darts to Albert's camp, where he finds freshened sugar water, and to Mary's home and Chris's camp and AJ's camp, and in each place he hovers and inserts his beak in freshened sugar water and withdraws, and finally he darts to Cosme's camp, where he comes face to face with such extraordinary nectaries, who tell him to remember sweetness must be stationed in the world.

In the morning, which begins the seventh day of the collective diet, he leaves the vestibule in pouring rain. His lenses bead and streak. He takes his glasses off and folds the temples. For a moment, Harold motions toward the left side of his chest as though to stow the glasses in the pocket that would normally be there. He sets them in the vestibule and takes with him the small knife and the tripod pot, which he holds by the wire handle like an unencumbered person going berrying in perfect weather down a path that he can follow with his eyes closed.

Harold's odor coats his tongue like mildew. He has grown accustomed to this force's strange immunity. He licks his lips, and thirst recalls him to necessity. Before he heads in the direction of the fiddleheads and chaga, he goes to the brook, a roar that drowns out birdsong and the rest. He dips the pot into the rapids, and he drinks without considering impurity or sediment. The far bank is a textured blur. He dips the pot again and drinks. Beneath the raised pot, Harold's body phosphoresces. Unintelligible voices struggle to be heard above the roar. He listens, puts the pot down, leaves the small knife, steps into the rapids, mooring each foot as securely as he can on bed rocks as he goes. He looks upstream for flotsam and lies down, his bare feet braced against depressions worn smooth in protruding ledge. The water volume threatens to upend him. Harold's head and shoulders riding higher than the rest of him, his body and the brook achieve a fragile equilibrium.

He cannot hear the soil woven through the roots of the expansive hemlock on the right bank loosening and after all this time together letting go. The hemlock branches shiver in the blur of canopy and shake a differential point of tropic coloration loose. The point descends with alien rapidity and hovers, wings outspread as if to colorize the crucifixion's bright side, inches from his nose. The hummingbird tilts left and disappears precisely. In its wake, the hemlock tilts and tilts, uprooting. Rain pours. Harold breathes. The canopy upholds for seven Mississippis, and the hemlock then falls through. His feet release from the arresting ledge depressions, and the water launches him, a luger with no discipline or form or luge, downstream. He feels the hemlock's downdraft on his scalp. The hemlock crashes in the brook where Harold was, a new span to the other side.

Harold hurtles through the straightaways and bends and tries to focus on the canopy, the interlocking form of life that makes a bower of his way. His head goes under and emerges, under and emerges, though, and it is all that he can do to reestablish respiration. Harold tells himself he cannot drown in water he can stand in and applies his tender soles with force to surfaces he shoots so quickly purchase is not possible. He flails and reaches for what will not reach for him.

At last, he tries to make himself as streamlined as an otter. He is battered still but less so. When his head emerges from the undertow again, he tries once more to focus on the canopy that drips on him in its detachment whether he goes down for good or not.

As Harold's head goes under once again, the brook bends sharply right. His feet smash into piled rocks, and he is headlong flung into an inlet where the overflow's propulsive force diminishes and in its place is mud-flat saturation.

Harold rises and spits water. He is bleeding and the bruising has begun. He does not wipe the mud from wounds. The rain drips from the canopy but does not wash the mud from him. As if he really has profoundly risen, Harold does not move. He blinks into the woods beyond the mud flat. Albert's cabin blurs two-hundred feet away. No movement's there. He does not call. He looks down at his muddy feet, his muddy legs, his muddy genitals, his muddy skin above where his urethra is, his muddy arms and trunk. He still has harvesting to do.

He limps upstream along the brook. As Harold had not registered immediately the hermit thrush's entry into silence several nights ago, so now he does not notice right away his odor's dissipation and departure. He smells pine and balsam fir and beech and river birch and fern and hemlock, but it's not until he makes his way across the fallen hemlock, finds the tripod pot and small knife, takes them to the fiddleheads and chaga, meditates and harvests, stands in rainfall in the clearing, and lies down in painful stages in the tent that Harold realizes he emits these fragrances, these essences. The awful odor is no more. He lays his hands upon the skin above where his urethra is and does not question what is happening.

Chapter Thirteen: Intentions

The brook is not torrential on the tenth day.

In the bend where Harold was ejected stalks a great blue heron, sinuous and lanky. Each stride enters a memorial stillness out of which a new stride comes to life.

The water babbles. Vapors shimmer where the sun shines through the fissures in the canopy.

Across the brook from Albert's cabin, just a stone's throw through the skewed and toppled woods from where the heron is, a stand of hemlocks soars above a needle-matted knoll that overlooks a burst of fern moss in the middle of an oxbow, which is puddled in the aftermath of deluge. On the stand side of the oxbow, four eyes stud a puddle and observe without a ripple a development unfolding on the knoll. The heron sees it, too, but strides upstream at an unaltered pace as though the riverine geography between her and the knoll is an acknowledged buffer state.

The hemlocks came to Cosme in a dream the first night of the diet. They looked as they had looked that morning when he passed the knoll: majestic, widespread, free of underbrush. In Cosme's dream, the ten of them drew water up from deep down in the earth, but what they drew was in retreat, withdrawing deeper each day. Cosme saw upstream a hundred well pumps sucking like mosquitoes. Downstream, toward the shambling reinvention of a lumber city, he saw tens of thousands more. He saw the water disappear, aboveground and below. This dream came each night of the diet to Cosme, and each morning after, even when it poured and water flooded through the oxbow, Cosme sat among the hemlocks on the knoll, attuning.

On the morning of the tenth day, Cosme sits, back plumb, legs crossed, feet bare, among the spirits of the hemlocks on the knoll. He senses the progression of the heron, but he does not turn his head or otherwise intrude. He is a statue, and in stillness do the hemlocks testify he is no stranger to this space. He sits for some time more, a student of the forest's energies. Neck craned, the heron stands high by the former outflow of the oxbow and observes with eyes whose central blackness and peripheral corona take in Cosme and approve of his reality. Her neck reclaims its natural sinuosity. She turns and wades her shallow way upstream, beyond the oxbow's former inflow. Then she disappears, a beauty he is grateful he cannot unsee. Unwinding, Cosme thanks the forest spirits and returns to his encampment, where the others are to reconvene this morning for the final preparation phase before the purge begins at sunset.

Albert is the first to show. His beard is longer, grayer for the elongation, but his eyes are bright. He smiles broadly, baring beige teeth he does not appear self-conscious of. He sets his folded camp chair, folded tent, and cookpot on the ground, approaches Cosme, and, without a word, does something that before the diet would have been out of keeping with his nature. Albert hugs him.

AJ, Chris, and Harold jangle in succession into the encampment shortly after. Each, like Albert, bears a superficial haggardness that does not dim the facial radiance, the sense that each is bursting with the secret of beatitude. They set their simple gear down on arrival and, without a word, hug Cosme first and then each other.

With the initial tactile business of reunion taken care of, they unfold their camp chairs, mill about and touch each other on the arm or shoulder, sit and touch each other on the knee. Repeated verification of corporeality seems necessary for a while.

They talk about the tribulations of the diet, about the storm and the diluvial expansion of the brook, about the living forest in the night and ancient fears, about the line between a vision and a dream and whether talk of such a line is pointlessly divisional, about how solitude at first played what they thought were mind games and then taught them how relational existence in the forest is and how ridiculous it was to think among such life and energies they ever were alone. They wonder if a force arranged it so they never crossed paths on their way to harvest fiddleheads and chaga. They are proud of how they harvested. They talk about what hunger is and what they thought it was, what silence is and what they thought it was, what real and unreal may and may not be.

The hermit thrush cascades.

"Her music helped me," Chris says, "not feel so, you know, in isolation."

Harold listens in agreement with the other lifted faces and betrays no indication of interior debate. His face uplifted still, he says, "I wouldn't normally confess this sort of thing to anyone." He pauses, giving the impression that he's reconsidering and maybe what he said is all he will say on the matter. Harold brings his gaze down and engages the assembly. "I saw Eva Desjardins." He pictures her. "Reclined against the river birch one morning. With a fresh wound. Ragged." With his hands upon his right thigh, he approximates the wound's circumference. "She was naked."

Cosme says, "This is a good sign. It reminds us to let go of our disguises. It reminds us to come clean with ayahuasca. There is nothing in us ayahuasca does not know. So to conceal or to be rigid, you may say, is just your ego trying to control the situation. Do not let your ego try to dictate. You may play the peacock in the world. But this is not the way with ayahuasca."

Harold estimates his ego's dictatorial capacity and says, "And *I* was naked."

Albert, Chris, and AJ wonder inwardly if it is possible that Harold has already been restructured, maybe has already found relief for his urethra, but they do not voice their private speculations and are not considering a way out of the purge despite their fears.

"Did she communicate?" asks AJ.

"Yes," says Harold, looking at his shoes. "She said I smelled. I looked up from my shoes," he says as he looks up from them, "and she was gone."

"This vision," Cosme asks, "has it affected your consideration of intention?"

On the first day of the diet, before they left for their encampments, Cosme asked them to consider their intentions. What did they intend in taking ayahuasca? Was it only to be healed of cancer? Was it only to preserve and heal the water and the land? Was there a more mysterious desire, a hope more difficult to verbalize? Did they intend in taking ayahuasca to recover something they have felt was long lost? Was urethra cancer but a symptom of a deeper longing or a deeper ill? Was depredation of the land and water but a symptom of a deeper longing or a deeper ill? Did they intend in taking ayahuasca to be healed of ills or longings so deep as to seem inherent, so deep that they only had the barest consciousness they suffered them at all?

Harold turns the question of intention over in his mind. The hermit thrush accompanies the turning over.

"Yes, of course it has," says Harold. "Yes. When I saw Eva…" Harold pictures her again. "Look. I intend to see what else there is to see. But I'm no visionary. I'm a Methodist. I don't know how to formulate intention for an ayahuasca ceremony. I want my urethra healed, that's true, but I believe there probably is more to all of this than healing my urethra."

"Do not think of it as formulation," Cosme says. "Just be receptive. Open."

Harold holds his forearm out to Cosme. "Smell me."

Cosme puts his nose to Harold's forearm and inhales. "The essence of the plants," says Cosme, smiling. "Yes, I smelled this when we hugged. You see that you have allies."

Harold offers up his forearm to the others. They inhale him and sit back. The essence of plants. They also smelled it when they hugged him but regarded it, if they regarded it at all, as an incidental application, an olfactory accrual after almost ten days with the flora. But it is a prelude to the purge. It is authentic emanation, and they feel for Harold an affinity they struggle with. They ask themselves if what they feel is envy.

"Please follow me," says Cosme, leading them a short way through the woods. As they approach the hemlock knoll, he says, "Intention is not a projection of control. It is a willingness."

They climb the needle-matted knoll and stand among the hemlocks. First the five of them are in a stationary cluster, taking in the space, imagining the lifespans and the intricate unfolding and the tapered reaching of the crowns. The five then separate and drift, the give of duff beneath their feet a shadow of flotation, a remedial peek at what it must be like to rise above the tendency to plod. Each visits each tree, touches each tree's bark, and stands flat on the duff above the roots as if in doing so a circuit is completed through which flows a power that is not content with circuitry and so becomes a power also in the general field. There is no visitation sequence, no reception time prescribed.

When the fifty visitations are complete, the five, attuned, sit with the tree they last laid hands on.

Cosme says, "Ten days ago I did not know the purge would take place here. I did not preconceive. The hemlock spirits came to me in dreams each night. Each morning I came here to them. A presence in their presence. You have touched them. You have listened. Through the diet they have been with you. This, their sacred space, they open to us. Please be grateful."

In the western distance, a machine bales hay.

His finger pointing in the sound's direction, Cosme says, "A farmer drives a farm machine a certain speed. He thinks he knows the time his job will be completed. He imagines this. It is not real. How can it be? It has not happened yet. A tire may leak air. A mechanism may give way. Then he is not where he envisioned he would be. The future says politely this time 'No' to his control. This is a common source of suffering. Remember this with ayahuasca. It is not for us to dictate terms."

They listen to the baler's faith in method, in compression, and in bondage.

"Harold," Cosme says, "you did not see yourself developing urethra cancer."

"No, I didn't. I felt fine when I first got the diagnosis."

"Albert," Cosme says, "you did not see a highway coming through here when you bought this property."

"It never crossed my mind."

"Chris and AJ," Cosme says, "you did not at the outset see so much of what you love endangered by this man and his associates."

They shake their heads.

"I did not see myself uprooted from my home. To walk so far I did not see," says Cosme. "Yet these things we did not ask for or envision, they have brought us here. The diet has given you such glows. Be grateful and be open. Please remember this in your intentions."

Chapter Fourteen: The Purge

The two frogs in the oxbow puddle venture up the needled hemlock knoll at sunset, slightly pressuring the fungi underground to signal to the roots the frogs are on the move. The frogs are bulbous emissaries, patient mystics. With them come the water from upstream, the water from the aquifer, the water from the canopy and sky. They climb up with the sediment, the mud, the moss- and lichen-covered stones, the stones as bare as fragments of the moon. They climb up with the apertures, the softnesses, the sinks, the areas of give. They climb up with the blacks, the greens, the grays, the browns, and in them swirls the tonal mixture. In the name of camouflage and no assumption, no obtrusion, they climb up with leaf and needle litter, toppled trees and castoff bark, decomposition, toadstools, loam, and all that loam conceals. They come with shade plants, keepers of the wisdom of the spore, with plants whose ancient lineage no human squint can narrow into view. They come with the abiding forms and beings who have helped and sheltered them. They come with presences and spirits who, since long before the fungi sensed the pressure of the first shoe, have been havens and abettors.

The underground mycelial reticulations carry particles of consciousness from root to root throughout the forest. Trees and plants who oversaw the diets for ten days recognize the signatures of the vibrations on the knoll. They sensed them when the people harvested the fiddleheads and chaga, when the people mumbled to themselves and sang and wept and snored and crouched beside the brook and felt the patience of the ledge, the patience of four-hundred-million years. The underground mycelial reticulations share the flora's recognition with the forest, all the beings of the forest, and this consciousness, this opening, intensifies the aura of the knoll.

The two frogs crest and wiggle-tuck their backsides in the needled duff beneath the nearest hemlock as the sun goes down. A fire in the lower half of a bisected black orb held up by three dingy silver legs illuminates the hemlock branches' underside, the shadows shifting with illumination's various intensity. Mosquitoes, oldwife underwings, and hemlock loopers leave their covers, loop and flutter, drawing closer to the irresistible attraction, to this burst of heat and light. Beside the half orb stands a black-haired man whose back is to the frogs. They have perceived him on the knoll for days. He is unlike the others, though the others have made progress. He perceives and knows he is perceived. His calves seem geological in their striation and extrusion. He begins to sing a song that is unlike the songs the frogs have heard before, and yet in it is the familiar, the suggestion of remembrance. As he sings, he lifts a stemmed glass from a knee-high cedar table and tilts back his head. His shoulders change. His voice goes still. Small pops resound inside the metal belly of the halved orb, launching sparks that flare and dim and blacken as they rise. He sings as he sets down the stemmed glass, now transparent, and refills it from a silver pot that flashes a reflection of the fire. The stemmed glass is opaque again.

The frogs contract a little more into their duff depressions as the firelight glints off the glasses of the bald man who has risen and stepped toward the man whose back is to them. They have seen him on the rapids of the swelled brook. They have seen him face down on the mud flat. He receives the stemmed glass, drinks its contents in two stages, grimacing at the completion of each stage, returns the glass, and sits back down, two spirits with him now instead of none.

The man whose back is to them sings. He's protected. His song lifts the frogs from their contractions in the duff. The frogs see spirits everywhere.

The forest feels another body, lighter, sprier than the first, put pressure on the duff, coordinate her mostly bare appendages, and rise. The two frogs do not shrink from her approach. Hers is a softer figure, yet, as she extends her hands to take the glass, her hands and wrists and forearms tell them in her is the cudgel quality of bone. The spirits that attend her are more numerous and guard her more familiarly than those the frogs see near the bald man. In a single stage she drinks the viscous liquid, briefly grimacing, and sits back down before a slender hemlock, listening to the unbroken song and tuning her intention.

He who rises next the frogs know. He has held each of them. He has communicated with them as he can. They peep as he drinks down the viscous liquid in a single stage, his grimace likewise short-lived. He returns the glass and looks in their direction, but he does not see them for the shadow of the roots. He smiles, though, and knows that nearby are their eyes and ears and bellies, closer always than are his to earth. He sits down, blessed with spirits they have seen with him before.

The only person who has not approached the man whose back is to the frogs has stood throughout the ceremony, leaning toward a hemlock, head bowed, hands laid on her trunk. He does not seem to notice that the man who smiled in the frogs' direction has sat down. No alteration in the song suggests his time has come. No voice calls out to him. No finger taps. The man whose back is to the frogs pours viscous liquid from the silver pot into the stemmed glass as he sings.

The man whose hands are on the hemlock trunk takes solace in this circuit: bare hands, bare feet, needled earth, mycelial reticulations, root hairs, taproots, heartwood, bark. A shadow lets go of the canopy, becomes a hue, becomes a hemlock sprig, and lands as softly as an owl feather on the man's bowed head. His body does not seem to register the new sensation right away. It does not seem to feel the field outside the circuit is unlimited. Each needle of the sprig becomes an energy, a presence, and above him now are many guardians. He registers a lightening, a reaching out. He lifts his head above the level of his hands. He lifts his hands and lowers them. He squats and picks the sprig up, taking it with him as he approaches and receives the stemmed glass from the singing man. His right hand closes on the stem. He drinks the ayahuasca in a single stage. No grimace. He upholds the stem and keeps his head atilt until the last drop coalesces on the glass's lip, elongates, and detaches, leaving just a shimmer and a slickness and an Adam's apple that goes still.

Before he hands the stemmed glass back, he hugs the man who handed it to him. For the duration of the hug, the song is still itself but a compression, slightly altered.

"Thank you, man," he whispers in the other's ear.

When he releases and returns the glass, the song recovers its essential pulmonary nature and expands. He goes back to the hemlock, bows his head, and sets the sprig securely in his hair. He lays hands on the trunk and reestablishes the circuit as the ayahuasca runs through him. He feels the field unlimited outside the circuit now. His guardians observe.

Before the moon has moved a half degree, the vomiting begins.

Two gray garden slugs contract and undulate their ways up to the knoll. They do not cross the shadow line. Their eyes atop extended tentacles observe the forms that retch in different zones of firelight. Each form after retching rises, wipes its mouth, and tries to regulate its breathing. Each form moves toward water, bends and rinses, bends and slurps from cupped hands, and returns to sitting in its zone of firelight. Each slug pans its tentacles a little, following the formal motions. Each form breathes as though a pressure at its core must be released.

The man whose back is to the oxbow frogs lays deadwood on the fire. He then lightly moves from form to form and sings to each directly, touching each, exuding calm. When he removes his touch and glides on, each form sees his song as spiral colors following him from form to form, resolving into psychedelic fractals. One form sees the eddy and the maelstrom, one the galaxy's arm unwinding, one the cosmic furl of fern and snail shell, one the embryonic universal curvature.

Another lunar half degree goes by.

The form that sees the eddy and the maelstrom takes its glasses off and drops them. It is wide-eyed, gaping upward at a white strand separating from the eddy and the maelstrom. Spiraling, the white strand tightens. At the center of its spiral is a horizontal darkness that in one direction branches into replicas of an intuited entirety and in the other thickens and goes vertical, extending into earth and sky, a corridor of capillarity, at each extremity reticulating, granting water molecules the necessary passage through.

The form that dropped its glasses looks down at its upturned wrists and sees no dermal mediation. Only blue veins branching. Only capillary action. Little fires slide in droplets down its cheeks and whiskers, leaping to the needled duff. The form drops, rolling as though answering a cry for an extinguisher. No little fires singe its skin or fabrics. Suddenly it stops, goes still, its back flat on the duff. The colors of the song are currents undulating overhead. The faintest sizzle of filtration levitates the form a needle's width above the forest floor. Its tears, which flow now from the corners of its eyes and leap past earlobes into soil, atomize and pass through root hairs, xylem, needles, rising. They transpire and evaporate. The form comes back to earth. The spiral overhead unwinds until its whiteness wraps around the horizontal darkness only once.

"I am not marginal," a voice in the direction of the unwound spiral says.

The form squints.

"You think I am marginal."

The form admits, "I thought that. I have thought that, but I do not think that now."

"It is no great accomplishment," the voice says, "being human."

"I have made attunements," says the form, "these last ten days."

The voice laughs. "What am I to you?"

The form squints.

"You see nothing but a dangled whiteness curled once," says the voice, "around a central darkness."

"I am trying," says the form, still squinting.

"What I am to you," the voice says, "is the narrow cure."

The form feels radiating pain in its urethra.

"Your urethra," says the voice, "is not the center of it all."

The pain arrives at all points in the form and presses frantically on its interior in search of a release. The surface of the form is ripple and pulsation. The potential for eruption shuts the crucial functions in the form down, one by one. The form gasps when its lungs shut down. The form convulses with the last beat of its heart. What floats up from the form observes the stillness of the form and tries once to reenter it and tries again and tries again and floats above a desiccated plain that had been forested and verdant in its day and teeming with exquisite variations on the theme of life.

Chapter Fifteen: Mother Bear

The form that has communicated with the oxbow frogs as it was able sees the galaxy arm unwinding and hears nothing.

Two coyotes, heads low, glide like spirits longways come through deadfall, over hemlock cones. Ears back, they lie outside the range of firelight, a bound away.

In the unwinding galaxy arm, three stars intensify. They outshine all the other bodies in the arm and in succession separate from it as if flung by the arm's unwinding. They turn black and hurtle earthward, sudden absences descending. In their wake, a superbloom lights up the sky.

A mushroom near the oxbow says, "The cosmos is a birth canal."

The form's eyes widen.

Grunts and bleats reverberate in sonic bursts across the sky, the sounds of premature detachment, of the infant search for mother.

The form's heart swells. It cups its ears to muffle its emotions. It lies back, expecting death to be a vaporizing flash, too quick to qualify as suffering, too thorough for the form to dream of afterlife reunion and atemporal togetherness. The form extends what it now sees are embryonic arms to welcome death. Its eyes shut tight and brace for transformation.

One, two, three explosions, almost simultaneous. Three mushroom clouds burst upward, raining rock and needle fragments, soil, microbes on the form's closed eyelids in such quantities that in an instant the entire form is buried, suffocating.

From each impact crater climbs a grunting, bleating black bear cub.

The buried form smells bared coyote teeth. The form grunts, trying to dislodge the particles of its entombment, and then feels three separate pressures on the mound. Each pressure delves and lightens, delves and lightens. Soon the form's face is exposed. Its eyelids flicker particles off and open. It identifies each cub and rises, quadrupedal, matted, clawed. It does not roar or charge at the coyotes sitting primly now in darkness, teeth uncocked.

The mother bear flares nostrils, taking miles in, and ambles through the forest. In her wake, three buoyant vulnerabilities approximate her sway. She teaches them to overturn and root, to lap and probe, to not turn up their noses at the forest's fecund secrets. The air is laden, close, the forest musty, but the knot of winter, months away, is in her. Mile after mile, teaching them the language, spoken everywhere, of death, she carries the contention that she cannot be their guardian forever.

Almost full, she leads them to a pocket of the forest free of human scent. The brook is nearby, sluicing through a minor gorge. They rub their backs against four hemlock trunks and lie in forest darkness on their backs, on earth that no one at this moment claims. The mother yawns, her tongue unfurling past the canopy, into the sky. She tastes the hemlock needles and the perspiration of the porcupine. She tastes the airborne particles of incomplete combustion and the lives of insects at high altitudes. She licks the nectar of the superbloom. Her heart is full. Her being hums. Her cubs send up their tongues and taste the laden breeze of hummingbirds and butterflies and honeybees, each pollen grain a cosmic integer. They lick the nectar of the superbloom. In each cub is entwined the fractal lineage, the patience to proceed from calorie to calorie, the knowledge that so many of the souls that will observe them through a window or bang metal to disperse them are not conscious of the kinship immemorial.

The superbloom begins to dim. Its fractal radiance resolves.

The bears take back their tongues and right themselves and huddle. Eyelids droop and spasm, droop and spasm. Sleep weighs in. Their lungs breathe on. Dreams come of low hives, purple berries studding bushes on untrammeled, sun-drenched ridges. Dreams of no serrated trap. No twisting missile. No machine. No vehicle. No mine. No powerline.

The superbloom goes dark.

Acuities attuned to this take over.

Time bends, but the moon is somewhere, sensitive, attractive.

In the outer reaches of the ursine auditory range, a tree frog peeps. And then another, closer. And another, closer still.

The mother's eyelids rise. Alarm.

From the direction of the peeps fly three points of green light. Each succeeding peep yields yet another point of green light flying closer. This linear formation passes just above the mother's ears and through the forest, banking steeply upward, paralleling the projection of an ancient hemlock through the canopy, into the sky.

Alarm.

The mother wakes her cubs and sees in the direction of the first peep a bipedal luminescence nearing at a pace that is escapable. The three cubs gallop, following the green lights upward, hooking claws and climbing quickly up the hemlock.

Then the mother sinks her claws in, climbing after them.

A rasping voice behind her says, "You're not their mother."

Still she climbs.

A firearm explodes, and she releases, falling backward as the cubs bleat, unseen, from above. She thuds, sees stars, and lies flat on the needled duff. Her wound weeps, blood extending from beneath her through a network of conductors.

Over her, the luminescence stands and rasps, "You're not their mother."

At its core, a bony form inside a workshirt smells like burning cherry wood. On each breast of the workshirt, in an alphabetic language, a partitioner of universal consciousness, are stitched the form's old physical identifiers.

"You are not their mother," rasps the luminescence.

Pained, the mother lifts a foreleg. In the luminescent glow, her black fur sheds like desiccated hemlock needles and her foreleg shrinks into an embryonic human arm.

"I'm still irradiated," rasps the luminescence, tapping on the letters stitched in cursive on the shirt's right breast, "from the reactors at the Lab."

"You shot me."

"It is not your time."

"You knew that it was me?"

"We each are in the other's care." The luminescence looks up at the hemlock. "Know that they are loved."

The form that has communicated with the oxbow frogs as it was able undergoes reversion to adult dimensions and observes that this is so.

"Where's mom?"

"She's here."

The form seeks the maternal presence.

The luminescence rasps, "Come here," extending to the form both hands. The luminescence hugs the upright form and heals its ragged wound. The form is luminescent.

"Know that you are loved," the luminescence rasps.

The form lets go to look the luminescence in the eyes. The luminescence is a meadow marsh beside a forest gamma radiation has bombarded since before the form was born. The form stands in canary grass and smiles at two tiger salamanders gazing at it from the water's edge. Its heart fills with the balm of their regard. The tiger salamanders' hearts beat, sending incognito ripples through the water toward the form. Across the marsh, beyond two frozen great blue herons, in the portion of the sky where physics says the sun should be, a man's esophagus is shortened and his stomach rises, blood-flecked, shining on the interwoven beings of the meadow marsh.

The taste of metal rises in the gullet of the form. The great blue herons fly. The tiger salamanders sidewind into what they think is shelter. From the form's mouth springs a pipeline. Over the canary grass it lengthens, casting as it goes a shaft of shadow. Katydids and spittlebugs arc over the canary grass and scatter. Where the surface water of the marsh begins, the pipeline ends, its mouth an outflow and an overlook. The form rigidifies and retches, spewing through the pipeline zinc and silver, chromium and lead, aluminum and copper, mercury and cadmium, beryllium and arsenic, barium and hepatitis viruses, which arc as one into the marsh.

The spewing ceases.

The retraction of the pipeline chokes the form, which grabs its throat and then its chest and drops to the canary grass. The form's mouth and the pipeline's for a moment perfectly align, and then the pipeline disappears into the form, which dry heaves, writhes, and flattens more canary grass.

The stomach in the sky is overhead and reattached to the esophagus.

The form goes still and squints as black flecks multiply on the esophagus and migrate to the stomach.

Dusk comes.

"Know the land my cancer lends you," rasps a voice, "is loved."
Black flecks metastasize like starlings to the sky.
In metastatic darkness wind the salamanders to the form. They scale its fabrics and its skin. Its ear hair shuffles and canal wax crackles. In its middle ears, the salamanders lie upon their bellies and their toes. The story of their harm seeps in.

Chapter Sixteen: Oldwife Underwings
and Hemlock Loopers

An oldwife underwing, its beacon eyes aglow, lands on the left eye of the sprier, softer form, which through the other eye still sees the cosmic furl of fern and snail shell. Then another oldwife underwing, its beacon eyes aglow, lands on the right eye of the form, which closes both its eyelids. Closure does not shoo the oldwife underwings. They only flutter and resettle on the eyelids, which have lost the power to reopen and are hidden under what appear to be two bark chips placed to pay the fare.

Signs of a cyclonic force descending are apparent to the oldwife underwings before the pressure drops and breeze perturbs their feathery antennas. Fluttering, the oldwife underwings uplift the form, the pressure of ascent inclining the position of its head, and by its eyelids fly it to a cylinder of well stones, which they hover over with the dangling form, negotiating the logistics of descent.

The form's feet cross the threshold. Cool air sheathes the form. The well stones speak of condensate and agency.

By wingbeat and by breath, the oldwife underwings cross over and descend. The well-stone rim recedes, a circle slowly closing on the whirlwind in the forestland.

The oldwife underwings, now deeply subterranean, fricatively respire. Their fluttering is strained. They struggle to fly laterally, descending as they do. The form's chin rasps against a well stone and slides down. It rasps against another and slides down, accelerant until the form's right forefoot lands on a protrusion that the form knows at the touchdown instant is a turkey tail. This mushroom's barnacle tenacity arrests descent.

The form's left forefoot sweeps old well stones, dips and sweeps, the right knee bending, and finds purchase on another turkey tail made manifest. The fingers of its right hand grope and trace the well-stone joints within their range until they climb a turkey tail made manifest at their extension limit and hold tight. The fingers of its left hand grope and trace, first high, then lower, lower. When the fingers touch a turkey tail made manifest and clutch, the oldwife underwings, their wings and spiracles unburdened, let the splayed form's eyelids go.

The form's eyes open and gaze up at iridescent orange flashes beating from the underwings. The form's hands tense. The mushroom cuticles compress. The fear of falling rushes in.

"Attune," the oldwife underwings, now perched beside each other on an upper well stone, whisper to the puffing form. The wingbeats and the iridescent flashes slow, the drawing out of intermittence's devotion to arrangements in relief.

The mushroom gills exhale a mist of spores.

A flare of nostrils, and the form breathes in a billion buoyant spores. Its right cheek, downy, presses hard against a well stone, craving contact, an assurance that the body will not be let go.

The oldwife underwings perform a half-rotation dance and beam their beacon eyes down on the form.

"You are not listening," they whisper.

Pressed against a well-stone joint, the spiral middle of the form's right ear hears deep interior transmissions on the way. Mycelial reticulations tell the forest of the frightened fingers and the pressed ear.

The forest tells the form to find the mushroom foothold to the lower left of where its left foot is positioned now, to find the mushroom handhold to the lower left of where its left hand is positioned now, to find the mushroom foothold to the lower left of where its right foot is positioned now, to find the mushroom handhold to the lower left of where its right hand is positioned now. The forest guides the form this way from turkey tail to turkey tail until the form is purely guided by the textures and the scents that spiral to the bottom of the well-stone cylinder where water tells the form that it must let the mushrooms go.

The form dips one foot in the water and withdraws it before deciding on immersion, but the foot is there no longer, only the protuberance of ankle and a smooth stump dripping echoes in the cavern of an aquifer. The form squints, scanning, but there is no foot afloat, no fish-white glow rotational below the surface saying *Here*. The form withdraws the stump and ankle farther from the water, farther from the poison or bacterium that must have taken from it what has been a part of it from the beginning.

Loss engulfs the form. Deformity and absence overwhelm it as it tries to keep the stump from sliding off the mushroom cap.

The form, in tears, at last concedes to self-deception, unaware that from its earlobes hang the oldwife underwings, and reaches for a higher turkey tail, experimenting with the possibility of following a clockwise spiral path back up the mushrooms to the well-stone rim and woods transformed by whirlwind.

When the oldwife underwings aim toward its middle ears and whisper, "Why? Let go. You're mostly water anyway," the form, extended, stops and looks down at the water. It releases both hands and falls backward, tensing for the splash.

The oldwife underwings release its earlobes and twirl upward. From each beacon eye, a water spirit flows and girds the form, which lands as lightly as a frond upon the water. As the form floats, it untenses and observes the oldwife underwings receding, growing smaller, fainter, more dependent on their fleeting, fractal afterimages to prove they ever were; and, as it watches, it dissolves, unfazed by dissolution. It is hairless, headless, skinless, bloodless, boneless, gutless. Water sticks to water, and the form as it has known itself, as it has understood itself in memories, in person, and in heavens high and low, has ceased to be.

The water, pressured, seeps through pores and fissures, fits inside the capillary seams that compression leaves between the granular and gravelly. Deep attractions draw the water. In it is the sense to scour hardness. In it is the wisdom of adhesion and of time.

Three inches is a day. Two hundred lunar years go by.

The water springs and trickles first downhill in hemlock shade, then flows in dappled sunlight, crooning of each grain of sand, each pebble, crooning of each particle of clay and silt, each particle of soil, each pore and fissure, each deposit that sloughed from it all impurity.

The water pools in a nitrogenous impoundment pond beyond a mooing barn and circles twice, escaping pumps, before a spillway lets it go. It flows past scattered beeches and a beehive humming in the sun and dips into a dirty culvert underneath an asphalt road, emerging into pine and hemlock woods and deep shade, nearing darkness, sluicing over ancient ledge and misting, like a serpentine sporangium, the fungi and the ferns.

Two hemlock loopers rise like shards of bark from separate branches of a bifurcated trunk and drift like new disciples of the mist. A bead of mist detaches from the fluid constellation and attaches to a hemlock needle that the loopers intimately know. The bead is brilliant, and the needle tries to take the bead and brilliance in. The hemlock loopers see the bead is slipping, getting longer, so they hover upside down beneath it. Wingbeats will the brilliant bead into the needle.

The hemlock loopers right themselves, intent on drifting with the mist. But suddenly the branches of the bifurcated trunk entwine, and the entwining tells the hemlock loopers it is in them to do more. They will themselves into the needle and become the heralds of the bead. They spiral upward, and their draft makes spirited the bead's rise up the spiral way. They reach the highest needle underneath the moon, and one by one the hemlock loopers and the bead transpire, rising in their new states to a cloud that drifts in the direction of the brook and the mist.

The cloud enshrouds a golden castle lit by forces powerful within. A turret mollusk on a battlement embrasure waits until the hemlock loopers and the bead in their new states get close and says, "With one compassion gene I seed this cloud," expelling from its aperture a single gene encoded for compassion that transcends the species lines. The gene wafts, serpentine, rotational. Inside the pressure of the cloud, the hemlock loopers and the bead condense. The cloud is saturated. Light rain falls. The loopers and the bead encapsulate the gene as it descends.

In darkness on a needled knoll below, a dead form's lips are slightly parted like a vole's as though another shallow breath is possible. The spirit of the form recedes. It hears on the invisible horizon the approach of chainsaws and machinery. It tries reentering the form again and, failing, thanks the air for all the air has done.

The buffered gene falls through the spirit, offering its draw and passing through the parted lips at original velocity.

The form convulses, and the gene locks in. The bead releases, leaving what it learned. The hemlock loopers whisper to the dead form their support. The spirit flows in, and the form convulses, coughing out the bead and loopers.

Stunned, the form lies mostly still.

A shaft of moonlight lights the knoll.

The oxbow frogs climb on the breathing form and up and down in unison they say, "Rewild."

The gray garden slugs climb on the breathing form and up and down in unison they say, "Rewild."

The hemlock trunk, against which leaned a form, its head bowed, hands flat on her bark, leans toward the prone form, dropping cones and needles that the form absorbs into itself, and says in earthy breaths, "Rewild, man. Let go. Rewild."

The bead rests on the needled duff and marvels at its forearm's underside, a date tattooed above a blue vein curving toward a terminal thumb.

Chapter Seventeen: Rewild

Albert fills a clear-glass feeder with a clear solution, one part sugar, four parts water. It has been two days since he has seen a hummingbird. October has been warm. He hopes he has not seen the last of them pass through this flyway.

Albert does not spill a nectar drop. He sets the sweaty Mason jar beside its screw top and the feeder's plastic bottom on the grass. He turns the bottom upside down and lines its threads up with the glass's threads and spins. He tightens the connection with a quarter turn and rights the feeder, sugar water dripping from the yellow florets and the lower petals of the four red plastic flowers.

As he hangs the feeder on its shepherd's hook, he thinks about the glorious arrival season on the Yucatan Peninsula. He would like to be among the southern welcomers one day.

He screws the top back on the Mason jar and walks with Charlie Watts back to the house.

A Forester pulls in the driveway. Harold Brown gets out. His left hand grips the rolled top of a paper bag.

"Good morning, Harold. How'd your three-month checkup go?"

"Well," says Harold, frowning, "I'm no longer in remission."

"Shit. I'm sorry," Albert says. "The cancer's spread?"

Harold squats to pet Watts for a while, wordless, and is beaming when he looks back up.

"The doctors don't know how," says Harold, "but the cancer's gone. Not in remission. Gone. I'm cured." He stands. His eyes are watery. "I'm cured."

"No chemo," Albert says in wonderment, "no radiation."

Harold shakes his head. He takes his glasses off and wipes his eyes.

"I owe you," Harold says.

"Not me," says Albert. "Cosme. Ayahuasca."

"I still owe you all. But yes," says Harold. "Cosme. Ayahuasca." He looks down at Watts as though in Watts resides his deepest obligation. "Whether it was Cosme's healing, or the diet and ayahuasca, if those even can be separated from his healing, or the turkey tails that Cosme said the vision said I had to take, or whether all of it is intertwined according to some cosmic pattern that is presently beyond me, I don't know, but I'm restructured, Albert. I'm attuned. Attuning." Harold puts his glasses on. "Forgive the outburst."

"Such good news," says Albert as he hugs him. "Such good news."

The three of them head for the house.

"Still getting death threats?" Albert asks.

"Oh, yes. Eva, too. When we came out against the Corridor in that opinion piece, we made some enemies. At least she's in Peru with Chris and Cosme," Harold says, "attuning, making her amends."

"What's next?" asks Albert.

"Litigation."

"You think you'll be sued?"

"Probably for breach of contract," Harold nonchalantly says.

"That doesn't bother you?"

"I used to see existence as a grid," says Harold. "Now I see the wild opening before me."

"You think the Corridor is dead?"

"My energies no longer flow that way," says Harold.

"Which way do they flow?"

"Toward this," says Harold, holding up the paper bag, "and The Rewilding Trust."

The screen door yawns and stretches as though summer is in full stride.

In the narrow kitchen, chaga simmers in a lidded pot. The low flame hulas as they enter.

Nothing has been quite the same since ayahuasca.

Watts jumps on a brown recliner in the next room, circles six times, orients, and lies down, basking like a sphinx in slatted sunlight. Harold sets the paper bag upon the table. Albert puts the Mason jar in the refrigerator and pours two cups of chaga tea. They sit and sip and listen to the boys and Mary pestling chaga in the back room.

Wordless minutes pass.

"When people talk about rewilding," Harold says, "they often have in mind a scale that's continental. It's about creating wild cores and corridors and reconnecting what is wild."

Albert sips and nods.

"The obstacles are monumental. The logistics are complex. Far more complex in some ways than the Corridor logistics," Harold says.

"Of course. The Corridor," says Albert, "only had to go a couple hundred miles."

The phone rings. Pestling ceases. Mary's muffled voice is clearly happy with the call.

"In some ways, though, if one recalibrates the scale," says Harold, "the logistics of rewilding are, all things considered, relatively simple."

"Simple how?"

"In terms of largely being just an exercise in raising money and then buying what is out there to be bought."

"That doesn't sound so simple, Harold."

"It's a multigenerational endeavor, to be sure, but it's doable. Rewilding the human consciousness is possible. Just look at me. Unfortunately, we can't give everybody ayahuasca. So attuning will take time. But maybe this can speed things up," says Harold, holding up his tea.

"This Trust," says Albert.

"The Rewilding Trust."

"It raises money."

"Yes."

"Buys land."

"Buys with an eye toward stitching back together what has long been fractured," Harold says. "Remediates what needs remediation. Mostly, though, we let it be. No roads. No logging. No development. No farms. No recreation. Nature will come back. It will diversify."

"And you think this can happen?"

"It is happening," says Harold.

He removes a folded paper peeking from the pocket of his shirt and holds it out to Albert.

"What is this?" asks Albert, taking it.

"A copy of the deed."

"To what?" he asks as he unfolds it and begins to read.

"It isn't much, but it's a start."

"You bought the Thomas farm?"

"The Trust did."

"To rewild?" Albert asks, still reading.

"To rewild."

"You have this much money?"

"I've lived frugally."

"Eight-hundred acres," Albert says. "Four-hundred dairy cows." He leans back in his chair and looks up at the ceiling. "What about the cows? You can't just slaughter them." He levels and looks back at Harold.

"This is where it gets less simple. Half the land will be reserved to let them live their lives out unencumbered. Then the Trust will let those acres go."

"To be rewilded," Albert says.

"To be rewilded."

"That will take some years."

"We implement remediation measures in the meantime, mainly the impoundment pond's removal, and restore the brook's health and the watershed's. We graze the cows rotationally. We put in conservation tillage."

"This is really happening."

"I didn't want to tell you," Harold says, "until I knew that this was real."

"And this is real?"

"The Trust already has commitments."

"What commitments?"

"Patagonia has pledged support, for one," says Harold. "For another, Waterloo and Kirk, Eva's company, once it's restructured. There are others. They, and all the other ecosystem-restoration sympathizers out there, know this is the side of history to be on, even if it loses."

Albert sips and nods.

"Do you remember what you told me in July before the diet?" asks Harold. "You said you'd give up your land for nothing if it was a part of a coordinated effort to rewild."

"I remember," Albert says, imagining himself long gone two centuries from now, three centuries from now, the old-growth forest back. "I will."

"I need you on the board of The Rewilding Trust," says Harold.

"Chris, AJ, Mary, you. And Cosme, if in spirit only."

The door to the back room opens and then softly closes.

Watts's tail wags hard against recliner fabric.

Pestling resumes.

"Hey, Harold," Mary says on entering the kitchen.

"Harold's cured. No chemo," Albert says. "No radiation."

"Oh, my God," says Mary, hugging Harold, "that is wonderful, just wonderful. Does Cosme know?"

"He's not an easy man to get a hold of," Harold says, "but I'll call Eva later. She'll relay the message."

"I'm so happy for you, Harold."

Mary pours a cup of chaga tea. They listen to the pestling.

"Did you know," says Mary, sipping, "it's the same time in Peru as it is here?"

They visualize the time zones.

"That was Chris," says Mary, "on the phone before. She said it looks like there's momentum to amend the Water Law so allocations are more equitable down there. She said it looks like there's a framework for an upstream-downstream reciprocity agreement. Her company divested."

Harold hands the paper bag to her.

"I have a proposition for you."

Mary opens it and peers inside.

"You harvested these turkey tails?"

"I did."

"From where?"

"Right now that information is proprietary, but, if you were willing to take on a business partner, I suppose I could reveal my source."

"You want to partner in the chaga business," Mary asks, "with me?"

"I do. But not just chaga. Chaga, yes, but also turkey tail and lion's mane and hemlock reishi. I'm convinced the path," says Harold, "to rewilding human consciousness up here runs through the fungi. Let's invite as many people as we can to listen in on the mycelial communications. Let's remind them how the earth communicates with us. Let's teach them to reciprocate. To do for earth as earth has done for us. To speak for earth and with her. To converse. If you had said three months ago this would be me, I would have told you you were crazy. How's that for a testimonial?"

She looks at Albert.

Albert shrugs and says, "I'd purchase fungus from him."

"Let me introduce you to the operation," Mary says, preceding Harold to the back room.

Pestling stops and then continues.

Albert glances at the calendar beside the kitchen phone. He walks outside with Watts and finds a flat stone on a slight mound near the greenhouse. He picks up a garden trowel to unearth the plastic shopping bag whose lofty biodegradation claim offended him so deeply back in June. He squats and notices an anthill near the flat stone and three others on the outskirts of the mound. He lays the trowel where he found it, and he wonders if that's all there is between attunement and upheaval.

THE END

THE AUTHOR

John Popielaski is the author of the novel, *The Hollow Middle* (Unsolicited Press), as well as several poetry collections, including *That Special Something* (Sheila-Na-Gig Editions). His poetry has appeared in a number of literary journals, including most recently *Canary, Common Ground Review, Public School Poetry,* and *Gramercy Review.*